RACHEL MEEHAN

Water's Edge

Book One: Troubled Times Series

First published in 2013 by Cherry House Publishing

Water's Edge

ISBN: 978-0-9575946-8-5

www.cherryhousepublishing.co.uk

Other Titles

Power's Out (Book 2: Troubled Times Series)

Eternal Inheritance

To Ray

ACKNOWLEDGMENTS

Thanks to family and friends who read through the pain barrier...

ONE

The sun beat down on Nairne as she crossed the garden; her hair, damp with sweat, clung to the nape of her neck. She placed the steel watering can beneath the water butt and turned the tap. Lifting the lid of the butt she peered at the cool water; only the slightest ripple indicated that the precious liquid was seeping away. She filled the can three quarters full so it was easier to carry and there was less danger of spilling it. She watered the lettuce, carrots, tomatoes and finally the beans, but there was insufficient water for the potatoes; they would just have to take their chances.

Placing the spout close to the base of the plants she watched the dusty soil turn a chocolate brown. The liquid puddled on the surface then sank in slowly. Nairne liked this part of the day: better than hoeing, she thought, as hours had been spent shearing off the weeds between the regimented rows of vegetables. She glanced at her watch: it was six fifteen, but there was still no sign of her brother Zane, or Dog. Their stomachs would tell them it was time to come home. They usually spent the afternoon in the woods shooting rabbits but with the drought rabbits were scarce this year. So Zane would be fishing or more accurately lying on the riverbank dozing, with Dog resting patiently next to him; another of their favourite pastimes.

Nairne heard her father's pick-up truck rumble up the potholed driveway long before it came into view. He parked outside the front of the house and waved to her before taking a couple of shopping bags inside.

As she gathered the tools and returned them to the shed another car approached more cautiously, trying in vain to avoid the most damaging holes. It swung into view. The driver emerged first, a tall man with black trousers and a dazzling white shirt. From the passenger door, a young woman appeared; she put on her hat and together they marched up to the front door and rang the bell. Her father let them in.

Zane's in for it now, she thought. It wouldn't be the first time one of them had got into trouble, but the police; what has he been up to, she wondered? Several minutes passed before her father reappeared.

"Nairne, where's your brother?"

"How should I know?" she responded, but his expression showed this was not a time to talk back. "I'll go and find him," she added and ran off towards the woods.

"Zane! Zane!..." She raced through the trees towards the riverbank. Her instincts were right; she could see his prone figure, hat covering his eyes and fishing rod lying abandoned at his side. Her call startled him. Dog lifted his head, barked and bounded towards her.

"What's the matter?" Zane mumbled, having just woken. "What's all the noise for?"

"You tell me – come on, get your shoes on. We need to get back to the house. The police are here to see you!"

"Yeah, very funny...." He paused. "Really?" He could see from Nairne's expression that this was no joke. He slipped on his trainers and charged after her, while Dog ran backwards and forwards between them.

"Hang on Nairne, wait for me. I don't understand. I haven't done anything!"

"Well, the police are here and dad didn't look too pleased so you must have done something." Although she was desperate to know what he'd done, she was also very protective of him. Zane was fifteen and a half, older than her by almost two years, but much younger than her in many ways. He was simple; at least that's what the other kids at school said. Dad said Zane was special. She liked 'special' better.

"Oh come on, it can't be that bad." She paused to let

him catch up. She could see he was scared.

As they entered the house, Zane grabbed her hand. The policewoman was in the living room with their father, who was leaning against the mantle shelf. He did not turn round. The other officer was in the kitchen making tea. No one spoke. Nairne glanced at the female officer. She was young with a plain face, which wore a look of professional concern.

"What's wrong?" Nairne could feel her stomach knotting and a rush of anxiety. "Dad, what is it?"

Zane squeezed her hand; she could feel his breath on her neck. Their father did not move. The policewoman spoke.

"Nairne, Zane, I'm sorry, we have some very bad news for you, why don't you come over and sit down?"

"No, we're fine here. What is it?" Nairne replied curtly.

"I'm sorry to tell you - it's your mum - I'm afraid she passed away yesterday." The silence was broken by the sound of Zane's sobs. He rushed to their father who hugged him tightly.

"How did she die?" Nairne asked.

"It was a fire; you might have seen reports on the news. The block of flats where she lived had been quarantined; it was at the centre of a dysentery outbreak. Several residents had already died; your mum was on the list of those infected and was due to be taken to hospital the next day. Unfortunately a rumour started circulating that infected people were trying to leave the building and there was a disturbance. Local people took matters into their own hands and someone set fire to the building. Your mum is one of those reported missing, presumed dead. The blaze was ferocious." The policewoman's voice was soft. "I know it's a terrible shock, but it's okay to cry."

"I'm not going to cry. As far as I'm concerned my mother died years ago," Nairne replied.

Nairne could feel the officers' relief when she showed

them out. She returned to the living room, followed by Dog, who could sense there was something wrong. Nairne went through to the kitchen and prepared the evening meal. She flicked on the radio; the news was still on.

"The London death toll in the arson attack at the Hanover flats in Kensington, which were linked to the latest dysentery outbreak, has been confirmed. Seventy-two people perished in the blaze. An official spokesman announced that the outbreak had been contained. The fire was started during a disturbance late last night. Police have not yet made any arrests in connection with the attack.

The high temperatures, which have been affecting the capital for the last two weeks, have exacerbated the spread of dysentery. Doctors expressed concern that due to the increasing costs of metered water, people are trying to save money by not flushing lavatories and not washing their hands thoroughly. This, the third outbreak in London this summer, has seen the largest loss of life."

She turned it off. She'd heard the reports earlier in the week, but unlike her father, she had not paid much attention. He always listened avidly to the news, especially anything to do with climate change, which he was obsessed by. This summer, the hottest in ten years, the news had been dominated by climate related stories including outbreaks of typhoid and dysentery, especially in the South.

Nairne had never seen her mum's flat, but from the descriptions on the news it was a block of luxury apartments, just the sort of place she imagined Angela, her mum, living. Dad couldn't understand how Angela could have been caught up in a dysentery outbreak; they normally happened in poor areas, where people couldn't afford to use too much water. The policewoman said that migrant workers, who cleaned the buildings, had introduced the infection. Their houses were far from luxurious. Several of the cleaners had also died.

Nairne placed the food on the kitchen table and called through. Her father and Zane came in and sat down. No one spoke or ate much. After dinner they returned to the living room. Zane had managed to stop crying, but he was pale and his eyes were swollen and raw.

"Dad," his voice was hoarse. "Can we look at the pictures?"

"Okay son, if that's what you both want to do.... I'll go and fetch them."

Nairne said nothing. She didn't want to look at them. She didn't want to think about Angela. Their father returned with a slender photograph album and sat down next to Zane.

"Nairne, why don't you come over here?" He gestured to the space on his other side. Reluctantly, she sat down but made no effort to look at the photographs. As he turned the pages Zane pointed out all the things he could remember.

"That was my birthday party. What age was I?"

"Seven," replied their father.

The picture showed Zane standing next to his new off-road bicycle. He was smiling. Nairne, who would have been five, was standing next to him, wearing her best dress, ankle socks and sandals. Angela was behind them, laughing; her arm draped around Zane's shoulder while her dark wavy hair framed her face.

The last picture in the book was of all of them standing outside their current house. Nairne remembered that day: she was nine and her hair was long then. Zane was standing next to her, behind them stood Angela. She looked older, the strain clearly showing. Next to her stood Daniel their father, his left hand rested on Zane's shoulder. They all looked at the picture in silence and then he closed the book.

"It's late, time you two got some sleep."

Zane was reluctant, but Nairne couldn't wait to get to her room, to get away from the pictures of Angela and the tears for Angela.

She lay in bed. The air was stifling although the

windows had been opened all day. Covered by a single sheet she listened to the noises outside and to the sobbing from her brother's room. Dad was still downstairs having a drink and no doubt thinking about Angela. Even after four years she could just come right back into their lives and ruin everything, thought Nairne, rage filling her chest. She watched the minutes tick by on the clock; hours passed before she heard her father climb the stairs.

Nairne was sitting on the stairs; the rough bare wood scratched her legs. The paint had been scraped off them, but they were yet to be sanded and varnished; like everything in the house, they were unfinished. She pulled her thin nightdress down over her knees and feet: She was shivering. The hallway was dark, except for a sliver of borrowed light from the kitchen. The voices had woken her so she had crept down to find out what was wrong, but as she neared the bottom of the stairs, she could tell it was something bad. Now she was too afraid to go in, but she was even more afraid of the darkness upstairs.

She had never heard her father shouting like that; then her mother's voice cut through.

"You can't expect me to live like this! The constant jibes and those bloody looks.... you think I haven't noticed the way you look at me. It was an accident for Christ's sake; an accident and I've done everything. I gave up our house; I came here to live in this God awful dump. I don't see my friends; my parents won't visit. Even the neighbours think we're mad."

"What? So because the neighbours don't like the fact that I'm getting ready for what's coming you're going to leave me? God forbid the neighbours don't approve. I know Angela, why don't you invite them round and they can tell me how to live my life? Or better yet, why not invite your good friends from the estate? We haven't seen much of them since the accident; we don't fit into their cosy little world anymore, do we? *Poor Angela with the spastic son and the crazy husband, maybe it would have been better if the boy hadn't survived.* Isn't that what they say behind our backs? But he did survive, so you'll just have to live with it."

She could hear her father pacing backwards and forwards.

"No Daniel, I don't have to live with it. It's not Zane. It's you and this end of the bloody world obsession. You're scaring me. You don't want me to go out, or have friends. We never go anywhere, we don't have any money and you spend every waking moment fortifying your little empire to keep the rest of the world out. I can't do it anymore! I'm leaving and I'm taking Nairne with me. I'm going to stay with a friend. It'll be better for all of us."

"Nairne? You'll take your daughter but not your son. Why is that then? Who's the friend Angela? One of those vipers you used to hang around with?" There was a silence, Nairne held her breath.

"Wait a minute; it's a man isn't it? - I should have seen it coming."

"Yes, it's another man. His name is Martin. I met him…."

"I don't give a shit what his name is, where you met him or what his sodding star sign is. If you want to leave then go ahead, but you're not splitting our kids up."

"Daniel please! I can't take them both….let me take Nairne."

"So why can't you take them both? Does Martin not approve of the spastic son? Is that too much effort for him? God it must be love!"

Nairne felt sick; she was shaking with the cold and with the sounds of anger. She could hear her mum sobbing.

"Oh don't start with the tears. You don't give a damn about those kids, you never have; it's just too difficult isn't it? It was fine when we were the perfect little family, but at the first sign of a problem, Angela can't cope. The best of it is if you had been a half decent mother none of this would ever have happened and you'd have two perfect children."

Nairne closed her eyes tightly as tears squeezed out from under the lids. She pressed her hands over her ears and blocked out the sound.

She opened her eyes. She was standing outside Mrs Allen's, two streets from their house.

"I'll not be long, so behave yourselves, stay in the garden and no wandering off and Zane, look after your sister." Her mother ruffled his hair and walked round to the back of the house.

Zane ran across the front garden and kicked the football to Nairne; she kicked it back. It was a blistering July day and they could hear the babble of voices from the back garden; Mrs Allen and mum's other friends were sitting on the decking drinking wine and gossiping.

They continued to play; half an hour came and went and they were bored.

"Kick it harder Nairne, see if you can score," Zane shouted. Nairne charged towards the ball and kicked it as hard as she could; it sailed into the air like slow motion, higher and higher, it flew over Zane's head and the garden fence onto the road. It bounced, again and again and again, each bounce slightly smaller than the last until it came to rest against the opposite curb. Zane raced through the gate across the road and picked up the ball. He turned and smiled.

The Range Rover turned into the estate. Peter Evans held the wheel with one hand and clutched his mobile phone in the other.

"Yeah Angie, I'm just at the end of the street, get a beer ready for me....."

He didn't see the boy, but he felt the impact, the dull thud of flesh and metal. Then he heard the scream. Afterwards that's what everyone said; they all heard the scream.

Nairne was screaming as her father rushed into the

room. She woke confused, soaked in sweat and then she was crying so hard she couldn't stop.

TWO

Nairne despised school: she was going into third year and Zane was going into fourth. He had been held back for a year after the accident. He had spent eight long months in hospital much of it slipping in and out of consciousness. Nairne found it difficult when he finally came home. He looked like the old Zane, except for the scar on his head, which was soon covered by his thick blonde hair. But he was different.

He couldn't do things that he did before; in fact, he could hardly read or write even though he'd always been much better at that than her. Her granny said he was slow and the other kids called him spastic and retard. Nairne asked her mum what spastic meant; her mother cried and told her never to use that word. The next time Nairne heard Johnny Simpson, a boy in Zane's class, utter the S word she launched herself at him punching and kicking him until he said sorry. She was sent home.

This year would be different, Nairne thought. Anything to get away from the house had to be good. Ever since Angela's death, the place had been unbearable. Zane cried at the slightest provocation and all he wanted to do was talk about her, while dad had buried himself in his work. Nairne just wanted it all to be in the past, for things to have moved on; for something exciting to happen. She didn't want to think about Angela, not now, not ever. Angela had betrayed them; she'd wanted to leave Zane behind.

It was a small school with only seven hundred pupils, but then Kelso was a small town. Although Nairne didn't know all the other pupils by name, she recognised everyone, so she was surprised to find that there were twelve new pupils in her year alone. Something is up, she pondered and by morning break she could see that all the classes were much bigger. Nairne could hardly contain her excitement; with all these new faces, she might make some real friends.

Nairne was what teachers called a loner. Her previous form teacher, Ms Kelly, two years out of teachers' training, and desperate to be the most popular teacher ever, had worried about her. Nairne became a regular topic of staff room conversation. Ms Kelly found out all about Zane's accident and how Mr Grear had sold the house, moved the family into a dilapidated small holding outside town and started up an odd job business. Apparently, Mr Grear believed modern civilisation was on the brink of collapse. Ms Kelly was intrigued. They also said that he let his children run wild and that after a year or so of this back to nature lifestyle Mrs Grear had run off with another man. It was the children she felt sorry for.

Nairne was a difficult pupil. She was extremely protective of her brother, which was admirable; however, she would use her fists to settle an argument before her tongue, although she was known for being quite cutting in that department as well. Ms Kelly was not deterred; she decided she would befriend Nairne and become her mentor. She confided in Mrs Walsh, the physics teacher, a stern old fashioned teacher respected by the staff and pupils alike, and who also had a soft spot for Nairne. She listened patiently to the young teacher's plan and advised against it; Mr Grear was always polite, but she sensed he would not take kindly to being advised on how to raise his children.

When parents' night came Ms Kelly waited expectantly for Mr Grear. He was younger than she expected, late thirties, well built and tanned from working outside. His brown hair was naturally bleached by the sun and with his bright blue eyes she could see where the boy got his looks. His accent was Scottish, a softer lilt than that of the Borders. They discussed Nairne and how she was getting on and then Ms Kelly asked if there were any female influences in Nairne life.

"Why?" he replied.

"She is a lovely girl, Mr Grear, but I sometimes think she has problems fitting in with the other girls in the class. For example, when was the last time Nairne got her hair styled or got new clothes for going to parties?"

"Nairne doesn't get invited to parties Ms Kelly so she would have little need for them."

"That's what I mean. The other girls think Nairne is a tomboy and so they don't invite her, but if Nairne were to make a bit of an effort then I'm sure they would realise she's just like them."

Daniel Grear sighed.

"The other girls don't think Nairne is a tomboy, they call her a gypsy. Luckily, Nairne isn't anything like them; she is an articulate and intelligent girl who knows her own mind. She doesn't hang around with the other girls because she has better things to do with her time. Tell me Ms Kelly, these girls, who could learn to tolerate my daughter, do you think any of them know how an electric motor works? Could they change a tyre on a car? I doubt it. They could, no doubt tell you who this week's celebrity is sleeping with, which pop star has lost or gained weight. I think Nairne's doing just fine without friends who think they can call her names because she doesn't wear the right clothes. I'm sure your heart's in the right place, but when I need advice on raising my kids I'll ask for it." The conversation was over.

Ms Kelly was mortified. He had looked at her as if she was as vacuous as he obviously thought the girls in Nairne's class were. She knew as Nairne got older it would get more difficult; what boy would ever ask her out? Most of them were too scared to speak to her. Now on the first day of the new term, Ms Kelly, still full of enthusiasm looked round her new class to see if there was a special pupil she could help this time.

A special assembly was called after morning break. The pupils filed into the school hall and the headmaster, Mr Watson, addressed the expectant audience. He explained about the influx of new pupils and issued a letter for parents. The hall was buzzing with chatter as the pupils returned to lessons.

At lunchtime, Nairne sought out Zane. She wanted to talk to him about Mr Watson's announcement. He was with the usual gang from his class plus a couple of new boys from London who were being interrogated.

"So what made you come here?" asked the aptly named Spud, a plump, gormless boy.

"My dad said we'd be better off here so we sold our place near Crystal Palace and bought a house on that new estate, next to the garden centre. It's all right I guess, but there's nothing to do here."

"So what's it like in London? Is it true you don't have running water?"

"No, but you have to pay for it and it's getting expensive. My dad said it's going to get worse; that's why we moved. What with that and all the foreigners; they're everywhere. We need to stop letting them in, that's what my dad says."

"Climate change, that's what it is," said Zane authoritatively.

"Yeah yeah," laughed one of the other boys. "You know all about that don't you Zane? Zane's dad's a nut case; he believes the worlds going to end. All the ice is going to melt and the water's going to rise and we're all going to drown." He mimicked the act of drowning, holding his nose with one hand while the other flailed around his head. The others laughed.

The newcomer chipped in.

"My dad says this global warming stuff is all crap. He says the problem with the water supply is down to the company that own it. They're French and my dad says the French are crap at running anything. How can we be short of water when we had all that rain last winter? It's all bollocks; it's bad management, that's what my dad says."

"Anyway, your mum lives in London with her fancy man, doesn't she Zane? She could tell you all about the place if she ever gets in touch," said Spud.

The others laughed. Zane started to go red as Nairne butted in.

"Our mum died last week."

The words halted the conversation instantly; the boys glanced at each other and then at the ground.

"Come on Zane, let's get lunch." Nairne took her brother's arm and they walked away.

As the afternoon dragged on Nairne tried to strike up conversations with two of the new girls, but it soon became obvious they'd been told not to speak to her. When the bell rang, Nairne joined the crush of bodies in the corridor as the pupils fled into the warm afternoon air. She sat with Zane on the bus home and forty minutes later, they alighted and ran up the driveway to the house. The two storey stone building had seen better days. Their father had reroofed the right hand side of the building, which they occupied. The remainder of the property was single storey. His plan had been to renovate it and rent it to holiday makers in the summer months, but he never quite had the money or the time to finish the work.

"Come on let's get the chores done," said Nairne, unlocking the front door.

"Oh, do we have to? I'm tired; let's go down to the river."

"No, Zane I'm not doing everything. You check the animals and I'll water the vegetables, deal?"

"I suppose so. Have you read the letter from school?"

"No, it's in my bag. Dad will read it when he gets home."

"So how many more people can fit in the school?"

"I don't know, I can't imagine there will be many more. There are lots of other places people can move to. Besides, there won't be enough houses to go round, will there?"

When he arrived home, Daniel Greer was surprised to see both his children hanging about in the garden enjoying the last rays of sunshine.

"I thought you two would be running about in those woods or be down at the river. How was school?"

This was met by a barrage of information from both of them.

"Look, we got a letter for you." Nairne thrust the envelope towards him. "There are eighty-three new pupils in school, from the south of England."

"Yes, and more and more are coming. The school is bursting at the seams," Zane butted in.

"All the new houses at the park have been sold and some people are living in caravans because their houses aren't even finished," said Nairne

Daniel read the letter.

The school had recognised that more people would be coming to the area and there were plans to construct an extension, but that would take time and cost money so more temporary units would be erected on one of the school playing fields.

"I guess this is the start," said Daniel.

"What do you mean the start?" Nairne asked.

"As I've said before, there are too many people in the south and with these hot summers and the winter storms we're going to see more and more of this."

"One of the new boys told me that his dad thinks climate change is rubbish, he said it was bad….." Zane hesitated.

"Bad management of the water companies," Nairne interjected.

"He may have a point," Daniel replied. "I'm sure most of our resources aren't well managed and people are wasteful, but climate change is here to stay. I remember in two thousand and four and five there was uproar when London had summer temperatures of one hundred and five, now that's normal. People always find other things to blame; they can't comprehend that we have damaged the planet and now we have to suffer the consequences. Anyway, let's have dinner and then we could go for a walk."

Nairne felt like time had slowed down; each glorious August day spent in a classroom seemed longer than the previous one. By the following Wednesday afternoon it was as if the holidays had never happened. It was double biology and they split into groups of three to look at samples under the microscope. Nairne was teamed with Laura Howard, one of the self-appointed class beauties, and Tamara Potter-Smith, a new girl. Nairne set up the microscope and loaded the first slide into place; she examined it and stepped aside for Laura.

"I don't want to look," said Laura pointedly.

"Nor me," chimed Tamara.

Nairne made notes of what she had observed and loaded the next slide; once again the two girls did not participate. Mr Cunningham, the biology teacher, became aware that only Nairne was taking part while her team mates stood idly by, whispering to one another.

"Is there a problem Laura? Nairne, make sure you all get a proper look at each sample."

"They don't want to look sir," said Nairne.

"Laura, do you know the answers to this lesson without taking part?"

"No sir."

"Then why won't you look in the microscope?"

"We don't want to share, Mr Cunningham."

"You heard what Mr Watson said, with so many new students we all have to make allowances and share some of the equipment. All right?"

"We don't want to share with her! Can we join another group?"

Mr Cunningham paused, he knew that Nairne was unpopular, but he hated the petty squabbling and bullying that went on in school and he would not tolerate it.

"No, you will stay exactly where you are and participate in the lesson or give me a good reason why not."

"It's her sir, she's dirty, I don't want to touch that thing not after she's touched it, and you can't make me. She's a dirty gypsy; she shouldn't be in the class with other people." Laura's face was flushed with excitement as she spat the words; Tamara stood behind her giggling nervously, as a hush descended on the room.

Mr Cunningham removed his glasses, rubbed the bridge of his nose and rose to his feet.

"Laura, come here right now!" There was an edge to his voice. The girl walked forward, stopping a few feet from him.

"You will report to the headmaster's office at the end of this lesson, but first, you will apologise to Nairne."

"I won't," she said defiantly, looking to the rest of the class for support. "It's true, everyone knows it; her mum had dysentery. And you get that from being a dirty gypsy. They just have to touch you, I saw it on the news and you can die from it. She shouldn't be here; she should be sent home."

Mr Cunningham was speechless. Nairne closed her notebook and placed it in her bag. She swung the bag over her shoulder and walked to the front of class towards Mr Cunningham and Laura.

"I think I need to go home," she said to Mr Cunningham.

"Nairne, it's okay. Laura will apologise or we will take

this matter straight to Mr Watson."

"Oh it's okay sir, it is true. My mum did have dysentery, so maybe Laura's right to be scared." With this she spun the other girl round grabbed her head tightly between her hands and kissed her hard on the lips. Whoops of disbelief from the class filled the air. "Let's just hope I'm not that infectious."

Minutes later Nairne was out of the school gates and running along the street, her heart pounding as tears of rage ran down her face. She never wanted to go back.

An hour later Daniel Grear parked his pick-up outside the school gates, leaving Dog sitting patiently on the passenger's seat. He located Mr Watson's office.

"She kissed her, kissed her for goodness sake! What kind of upbringing has she had? My Laura was horrified; to be kissed like that in front of the class, by another girl!" Mrs Howard shrieked.

Mr Cunningham did his best to explain what had happened, but she wouldn't listen.

"There can be no excuse for that sort of behaviour, she must be expelled or at least suspended. I know she comes from a difficult background, but this cannot be tolerated."

Mr Watson sighed, Mrs Howard was always complaining about this or that: Laura should be doing better; Laura should get the lead in the school play; Laura should be the soloist in the choir even though she couldn't hold a note. On and on it went.

Mr Grear was much more of an unknown quantity. Nairne was not new to trouble, but she had certainly been provoked.

"So what's going to be done then, Mr Watson? I need reassurances," Mrs Howard demanded.

"Firstly, I think we should hear from Mr Grear." He indicated to Daniel.

"Thank you. Firstly Mrs Howard I do feel that I need to clear up a couple of points. Nairne comes from a very loving home. Admittedly, she has only one parent, but she knows the difference between right and wrong and she knows how to behave. I understand that your daughter suggested that Nairne would give her dysentery and that she was, let me quote, 'a dirty gypsy'. Apparently your precocious daughter believed that my child could have a highly contagious infection because two weeks ago her mother died." Mrs Howard nodded in agreement. "The problem is Mrs Howard my wife had been living in London for over three years and has not been in contact with my daughter. My wife was suffering from dysentery when she was brutally murdered in an arson attack in Kensington, a victim of ignorance and prejudice, traits you and your daughter appear to be familiar with. So to compound the fact that my daughter has just lost her mother, insult is added to injury by misinformed ignorance from your child. Ignorance I can only imagine she picks up from her parents."

Daniel had been home for almost two hours before Nairne showed up. After walking home Nairne had gone down to the river. Zane had come looking for her when he arrived home from school. No doubt he would have heard all about it, but she didn't respond; she didn't want to speak to him or anyone else. She knew dad would be furious; he hated being called to the school. Eventually, she tried to sneak into the house, but he heard her creeping up the stairs.

"Nairne, get yourself in here right now." His voice was stern. She walked back down the stairs and into the kitchen. "Sit down and explain yourself."

"I knew you'd be like this, but she was asking for it, you should have heard what she said. You've no idea what it's like. She's a stuck up little bitch."

"Nairne, you know better than that. Yes, her behaviour was terrible, but you shouldn't rise to it."

"That's easy for you to say. You don't have everyone in

the class talking about you and calling you names. Anyway, it's not as if I hit her, although I wish I had."

Daniel could hardly maintain his composure, for although he knew he had to reprimand her he also knew the other girl deserved it and deep down he was impressed she had held her temper. As Mr Watson had said, what is an appropriate punishment for kissing someone? It showed a certain maturity of response that he didn't expect from Nairne. She was impulsive, just like he had been at that age; she led with her fists and thought about the consequences later.

"I've been to the school and you have to stay off until Monday."

"That's not fair; can I stay off too?" Zane interjected.

"No, not unless you kiss Laura Howard as well," said Daniel, stifling a laugh.

Zane looked horrified at the thought.

"And what about her?" Nairne demanded.

"Laura will be suspended for a week and a note of her behaviour will go on her record permanently, so Nairne, think about it. Using your fists is not always the best way." He winked as he spoke.

THREE

The next few weeks held little excitement; so much for all the new pupils, thought Nairne. All the extra kids at school had caused was more friction. Every week a few new faces appeared. Some stayed, some moved on again.

Although life was uneventful here, this was not the case in other parts of the country. The first floods hit in the last week of September. In the south of England, more than nine inches of rain fell in two weeks. Initially, the rain brought relief to the drought stricken farmers, who had experienced the third dry summer in a row, but by mid October it became clear that the rainfall was not the blessing people had hoped for.

The baked earth encouraged the downpour to surge into streams and rivers causing hundreds of flash floods. Massive landslides closed two motorways and destroyed extensive sections of the main East Coast rail line. The sheer force of the water washed away cars, roads, bridges and buildings; pedestrians caught unaware were swept away. Each night Nairne and her dad watched destruction and despair unfold on the news as householders, in wellington boots, muddy and wet, surrounded by the remnants of their lives, gave heartbreaking interviews. There were the obligatory images of firemen rescuing pensioners or family pets stranded in upstairs rooms. By the end of the third week, over one hundred and forty thousand people were homeless. Hundreds of thousands more were without power or water and billions of pounds of damage had been inflicted; businesses closed and insurance companies were in crisis.

"It's not even October. It was January last winter before we saw this kind of thing," Daniel remarked. "And God knows last year was bad enough."

"What will they do with all the people?" Nairne asked.

"I don't know, but this is only the start. If this weather continues for the next few months there will be millions looking for new homes. The Government has declared a state of emergency in Kent and troops are being mobilised to help with the rescue work."

"That couldn't happen here, could it?" Nairne asked.

"Oh no, we're too high up for this house to get flooded even if the river burst its banks. That was one of the reasons I chose this place."

"What, because you thought this might happen?"

"Nairne, I knew this would happen. Fifteen years ago, climate change was the news story. We'd had several extremely hot summers, then a couple of wet winters with floods and snow. Everyone agreed we needed to do something about it, so there were new laws about recycling and efforts were made to encourage us to be energy efficient, but then the temperatures dropped for a couple of years and people lost interest. That, combined with our victory in the Middle East which secured more oil for the West, made people think they would be all right."

"But how could they just lose interest? They hadn't solved anything."

"No, but people don't like being told what to do. The Government tried taxing energy use and putting up the price of petrol, but people didn't vote for that party again and with the China paradox things got worse."

"The China paradox?"

"Back then China was expanding rapidly, using coal for most of its energy production so people said 'why should we change? Our little efforts won't make any difference'. It was every polluter's perfect excuse."

"Mrs Craig, our geography teacher, says even if climate change does have an effect it won't be that bad. She says it will take another seventy years before a rise of one metre in sea level and that's ages away."

"I hope you and Zane will still be around in seventy years, and your kids, my grandchildren. In climate terms seventy years is the blink of an eye and these are only predictions, they could be sooner or later. Anyway, let's hope your dad's just a crazy eccentric and that nothing will happen." He pulled a mad expression as he spoke.

Nairne laughed although she did not think he was mad.

In mid October notices appeared in local newspapers. There was to be a meeting in the town hall. Nairne's father didn't usually take much interest in the town, but he thought they should all attend.

They found seats at the end of a row near the front. Zane hadn't been keen and after a few minutes he wandered off to talk to a couple of friends from school.

By seven o'clock the hall was packed. The four officials sat on stage beside a lectern and screen. Councillor Walker made the opening address. He was a portly man in his mid fifties, with a very cheery disposition, but tonight the perspiration was breaking out on his forehead and he scanned the crowd anxiously.

"We have two guests with us this evening to explain the situation: from the Department of the Environment, Dr Goldsworthy, and from the Department of Rural Affairs, Ms Whiting." He indicated towards two of the people sitting on stage.

"Dr Goldsworthy will give us an overview of what the weather has in store for us in the coming months. Then Ms Whiting will explain what the Government is asking each one of us to do. So I will hand over to Dr Goldsworthy."

The Doctor stood up and began.

"Good evening to all of you. I am going to give a short talk and will take questions at the end. As many of you will be aware, for the last four years we have experienced the hottest, driest summers and coldest, wettest winters in living memory. Older members of the audience will remember such dry summers in previous decades as climate change has been with us for some time and I am sure you are all familiar with the science." He explained how the polar ice caps were melting and sea levels were rising, slowly, so there was no reason for alarm. "However, the extra fresh water from the melting ice is also affecting ocean currents and this is leading to an increase in storms and extreme weather. We, in the UK, are seeing minor changes in comparison to some other areas of the globe such as the central African droughts and of course the flooding that the Asian sub continent has experienced." As he spoke, images flashed onto the screen showing the all too familiar faces of starving children in Africa, their bellies distended, followed by pictures of shantytowns flooded with raw sewage.

"So how does this affect us? You will be familiar with the floods in the UK earlier this year, and the problems London, Birmingham and other cities in the south are experiencing with water supplies." Now the images were of the UK. "The weather forecast over the next four months is poor. We are currently predicting greater rainfall than last year plus colder temperatures." Maps of various English counties flashed onto the screen with rainfall levels in graphs and charts.

"In light of last year's flood damage and the start of the problems this year it has been agreed that we will be evacuating some people to new locations across the UK. This is a temporary measure and it is hoped that many of them will be able to return to their homes within two to three years. This will give us time to improve flood defences, drainage systems, power and water supply systems. We are asking all areas of the UK that are not experiencing such severe problems to assist. For details of the actions required in this region I will now pass over to Ms Whiting, unless there are any questions."

There was silence for a few seconds and then the first hand went up; a microphone was handed to the questioner.

"Good evening, Douglas Livingstone, Community Councillor. Doctor, you said these incomers might stay here for two years, we have already seen a huge influx of people over the last six months driving property prices through the roof out of the reach of local people. Tell me where are all these folk going to live?"

The question was met with a murmur of approval.

"I think that may become clearer after Ms Whiting has presented, but rest assured the Government will provide support."

The murmuring subsided and Ms Whiting took her place at the podium. She spoke with confidence and authority. A map of the region was displayed with the major towns clearly marked with population numbers.

"As you are all aware this region has one of the lowest population densities in Scotland, or for that matter the UK. The area is mainly rural in character with four main population hubs. She indicated these on the map. It is proposed that each area of the country takes in the same number of people in direct relation to their current population. The Borders region with a population of one hundred and twelve thousand will be expected to take an increase of ten percent, which means …"

"Over ten thousand people," an incredulous voice shouted from the audience.

"Thank you; yes, just over ten thousand people. This may seems like a large number. However, bear in mind these people will be dispersed across the entire region. The Government will provide temporary accommodation in the form of static caravans on managed sites. Temporary units will be provided at local schools where required. We hope some people will be able to work or to set up businesses, and for those who are unable to do so benefits will be provided. This is a massive undertaking, therefore we are also asking anyone with empty property who is able to accommodate a family, or anyone who has room in their home for an individual to consider helping. Rentals will be paid."

The crowd was positively restless, with the murmur of voices rising.

"Let's get this straight, you want us to take complete strangers in and let them live in our homes. These immigrants could be druggies or child molesters." The same questioner shouted out.

"Let me make this clear. These people are not immigrants," Ms Whiting sounded annoyed. "These are British citizens and this is a time of national emergency. We are not forcing anyone to take a stranger into their home. We are asking all of you to consider how it would be if this area was under threat and you were reliant on the goodwill and assistance of people in another part of the country. Are there any other questions?"

"Yes." A woman near the back of the hall stood up. "If we are able to offer someone accommodation what do we do?"

"Thank you, we will be taking people's details at the end of the meeting. Notices will also appear in the local press and staff at your local council office will be available to give more information."

"Dad." Nairne nudged her father. "We could take someone in to the other part of the house, couldn't we?"

"It's a bit basic; there's no kitchen."

"No, but they could share ours until you could get a second hand cooker and stuff. I bet it would be nicer than a caravan."

"We'll see, Nairne, we'll see."

Councillor Walker gave the closing remarks and the audience began to disperse.

"See if you can find that brother of yours, I want to speak to a couple of people."

Nairne searched the hall for Zane; she pushed her way round and between groups of gossiping locals.

"Take in even more of these incomers." She heard one disapproving voice.

"It's a bloody disgrace!" said another.

"How bad can it be? As for disease, that's only happening because of all the dirty foreigners they've let in…." replied the first.

Eventually, Nairne spotted Zane's fair hair. He was messing about with two other lads from school. She tapped him on the shoulder.

"Dad says it's time to go."

He said goodbye to his friends and followed her through the crowded hall. Their father was talking to Dr Goldsworthy; the discussion looked quite heated.

"I understand what you're saying Mr Grear, and yes I would have to concede you could be right, our estimations could be on the low side."

"So if I am right, how long will it be before we are forced to take people in?"

"I don't know. That would be a policy decision, but I think you might be surprised by people's willingness to help. After all, it's merely chance that they're not in the same situation."

"Looking at the mood of this lot I doubt you'll get enough volunteers, but I hope I'm wrong. And thanks – it was very interesting."

They shook hands and Daniel turned round.

"All right time to get the two of you home."

Five minutes later, they were sitting in the front of the truck. It was a miserable wet night and the rain lashed against the windscreen.

"So are we going to take in some people?" Nairne asked again.

"Why are you so keen? You normally hate it if we have visitors. Anyway, we don't have to decide tonight. I think we should sleep on it."

FOUR

Every day when Daniel got home from work Nairne would ask again.

"Have you decided yet? Will we take people in?"

"I'm still thinking about it," Daniel sighed. "I'm proud of you for wanting to help, but we need to think it through."

"What is there to think about? We have the space. People don't have anywhere to go. What are you worried about?"

"It wasn't in my plan, for us, for this place. After Zane's accident, I had a plan: moving here, keeping both of you safe, and providing for your future.... I chose this place carefully. It was large enough to provide for us as a family, it has its own water and now we have our own power. I wanted to keep us safe, separate from what was going on out there. I know everyone thinks I'm crazy, but when Zane was in hospital I had all that time to think about what was really happening in the world, about what was going to happen. Taking in extra people didn't figure in the plan. But I know you're right, if we can help other people then we should and it's not like they will be here forever, right?"

"So should we call the council offices?" Nairne asked excitedly.

"Better still let's go in tomorrow and speak to them. Happy now?"

"Yes, dad, it'll be great, just wait and see."

Two weeks after the meeting in the town hall, Daniel and Nairne went to the council office and offered the use of the other part of the house.

"It has two bedrooms, a bathroom, living room and

space for a kitchen. The building is in need of decoration but it's habitable," Daniel explained.

The girl behind the desk took down all the details.

"Have you had much response?" Daniel asked.

"Yes, quite a few people have come forward and some people who own holiday homes have been contacted and have offered their properties until the Spring. However, we are always looking for more. Thanks for coming in today Mr Grear. We'll be in touch when we have suitable tenants for you."

"Oh, yes, I meant to say, they need to have their own car, it's a fair walk to town and the buses are pretty infrequent."

"Okay, thanks again Mr Grear."

They left the office.

"Satisfied?" Daniel asked.

"Yes, I think we're doing the right thing," Nairne replied.

"Let's hope you're right. Anyway, the rent will come in handy; the way prices are going we need to save as much money as possible over the winter."

Nairne was so excited at the prospect of new people to stay she talked about it all the way home.

"We'd better get the place ready," she exclaimed. "We don't want people turning up and finding it in a mess."

"You heard what the girl in the office said, it could be weeks or months before anyone needs it."

However, Daniel Grear had spoken too soon and over the next twenty-four hours everything changed.

Zane was in the living room flicking the television remote from channel to channel.

"Zane, if you're not watching it switch it off." Daniel was sitting at the dining room table drawing up his invoices for the week. The film was interrupted by a news flash. Daniel looked up as Zane increased the volume. The newscaster looked solemn.

"I repeat, at seven fifteen this evening, during some of

the worst weather that London has experienced in recent times, a high tide surged up the River Thames and breached the Thames barrier. Initial reports suggest the flooding in the city centre is extensive and includes several underground tube stations. Emergency services are on hand, but their rescue efforts are being hampered by the severe weather conditions with winds of over seventy miles an hour in some areas. There is widespread damage to properties, many roads are closed and it is feared many people may have lost their lives. We now go live to our correspondent Damien Clarke in Westminster."

The picture on the screen changed to one of a reporter, clutching at his flimsy coat. Rain lashed against him as he shouted into the microphone.

"As you can see there are scenes of devastation here, with water up to two metres deep in some places. Traffic is at a standstill and we have had reports of fire crews battling to rescue people trapped in underground stations. Ambulances are struggling to make it to the scene of the worst floods, as roads are impassable. St James' hospital in Westminster has closed its doors to new admissions and casualties are being taken to other hospitals. The unconfirmed death toll is over two hundred and fifty and is expected to rise. Now back to the studio."

"Once again the headline – a major breach of the Thames barrier has flooded central London. For ongoing coverage please switch to the BBC news channel."

"Zane, flick over to the news channel," said Daniel. "Let's see if there is any more information." The news channel was showing live broadcasts from various reporters at locations along the East Coast. It seemed London was only one of the areas affected. The heavy rain was set to continue for the next few hours with more forecast for the following three days. Daniel reached over, took the remote and selected the Scottish news option.

On the east coast, North Berwick and Perth were flooded and in the west, the river Nith in Dumfries had burst its banks and there was localised flooding along the Solway Firth. Next, he selected the north of England; Northumbria had escaped the worst of it, but further down the coast, at the Humber estuary, the damage looked significant.

The newscaster gave lists of the road closures, traffic warnings and continued weather warnings: the Government had announced a state of emergency in three regions, including central London. The army was mobilising and starting to help with rescue work and civil disorder. People were advised to stay at home and tune into their local news for further information. Evacuation of some areas was inevitable and this would be set in motion as soon as the weather subsided.

"It looks like our house guests could be arriving sooner than we thought," said Daniel. "Tomorrow, if it's dry enough, we'll give the place a good clean."

They spent Sunday preparing the other part of the house.

"I'm not doing all the housework, just because I'm the girl," said Nairne defensively.

"Would we do that?" Her father teased. Zane, as usual, pulled a face.

"Right, for that useful contribution Zane, you have just won the prize of doing all the vacuuming, and that includes high up round the ceilings; let's get rid of all those cobwebs. Remember these are city folk so they'll be afraid of spiders. Nairne, can you wash the windows and clean the bathroom? I'll see if I can pull together some basic furniture for the kitchen. Oh and Zane, bring in some logs; there are a couple of old wicker baskets in my workshop. We'll light the fires and get some heat into the place."

"We need to put up curtains," said Nairne. "I think we might have some from our old house in the attic."

"All right, can you look those out? Give them an airing and we'll put them up."

The work took all day, but by four o'clock they were

sitting in the newly cleaned kitchen. Daniel had found an old table in his workshop and some fold away chairs. The window sported a second hand blind and a length of worktop, left over from their kitchen had been installed next to the sink.

"Next week I'll go into town and pick up some second hand units, a cooker and fridge. Anyway, I suppose they can always come to ours for their dinner if they need to. Well done, the rest of the place looks great."

"What about bedding?" Zane asked.

"I hope the council will provide them with some and I suppose they may bring some things with them," Daniel replied.

That night, after supper, they sat and watched the news. The weather for them had been wet and windy but nothing unusual. However, torrential rain continued to batter the east coast and much of the south of England. The death toll in London had reached over four hundred and was still rising. The wind had subsided during the day, but returned as darkness fell. News footage showed the centre of London as a ghost town; the only vehicles were army trucks. Young soldiers, armed with tear gas, chased looters from shops. In some of the estates affected by flooding people had taken to the streets to protest at the lack of water and power and to demand that the Government take action.

"Dad, what's going to happen to all those people?" Zane sounded worried.

"Oh, the Government will help them; they'll be relocated to different places until their houses can be fixed."

"But what if they get flooded again and again? They can't keep fixing the houses can they?"

"No, I suppose they'll have to stay in their new places."

"So does that mean the people we get might stay forever?"

"Oh no. It's temporary accommodation, until new

houses can be provided. They'll only be here for a few months," he replied. Nairne felt his statement lacked conviction, and she began to have a niggling doubt about their generous offer of help.

"Do you think that we've made a mistake offering our place?" she asked, when Zane was out of earshot.

"No, to be honest if people don't offer I'm sure the authorities will force us to take people in. It's better to do it on our terms than be forced to take part later. You were right to persuade me. We are very lucky. Just look at those poor people; what must it be like to lose everything?"

FIVE

Daniel arrived home soaking wet and exhausted; his boots and overalls were caked in mud. He'd been working next door at Mr Cranshaw's farm helping repair two of the barns. The high winds at the weekend had wreaked havoc and old man Cranshaw was worried if they didn't repair the holes quickly, one strong gust might tear the entire buildings apart. Being on top of a barn in driving rain was not Daniel's idea of fun, but Mr Cranshaw put a lot of work his way and he'd been a good friend to Daniel when they first bought the smallholding.

"Ah, the best smell imaginable, homemade soup. You read my mind. I'm going to have a quick shower." He ruffled Nairne's hair on the way past and shouted a greeting to Zane, who was sitting puzzling over his homework.

Nairne handed him the letter after he had eaten. She knew what it contained and although part of her was pleased, she knew dad would be concerned.

"So what's this then?" he asked as he tore the envelope open and scanned the contents. "After the Christmas break the school will be open four days a week until further notice. So how are the two of you supposed to get a proper education?"

"Mr Watson spoke to all the older kids today. He said they didn't want to do it, but there wasn't any choice. He said there was a problem with fuel for the school buses and they're expecting even more pupils in January. They're having a meeting at the school next week," Nairne replied.

"Well I'll be going along to that."

"Dad, one of the boys in my class said they were getting two old people from London to stay with them. She's over eighty and he's ninety. They're arriving on Saturday. Will we get an old couple?"

"I don't know, Zane, where does this boy live?"

"In town. Their house has a granny flat, but his granny's dead so it's empty."

"I think for old people they'll try and house them near to all the facilities. I did say we need people with a car, otherwise they'll be stuck here; like you when you're off school."

"We're supposed to do school work at home and you're supposed to supervise us," Nairne laughed.

"I'll be out at work, but that won't stop me popping home unannounced to check up on you."

"Oh dad, do we have to? Can't we do stuff round here instead? I could come to work with you. That would be much better." Zane was desperate to finish school and start work, although his father doubted he'd be quite so keen at getting up early and going out in bad weather.

Zane was a good worker if the task wasn't too complex and didn't take too long. He showed a natural ability to work with wood, while Nairne was very quick with anything electrical or mechanical. Daniel often thought she'd make a good engineer. Zane, on the other hand, would be unlikely to pass any exams so it was important that Daniel taught him sufficient skills to make a living. He'd always intended that Zane work for him; that was one of the reasons he started the business. It offered Zane a chance at some sort of job security.

The next morning Daniel was on his way to work when he got the call from Cheryl Brown at the council offices. Over two hundred people were arriving in the town over the next two days requiring accommodation. Cheryl suggested a family: a man, woman and teenage boy who had their own transport.

"Would they be suitable?" she asked.

"Can you tell me anything about them?"

"No, I'm sorry Mr Grear; we only have their names: Mr

Unwin, his teenage son Paul and his partner Ms Groves. Mr Unwin is a business man. They are making their own way here from London so we know they have access to a car. They hope to arrive on Friday afternoon, so if you're happy to take them they'll register with us and we'll give them supplies and directions to your place."

"OK, that's fine; I'll make sure I'm at home to meet them."

"Thanks Mr Grear. If you have any questions please give me a call."

A family with a teenager it would be great, thought Nairne.

"We'll need to get some food in for Friday and cook them dinner."

"Remember Nairne, they're going to be here for some time, they aren't guests. They'll have to get used to making do next door, but it's a kind thought, I'm sure they'll be exhausted after such a long drive. You give me a list and I'll pick up some food in town tomorrow."

School was torture. Nairne was the first out of her class when the bell rang and was waiting impatiently at the bus stop when Zane, his hands thrust into his pockets, sauntered over to join her. The bus journey took ages and when they arrived they tore up the winding drive to the house. A black Range Rover, stuffed with bags and boxes, was parked outside. Zane flinched at the sight of the gleaming bull bars. At least they managed to salvage some possessions, thought Nairne, as they ran past it and into the house.

Nairne and Zane burst into the living room. The man and woman stood up to greet them as their father introduced everyone.

"Nairne, Zane, this is Mr Unwin." The man leaned forward and shook hands with both of them. His grip was firm and his nicotine-stained fingers were warm and soft. Nairne had not imagined he would be so old, as his son was their age, but she guessed he must be at least fifty. He was dressed casually: open necked shirt, slacks and a light weight jacket. Three thick gold rings decorated his fingers, complimented by a gold chain around his neck. His slicked back hair was greying slightly at the temples and receding on top.

"Please call me Garrick," he smiled. "We're going to be next door neighbours after all." He introduced Pamela, his partner. Pamela was a little younger than their dad. She was all curves, peroxide and lip-gloss and her handshake was limp and ineffectual. Nairne guessed they had packed in a hurry, as Pamela was hardly dressed for an evacuation. She wore a fitted blood red dress, sheer nylon tights, stilettos and a soft cashmere wrap draped over her shoulder.

"Nairne, what an unusual name. Is it Scottish?" she asked as she shook Nairne's hand.

"Yes, it means 'of the river' or 'water'," said Daniel, as Pamela moved over to Zane. He was captivated and she held onto his hand just a moment longer than necessary.

"Why Daniel, he is so like you, look at those beautiful blue eyes." Zane went scarlet with the compliment.

"Pamela, you're embarrassing the boy. Just ignore her, Zane. She's a terrible tease," Garrick said, turning to face the armchair where a young man was lounging.

"And this is Paul. Paul stand up and say hello properly." The boy reluctantly dragged himself from the comfort of the armchair and nodded to each of them. He was taller than Zane but lankier, with a severe haircut and a gold stud in one ear. His complexion betrayed an indoor lifestyle and his clothes an interest in this week's fashion.

"God, sorry about this. No manners these days. Isn't that right?"

"Don't worry, mine can be just as bad, believe me," Daniel responded. Nairne thought that was a bit unfair. Zane was always polite to visitors or so shy he was silent and so was she, most of the time, but perhaps her dad was trying to make them feel at ease.

"Now Garrick, why don't we give you a hand unpacking the car? Nairne has offered to cook us all up some supper so we would be very pleased if you would join us."

"That's very civil of you, we'd love to."

Nairne and Zane charged upstairs and changed out of their school uniforms while Daniel took the new arrivals round to their new home. Unlocking the door, he handed the keys to Garrick.

"It's pretty basic and as you can see there's no proper kitchen, but I thought we could pick up a second hand cooker and some units tomorrow. To be honest we didn't think anyone would need the place until after Christmas. We've put in some furniture that we had, but we're a bit short of bedding."

"Oh that's okay; we were given stuff at the council centre in town when we registered and they said they could provide us with basic cooking equipment if we need it. Anyway, Pamela's not a great one for cooking, so as long as we have a kettle and microwave I'm sure we'll manage," Garrick replied.

Pamela could not disguise her disbelief as they went round the rest of the property. She had never lived in a house without central heating and had never lit a real fire. Paul tagged along behind, teenage disinterest emanating from his very being until they reached the living room.

"So where's the television?" he asked.

"We don't have a spare one," said Daniel. "My two don't watch it that much, but you're welcome to come round and watch ours until your dad can pick one up."

"So what package do you get?"

"Package?"

"Yeah, satellite packages. Do you get all the sports?"

"No we don't have satellite; we only get the free channels. As I said mine don't watch it that often." Paul sighed, his glum expression deepened; Garrick glared at him.

"Less time spent staring at the television would be no

bad thing. It's all he's interested in, getting out and doing some exercise would be a better use of your time."

The car was crammed full and had been packed in a hurry: clothes and other possessions were stuffed into cases and carrier bags. On the back seat were two large plastic bags from the council offices, containing duvets, sheets, pillows and blankets. Zane brought them in.

"Ah, Zane, why don't you give Paul a hand with his stuff and help him make up his bed," Daniel suggested.

"Okay, will do." He took one of the bags of bedding through to the smaller of the bedrooms. Paul was throwing his clothes into the wardrobe, carelessly.

"Dad says I've to give you a hand with the bed." He ripped open the plastic bag and spilled the contents on to the mattress. Paul made no effort to help or to communicate.

"I can't wait to hear all about London, I've never been; I've been to Glasgow and Edinburgh but not London, my mum lived in London, in Kensington, do you know Kensington? Anyway, she doesn't live there anymore. Where was your house? Was it near Kensington? You might have met her, my mum, her name was Angela, I've got pictures of her next door, I could show you if you like." Paul did not respond; he watched Zane struggle with the unruly duvet and cover. "It said on the news lots of London is under water now, was your house flooded? Is that why you had to leave?" On and on he went, barely pausing for breath. Zane tended to chatter when he was nervous and he was nervous of Paul. Although they were the same age, Paul seemed older. Zane often felt like that with other boys of his age: the way they would answer adults back, the way they chatted up girls, he could never do that. He had his female admirers as he may not have been the smartest boy, but his good looks did not go unnoticed.

Daniel's voice interrupted the awkward silence that descended once Zane ran out of verbiage.

"How are you two getting on in there? Do you need a hand?"

"No dad. We're nearly finished," Zane replied.

They returned to the living room where the others were waiting for them.

"Let's stoke up the fires so the house will be warm when you get back after supper," said Daniel, placing a large dry log on the living room fire and replacing the guard.

"Is it safe, leaving it like that?" Pamela enquired. "Since we'll be next door?"

"Yes, it's fine if you've got the guard up. Anyway, I've fitted smoke detectors, just in case, so we'd hear it before the whole place burns down." For a moment she looked concerned.

"Oh, you're teasing us city folk," she giggled like a schoolgirl and flashed her impressive smile.

While the others unpacked, Nairne dashed round the kitchen. The chicken was in the oven along with the potatoes. She prepared carrots and parsnips from this year's harvest. For starters, there was homemade soup and for pudding, a cake from the bakery. Her father had bought wine and some cans of coke for Paul. She felt nervous. They rarely had visitors and she wanted the evening to be a success.

She mulled over her first impressions. Garrick made her think of a flash television character from one of the soaps. She half expected a medallion to pop out from his open necked shirt and she would bet he had tattoos on his arms. Pamela reminded her of a blonde from the adverts, all giggles and heels. How could anyone walk in those? Nairne mused. More importantly why would anyone want to, especially if you were fleeing from a flood? *Oh, hang on while I put on my stilettos;* even the thought made her giggle. And as for Paul, she wasn't sure what impression he had made; he seemed a bit unfriendly, but maybe he was just shy. He was quite nice looking in an unassuming way and certainly well turned out. He'd fit right in with some of the rich kids at school. She heard them arrive back, and Pamela appeared at the kitchen door.

"Oh, darling, it smells divine, do you need any help?"

Nairne glanced over at Pamela in her blood red dress, with matching fingernails; a variety of sparkling rings decorated her fingers as she rubbed her hands together nervously.

"Thanks, it's nearly done. You could ask my dad if he can come and open the wine and get the drinks out."

"Okay, dear." Pamela retreated from the kitchen and moments later Daniel appeared.

"Is everything okay?"

"Yes, I'm nearly ready to serve the soup. I need you to sort out the wine and stuff?"

"Certainly chef. Anything else chef?"

"Yes, don't be cheeky or you'll not get any supper," she laughed.

Nairne had been worried that she'd made too much, but there was no reason, Paul and Garrick ate huge amounts, both asking for seconds. Pamela, as suspected, pushed her dinner round the plate, teasing it with her fork and insisting she should only have baby portions.

"I must watch my weight; a girl's got to take care of her figure you know. Nairne's too young to have to worry about that. I remember when I was her age I was all arms and legs, positively skinny." Nairne could not imagine that Pamela was ever skinny. It seemed amazing to think that puberty could do that. She certainly hoped nothing like that would ever happen to her.

"If my Pam could cook like your daughter I don't think I'd ever leave the house. That was lovely, exactly what we needed, wasn't it Paul?" said Garrick. Paul grunted what sounded like a yes; he had hardly spoken except to ask the occasional question about how long they would have to stay and how far away town was.

"You have a very talented daughter, Daniel, very

talented indeed."

"Oh I know," Daniel replied. "She's a good cook, but she has plenty of other talents." She blushed, it wasn't like her dad to compliment them; he was usually quite reserved.

When everyone had finished Zane and Daniel cleared the table. Pamela went through to the kitchen to help with the tidying up only to return moments later aghast to have discovered there was no dishwasher.

"That's what I keep dad and Zane for," said Nairne. "Anyway dishwashers use lots of water and electricity."

"So do you do all the cooking? It must get to be quite a lot of work on top of all the housework and school," Garrick asked.

"Oh, I don't do all the housework or all the cooking. Tonight's dinner was my idea and Friday's my turn. Just be grateful you didn't arrive on a Thursday or you would have had Zane's speciality, omelettes with everything. We all take turns at everything: looking after the animals, the vegetable plot, fixing stuff around the place. After all, why should that be my responsibility?"

"Quite right, dear," said Pamela. "We girls have to stick together."

"When was the last time you did any housework or cooking?" snorted Paul sarcastically. "I doubt you even knew where the kitchen was in our old house."

"Enough of that lip young man." Garrick's tone was light hearted, but there was a hard edge.

"Yeah, whatever," Paul retorted, and sunk into silence again.

Their visitors retired to their new home at half past ten. Nairne was glad there was no school tomorrow as she was exhausted. It was hard work spending an evening with strangers. Dad was more relaxed than she had imagined he would be; surprisingly he and Garrick appeared to have a lot to discuss. They had arranged to go into town and pick up some more equipment for the kitchen and there was also the matter of a television for Paul.

"Why don't you and Paul come in to town with us tomorrow?" asked Daniel. You could show him round, introduce him to some of your pals from school then next week he won't feel so strange going in on his first day."

"I suppose," said Zane. "If he wants to."

"I'll come with you," said Nairne. She could see Zane was unhappy about something.

"No it's okay," he responded, putting on a not too convincing smile.

"Right, time you two got some sleep. It'll be a busy weekend helping our new neighbours settle in."

Nairne and Zane went upstairs, while Daniel finished clearing up.

"So what's up?" Nairne asked when they reached the top landing.

"Oh nothing, it's just, he's not very friendly. I don't think he likes me."

"Of course he does, he's shy; think what it would be like going somewhere totally new where you didn't know anyone. Of course he liked you, especially those baby blue eyes. Let's face it, what's not to like?" she teased. "Don't be such a worrier, Zane; you'll see, he'll turn out to be your best friend."

SIX

Nairne opened the curtains; the sun had not yet risen, and even if it had, a thick blanket of grey cloud covered the sky. It was drizzling, but at least the wind had subsided. Her dad was already up and making breakfast when she entered the kitchen.

"Give that brother of yours a shout. I told Garrick we'd head into town at half past nine and you know how long Zane takes to get organised."

She shouted up the stairs until she could hear Zane emerging from under the duvet and stumbling to the bathroom.

"Are you okay staying here Nairne? I don't think it would be fair to leave Pamela alone."

"I suppose so, as long as I don't have to entertain her or anything."

"Why, didn't you like her?"

"She's a bit…. you know...."

"No, what?"

"Blonde," said Nairne scathingly. "There are girls like her at school; they think if they smile and giggle everyone will run after them. What's truly weird is it seems to work."

"That's a bit harsh," he replied. "I think she's simply from a very different background; she's used to having money and nice things and people to look after her. Garrick said they had a housekeeper in London who did all the cooking and cleaning, so this must be a bit of a shock."

Nairne was amazed; her dad always disapproved of people who lived like that.

"So what did she do all day?" Nairne asked.

"Oh I don't know, I suppose she would go shopping and Garrick said they did a lot of entertaining, so I suppose she had to do that."

"Yes, but they had a cook, so all she had to do was turn up and eat. The only challenge there is sticking to baby portions."

"You shouldn't be so judgmental Nairne, she seemed nice, and Zane certainly liked her. You know, I think it'll be good for you to have a woman's influence."

"God, you sound like Miss Kelly, maybe you're right. Maybe I should study *Pamela*," she said the name with feeling. "Then I could let my brain turn to mush, concentrate all my efforts on wearing this month's shade of lipstick, leave school, move in with an older man and do bugger all every day."

"Language Nairne and you know that's not what I meant." Sometimes Daniel thought his daughter was a bit too smart for her own good. She could be very abrasive and although only fourteen, she was so set in her ways. Pamela was certainly not the practical type, but there was no harm in her.

By nine forty-five, everyone had set off to town. Daniel and Zane went in the pickup followed by Garrick and Paul in the Range Rover. Paul seemed unhappy about being up so early, so did Zane; at least they have one thing in common, thought Nairne.

There was no sign of Pamela yet. She had overheard Garrick telling her father that Pamela wasn't really a morning person. Nairne wondered what sort of person that made her, other than lazy. Nairne took the opportunity of having the place to herself to get on with some of the days' chores. She cleared away the breakfast things, got the school clothes into the machine; which meant entering Zane's room and rifling through the dirty washing, not one of her favourite tasks. At this rate, she would have all her stuff done by lunchtime and could spend the rest of the day reading. Nairne loved to read, especially books that involved travel to foreign lands. She had never been abroad; air travel was expensive and her dad didn't approve. He said it was unnecessary for people to fly round the globe to sit on a beach. Nairne would not have wanted to sit on the beach, but she would have loved to go exploring. By ten thirty, the indoor tasks were completed and the rain had eased off. She donned her coat and boots and went out to the hen house to check for eggs. It had been a wild, wintry night so she checked on the goat and took the leftovers of last night's dinner down to the pigs. They rushed over to greet her snorting and banging into one another. She emptied the bucket into their trough and they tucked in, delighted with the peelings and scraps from the table. Pamela emerged from the house. She spotted Nairne and tottered over to see what she was doing. She was wearing a different outfit today: a long, snug, cobalt blue skirt and a grey mohair jumper with a man's outdoor jacket slung over her shoulders.

"Oh, pigs!" she exclaimed. "Aren't they adorable?" The pigs continued to snort and gobble. "Look at the mud, poor things; it must be cold out here trampling around in that."

"Yes, but they have a pig arc." Nairne indicated over to the corrugated shelter. "We put them in the outbuilding when it's very cold and they get straw to bed down and when the weather's better we open the gate and they can wander about in the woods."

"Don't they run off?"

"No, the woods lead down to the river on one side and there are fences so they can't go anywhere. Once, a couple of years ago, one of them went across the river in the summer when the water was low, but Mr Cranshaw, who owns the farm next door, brought her back."

"So what are their names?"

"The big one is Mona and that's Lisa, her daughter. Mona had a litter of eight this year."

"So where are they?" asked Pamela innocently.

"In the freezer," said Nairne. "We sold them to the butcher, he slaughters them and we get a share of the meat."

"But don't you get upset?"

"No, that's what they're for. The first year we gave all the piglets names, but that makes it harder when the time comes. You must be cold, let's go in to ours, it'll be warmer." Nairne felt sorry for Pamela, as she looked frozen. These were obviously her warmest, most sensible clothes and they were still impractical for here.

Soon they were ensconced in the warm kitchen. Nairne made tea and coffee while Dog lay in front of the fire soaking up the warmth.

"God, it really is bleak out here, isn't it?" Pamela gazed out the window across the gravelled yard and bare vegetable plot. "No offence intended, you've made the house lovely, it's very …. homely."

"None taken. It can be bleak at this time of the year especially when it rains, but when the snow comes and we're cut off from town and everything is white, crisp and silent it's beautiful. Spring and summer are the best though, when the vegetable garden is bursting with things to eat and the place is swarming with birds and insects. You can hear life going on all around, then you want it to stay like that forever."

"But what do you do out here? There must be parties and shopping and boys; don't tell me there isn't a nice young boy at school you've got your eye on?" Nairne blushed. She wasn't used to this kind of discussion with an adult.

"I don't particularly like shopping, I don't need anything and I'm not a great one for parties."

"But what about your friends, how do they get here to see you?"

"I see them in school," she lied; somehow, she couldn't bear to tell Pamela she didn't have any proper friends. It would make her sound like a failure and Nairne hated that.

"And what about Zane? Such a lovely young man, I bet he has all the girls out here visiting him, hmm?"

"No, Zane's … very shy with people, I guess some of the girls in school probably think he's cute, but he would be clueless. He's …. a bit immature."

"You should see Paul. He never misses a chance to chat up the girls, I'm sure he'll be able to teach Zane a thing or two. He's a bit wild that one, a bit of a leader; he takes after Garrick."

"I think Zane was nervous of him," said Nairne.

"He needn't be, Zane's a smart young man, and with that lovely smile he could charm the birds from the trees."

Nairne hesitated. She wasn't sure how much to tell Pamela, but it would be obvious to them soon enough that Zane had problems.

"No, Zane's not very smart. He got knocked down when we were kids. He suffered head injuries, that's why he's so shy. He has to go to the special classes at school so I don't think he'll ever be out chasing the girls."

"Oh, I'm so sorry…. I had no idea… that must have been terrible for your parents and you…. If you don't mind me asking, where is your mum?"

"Her and dad split up years ago," said Nairne. "She moved to London, but she… died earlier this year, in that dysentery outbreak in Kensington, in the fire."

"Darling, I'm so sorry." Pamela was mortified. "My big mouth, I didn't mean to pry or upset you, oh you poor things…."

"It's okay. We're fine about it. She'd been gone for so long. We were upset at the time, but we hadn't seen her in ages."

A few minutes later they heard the door open. The others had returned from the town, laden with bags and boxes.

"How did you get on?" Pamela asked, as they came into the kitchen.

"Not too bad," Garrick responded removing his jacket, which was dripping wet. "We got some more bedding and towels, food, a microwave and dishes, but we couldn't get a cooker."

"I've never seen the place so busy," said Daniel. "The supermarket had hardly any food left."

"What about the council offices?" Pamela asked. "Yesterday they said they could help us get settled."

"Yes, we went along there, but it was mobbed. I reckon at least thirty or forty families must have arrived in the last few days and everyone is on the lookout for spare furniture and appliances. Daniel got talking to, who was it?"

"Bill Neil, he's a local Councillor. He said there are another fifty families due at the end of next week. They're setting up a temporary caravan site at the agricultural park. They have a couple of toilet blocks and power supply for when they take in visitors in the summer. He said the council are getting in forty static caravans."

"Oh, I don't fancy that, not in the winter," said Pamela.

"No, we've been very lucky to get this place," Garrick said. "You know we are very grateful."

"Oh, don't mention it. "I'm sure you would have done the same for us," Daniel replied.

Nairne watched the exchange; she didn't feel quite so confident as her father.

"Wait until you see what we got you, Pamela." Paul went into the hallway and brought back a giant blue plastic bag.

"Just your kind of thing." He reached inside and pulled out a dark green waxed jacket. "Very hunting, shooting, fishing." He held it out to Pamela, who looked at it in astonishment. "Oh, and these." This time he pulled out a pair of green wellington boots.

Pamela took them. She put on the jacket, which was a little large and then she slipped off her shoes and struggled with the unwieldy boots.

"Not very flattering are they?" She glanced down at the rubber appendages. "But at least I'll be able to go outside without getting soaked. Thank you darlings." She leaned over and kissed Paul on the cheek; he pulled a face.

"And you, darling." She gave Garrick a kiss on the lips.

"So what did you two get up to?" Nairne enquired, looking over at Zane and Paul. Zane had been very quiet since their return.

"Nothing much, we had a wander round, met a couple of the guys from school, Spud and Eric. We think Eric will be in the same class as Paul."

"Isn't that nice," said Pamela. "At least on Monday there will be a couple of familiar faces."

"Yeah, great," said Paul. "Anyway, I'm going to take the stuff we bought round to ours."

"We'll give you a hand," Nairne volunteered, glancing at Zane.

The three teenagers carried the bags to the house next door. Nairne unpacked the food and put it away, while Zane and Paul brought in the other items.

"So what did you make of town then?" Nairne asked.

"It's a dump," Paul responded. "There's nothing to do, it only took fifteen minutes to walk round it, it's too small and this place is a dump as well. It's the middle of nowhere."

"We like it here," said Nairne pointedly. "After all, who would want to live in the city, it's so dirty and expensive and there's too much traffic. We find plenty to do here, don't we Zane?"

"Yeah, I suppose," said Zane. "Although it's not much fun this time of year. But in the summer it's good, you can go fishing and shooting and spend all day outside; it's great in the summer."

"We'll be long gone by then," Paul retorted. "This is only temporary; my dad's got loads of cash, so he'll be able to buy us something much better than here. He said property prices here are much lower than in London, so once he sells our place he'll be loaded."

"But who would want to buy a house in London? After all it might get flooded and thousands of people are trying to get away from there?" Zane asked, puzzled.

"What would you know about it?" Paul snapped back at him. "You've never even been to London."

"I was only asking," Zane's tone was subdued. He glanced at his sister. Nairne was furious. It had been a perfectly reasonable question. She decided at that moment she did have a view on Paul and it wasn't very flattering. She put away the last couple of tins of food.

"That's us finished; maybe we'll see you later. Come on Zane, we'd better get back." Zane hesitated but followed her back to their house.

They met Garrick and Pamela in their hallway, collecting their coats as Daniel showed them out.

"So about seven thirty. That's fine. We'll see you then." Daniel shut the door behind them.

"Are they coming round again?" Nairne asked.

"Yes, they don't have a TV or anything yet so I asked if they wanted to come round tomorrow evening for a drink and a chat. They'll make their own dinner."

"Are they bringing Paul?"

"Yes, if he wants to come. Why?"

"Oh no reason," said Nairne unconvincingly.

Sunday was a day of rest for Nairne and Zane. After the chores were completed, they entertained themselves for the afternoon; there was no sign of life from next door, but as dad said, they must be tired and would need time to unpack and settle in. After Sunday dinner, their neighbours arrived. Paul joined Zane in front of the television while Daniel opened a bottle of wine for the adults who sat at the dining room table chatting. Garrick examined the books on the shelves behind the table.

"I can see you have a pretty keen interest in all this global warming stuff," said Garrick.

"Yes, I've been interested for years," Daniel replied. "That was one of the reasons I bought this place."

"I don't understand," said Pamela. "What's special about here?"

"Several things: for a start we're way above sea level, we have our own water supply. The house came with enough land to grow most of our food and keep some livestock, plus the woods provide fuel."

"And the wind turbines, do they provide all the power you need?" Garrick asked.

"No, but enough for the essentials. When we're not using it, the extra power is stored in a battery and when that's full it feeds back into the grid, so the electricity company sometimes owe us money."

"But I've heard they're pretty expensive to buy."

"Yes, we bought the first one, but the other two I made myself with some help from one of the agricultural engineers in town. We also put in solar panels on the south side of the roof; they provide some of our hot water, especially in the summer when we don't have the fires lit. The stove in the kitchen heats the water and a couple of small radiators so it's fine in the winter."

"So you're pretty self sufficient. That's smart Daniel, very smart."

"I wouldn't say self sufficient, but we could get by if we had to."

Nairne watched the conversation unfold. Garrick didn't strike her as a man interested in the environment.

"So what do you think then? How bad is it going to get?" Nairne could see her father was in his element. He loved talking about this stuff.

"Put it this way, this is only the beginning," he said, his tone sombre.

"But the Government keeps saying that this weather is a cycle and that it will settle down. I remember the heat wave that started in two thousand and six, and the wet winters, but it didn't last," Garrick responded.

"Yes, but because it settled down we didn't change anything. There was lots of talk, but we didn't do it. Token gestures, all that fuel tax and Government campaigns, we needed to radically change how we lived. Look, the experts say that the planet can withstand a certain change in global temperatures, it has happened all through history. However, anything greater than one or two degrees a century is too fast. We'll exceed that even if we stop all the carbon emissions right now. It takes decades for their effects to dissipate."

"So is it too late to do anything?" Pamela enquired.

"No, it's going to get worse, but if we act now we could reduce the impacts for the future. It's too late to stop it happening completely, but there may still be time to save us."

"That's a bit melodramatic, isn't it? You say that as if it's the end of civilisation as we know it." Garrick chuckled.

"For lots of people it's already too late," said Daniel. "Look at Bangladesh, it floods every year, millions of people have been permanently displaced, and there are parts of Africa that haven't had rain for a decade. The tragedy is they're facing the consequences of our pollution, but it won't stop there. If the temperature rise continues the Gulf Stream could fail, then the weather we're having now will seem like a picnic. Never mind the occasional flood, the entire climate would shift. We could be facing winters with freezing temperatures and storm surges, large areas of the country could be abandoned and it won't just be the UK, the whole of Europe will be affected."

"But the Government must know about this, they'll have plans," Pamela replied confidently.

"Perhaps, but I can't imagine what. If it gets that bad huge amounts of the arable land in the world will be destroyed, we won't be able to import enough food. Look at the news this summer, we have a heat wave and people riot. That kind of thing is going to get worse, because everyone thinks someone else is to blame and that if they complain it'll get fixed."

Nairne listened in. She was amazed at how little Garrick and Pamela seemed to understand; it was as if all the 'unnatural disasters', as her dad always referred to them, had never happened.

"Anyway, I don't want to alarm you. I am describing the worst case scenario." He smiled reassuringly at Pamela.

"You've certainly given us something to think about," said Garrick. "But it's getting late, time we left you in peace, especially with school tomorrow. Paul, it's time to go home now." Paul grunted and struggled to his feet.

Daniel showed their visitors out.

SEVEN

The ground was hard with a fine coating of frost, the first of the year. At least it's dry, thought Nairne, as the three of them set off to catch the school bus.

"I don't understand why we have to leave so early," said Paul. "School doesn't start for another forty minutes and it's only a few miles away."

"Yes, but the bus doesn't go straight there, there are four other farms to visit on the way," Zane replied.

"God's sake, I'll need to get dad to take me in. I'm not doing this every morning."

"What, getting up early or moaning about it?" asked Nairne.

"Ha ha, very funny." He strode ahead of them.

"Why did you say that?" Zane hissed at her.

Paul and Zane sat together on the bus; Nairne was relegated to the seat behind. She didn't mind, it was good to see Zane with a new friend. He had mates at school, but most of them were complete losers, who went to some of the remedial lessons that Zane attended. He didn't have a best friend and it would be great if he and Paul became like that, even if she didn't like him.

They soon settled into a routine: Zane and Paul sat together on the school bus and at lunch times she would find them with a few other new boys. It meant her lunch periods were lonelier than before as she had not made new friends of her own. Part of that was due to Laura Howard; ever since the kissing incident she had gone out of her way to ensure new pupils were aware of Nairne's popularity rating.

Some days she felt quite low, but it was good to see Zane fitting in. If she did go and join them Zane would look uncomfortable. Let's face it having his little sister tag along hardly helped with his credibility, thought Nairne.

School felt different; with over two hundred new pupils. It was more of a crowd control exercise than a place to learn. Fights, previously a rare occurrence, were common place. The new caravan park was full; new faces appeared at school every few days. Nairne couldn't wait for the four day week to start after Christmas; anything that reduced the time she had to spend there was a good thing.

Life at home also settled into a routine. Garrick would visit a couple of times a week, sometimes with Pamela and sometimes alone. He and dad would talk. Zane would visit Paul. Daniel would suggest Nairne should go too, but she always had an excuse not to. She knew Zane wouldn't thank her for butting in, plus, she didn't like Paul. She felt the same way about Garrick although he hadn't given her any reason. Most evenings, she had company. Dog, who was originally Zane's soon realised he had been replaced in her brother's affections so Dog switched his allegiance to Nairne. He would follow her round the house, his expressive eyebrows furrowing and his low whining signifying when he needed to be patted. Nairne didn't mind; she loved Dog. He wasn't the brightest, but he always loved attention.

At weekends, after they finished their chores, Garrick usually took Paul and Zane into town. Her dad often worked on Saturday mornings, as he needed the money.

Supply and demand, that's what Garrick said, the more people the higher the prices. Garrick talked as if he knew a lot about business, although Nairne never quite understood exactly what he did for a living. He didn't seem to do much, although other men visited the house, business acquaintances according to Pamela. When the others were out, Pamela would call round for coffee. Nairne didn't mind as Pamela was obviously lonely; she didn't have any friends, she couldn't drive and they only had one car. Garrick took her out for dinner to one of the local restaurants at least once a week, but she was finding it difficult to adjust. For the last three weeks, they had eaten Sunday dinner together; Daniel thought it was a nice gesture as the kitchen next door was not exactly comfortable. Moreover, he guessed Pamela wasn't used to fending for herself.

Nairne was home alone and had settled down to read a book about the wildlife in the Amazon river basin. She was wondering how many of the animals still existed when she heard a knock at the door. Pamela stood outside, a shawl wrapped round her shoulders.

"Come in." Nairne stood aside to let her pass.

"Oh, thank you darling; I'm not disturbing you, am I? It's freezing next door and with my boys away I wanted to ask a favour." She handed Nairne a small cardboard box containing two chocolate éclairs.

"I know they're bad for us but what the hell."

"I'll put the kettle on; you go in and get heated up."

They sat in the living room; Pamela clasped the hot coffee mug and devoured her chocolate éclair.

"Hmmm, that was delicious. Honestly Nairne, if I spend much longer stuck out here I'll go mad. It's okay for Paul; he has you and Zane and school. Garrick has his business and your dad for company, but I feel completely lost. That's one of the reasons I came round. It's not long until Christmas and I thought, since you have been so generous, inviting us round so often that I should cook Christmas dinner and we could have it together. What do you think? Or do you have plans?"

"We don't have anything planned, but there isn't much room at yours. What if we ate here?"

"If that would be all right, but we'll provide all the food and I'd like to make the dinner. Between ourselves I'm not exactly a whiz in the kitchen, so I wondered, could you show me how to make some things? Garrick and Paul always rave about your cooking; it would be such a lovely surprise if I could make something for them."

Nairne was flattered. She could cook well enough to get by, but no one had ever asked her to teach them anything.

"Okay, I've got some recipe books that belonged to my mum; you could choose some dishes. We could make some soup this afternoon and then try a couple of dishes next weekend."

When Daniel got home that evening, he could smell the vegetable soup as he entered the house.

"Is that for tonight?" he asked. Nairne was washing some dishes; she looked very pleased with herself. It was good to see her look happy, Daniel thought, as he often worried about her. She spent too much time on her own with her head in a book, especially now Zane had Paul.

"Yeah, I made it this afternoon. Pamela came round and asked me to show her how to cook so we made a batch and split it. I noticed we're getting through the vegetables; I don't think we'll have enough to last until spring."

"Yes, I suppose we've given quite a lot to next door over the last few weeks. We need to make sure we plant more this summer."

"But they'll be gone by next winter, won't they? Paul said once Garrick sells their house they'll be able to buy somewhere."

"I don't think it'll work out like that. Too many people are trying to sell and with the threat of more floods their house is worth next to nothing. Last time they were lucky, there was no actual damage to their place, but who knows."

"So how long will they stay?"

"I don't know: Garrick's got some business deals underway, he says if they work out he should be able to afford somewhere better, but it'll take a few months. Anyway, even if they move, chances are we'll be asked to take other people in. I heard from Bill Neil at the council that they are expecting more arrivals in the New Year."

"But there's nowhere for them to stay."

"I know, but you saw those pictures on the news last

night."

Nairne nodded. The news had shown the mass migration of refugees in Holland. They had suffered substantial flooding and anyone who could afford to get away was on the move.

"Where's Zane?" Daniel asked.

"He's out with Paul. Garrick said he'd bring them home by about six thirty."

"Didn't you want to go with them?"

"Yeah, Zane's going to want his little sister tagging along. Honestly dad, you've got no idea." Daniel shrugged. The kids had always been inseparable and he knew Nairne always looked out for her brother but maybe she was right, Zane needed to get some independence and Paul was a good kid.

At seven o'clock Daniel went next door to see if Pamela had heard from Garrick. She tried his mobile; there was no answer.

"I'm sure they'll be here soon, I know Garrick was meeting some business contacts from back home, they've just arrived and were looking for somewhere to stay, but it is so hard. Maybe the meeting has run late."

"Is it another family who need housed?" Daniel enquired.

"No, just two young men. They're good boys, but the council have said they aren't a priority. Garrick is keen for them to find somewhere nearby. He's worked with them for years and it would be great if they could help out with this new business venture of his."

"Look, I could speak to Mr Cranshaw. He lives alone in that farmhouse and I'm sure he will be forced to take people soon enough if the numbers keep rising, so better the devil you know…."

"Daniel, that would be great. Garrick would really appreciate it. It would mean a lot to him." Pamela smiled. "Thanks, I'll let you know as soon as Garrick rings but I'm sure they will be back soon."

By eight o'clock, Pamela joined them. She had left messages on Garrick's answering services but there had been no response.

At eight fifteen her phone rang.

"Garrick where are you? We were getting worried....... Why, what's happened? Okay, I'll let them know." She clicked the phone off.

"What is it?" asked Daniel.

"Oh, they're all right. Garrick had a meeting at the Black Swan; the boys said they'd meet him there. Apparently, there was trouble outside the pub. A man was stabbed to death. The police wanted to interview everyone, so they've been at the police station. However, they're fine and they'll be back in about twenty minutes."

"God, what is happening to this place?" Daniel sighed.

The three of them arrived back shortly before nine. They filed into the house, cold and hungry.

"Stay for some supper," said Daniel.

"Thanks, that would be good. Sorry about this, I would have called earlier, but the police didn't give us much opportunity."

"As long as everyone's okay, what happened?"

"We don't know. I was in seeing a couple of old friends; they have just arrived."

"Yes, Pamela explained they're looking for accommodation. I'll put a word in with Mr Cranshaw next door," Daniel interrupted.

"Thanks, that would be great. Anyway, a couple of blokes got into a disagreement in the pub; one of them left. Later, when I came out to pick up the boys, there had been a scuffle outside, three or four men; next thing one of them is lying on the ground, stabbed in the chest. The police think it must have hit his heart. He was dead within seconds. Since the boys had been outside, the police wanted to interview them both. I sat in with each of them, as they're underage, I thought it would speed things up, rather than you having to come down to the station. I hope that was okay."

"Yes, thanks."

"Neither of them actually saw anything, did you boys?" Paul and Zane both shook their heads.

"It was all over so quickly," said Paul. "And there was a crowd so it was impossible to see what happened...... I don't want any supper. I think I'll call it a night." Paul looked ill; he excused himself and went next door.

Dinner was a quiet affair and at nine forty-five the visitors went back home. Daniel was perplexed.

"I can't believe the place has got so bad someone gets killed at six thirty on a Saturday night. It must have been a bit of shock, son."

"Yes," Zane mumbled. "I think I'll go to bed. I'm a bit tired after all that hanging around."

"Okay, are you all right?" The boy was pale, probably shock.

"I'm fine, dad. Goodnight." He went upstairs.

Garrick and Pamela sat in their temporary living room. The fire had died down and the house felt chilled. Paul was in his room; they could hear the constant beat of his music. Garrick poured himself a whisky.

"Do you want one?"

"No, darling, I'm fine. But you look like you need one."

"Too right. Bloody hell, what a night! I tell you, you can't turn round in a town like this without people knowing your business."

"Garrick, what happened?"

"Nothing for you to worry about, but the guy that got stabbed is local and there's enough bad feeling about us incomers. I told Stevie to take it easy, but no, he kept pushing the guy… and for Zane to see it, well..... In a place like this, you can't afford to draw attention to yourself."

"But I thought the boys didn't see anything."

"Paul got there after it was all over; apparently he was busy saying goodbye to some girl he's been seeing, two's company and all that. Zane had run on ahead and he saw the whole thing. He didn't get a clear look. They both told the police they saw nothing. I gave Zane some friendly advice."

"Garrick! – Zane's only a boy and not a very bright one at that. What if he tells someone?"

"Don't worry, he won't. I've explained to him that now he's made his statement to the police if he changes it he'll be in big trouble… social services and all that, he won't say a word."

"And Paul?"

"Paul didn't see and anyway he knows the score… he knows what's expected of him."

Zane slept late although he had gone to bed early.

"We'll let him sleep," said Daniel as he sat down to breakfast with Nairne. "I heard him get up during the night."

"Do you think he's okay?" Nairne asked. "He didn't seem himself last night."

"No, but it must have been pretty unpleasant. I'm sure he'll talk to us about it if he needs to."

Zane surfaced at half past ten. Nairne had already tended to the animals. He made himself some breakfast and came through to the living room.

"So what are you doing today? Are you going round to Paul's?" Nairne asked.

"No, don't think so, I think I'll stay in." He was sullen.

"Are you okay?"

"Yeah, why shouldn't I be?"

"Just asking." She left him sulking and went to her room. When she came downstairs at lunchtime he was still moping around.

"What is it? Is it last night? Was it awful at the police station?"

"No it was fine; I spoke to that policewoman, the one who came when mum died. She was nice, it's just…."

"What?"

"You should've seen him Nairne, the look on his

face..."

"What, the dead man?"

"No, the man with the knife; he was smiling.... like it was funny. The other one hit the ground, and there was this awful gurgling sound from his chest and all this blood poured out his mouth.... It was horrible."

"But I thought you didn't see anything."

"I didn't it was just.... never mind." He fell silent. Nairne attempted to get him to explain, but she knew better than to push him. He could be very stubborn; he didn't like pressure and could be quite aggressive.

"So what did you do yesterday, before then?"

"We went to Craigie's house; he's one of the new boys in my class. There were a few of us round and a few girls, including Laura Howard."

"What was she doing there?"

"Oh, she came with that other new girl with the weird name."

"Tamara Potter-Smith," Nairne spoke the words in an affected English accent.

"Yeah, she's going out with Craigie."

"No accounting for taste. Be careful with Laura, she's such a bitch."

"She was okay yesterday; in fact she was quite nice," Zane replied.

Nairne grimaced and raised her eyes to the heavens in disbelief.

EIGHT

Word of the stabbing spread throughout the school, making celebrities of Zane and Paul. At break time kids crowded round them.

"So what happened?" asked Spud excitedly. "I can't believe you guys saw it."

"We didn't get there until afterwards. He was already on the ground. But you should have seen the blood man; it was everywhere. Isn't that right Zane?" Zane nodded in agreement; he disliked being the centre of attention.

"All the same, it must have been awful," Laura twittered.

"In London you see lots of stuff like that." Paul was revelling in the attention.

"So how many people have you seen killed before?" enquired Nairne. She knew Paul was just showing off.

"I've seen things."

"Like what?" She wasn't going to let him off that easily. The rest of the group looked on expectantly.

"Gang stuff and that, you know."

"No. What?" Her tone was confrontational.

"Ignore her Paul, we know what you mean," Laura interjected. Paul's complexion was beginning to colour; he didn't like to be challenged.

"Zane, maybe you should tell your sister to watch her mouth." He walked off with Laura hanging on his arm.

"Maybe you should tell me yourself if you're so tough," Nairne shouted after him. Zane glared at her.

"Nairne, what did you do that for?"

"'Cause he's nothing but a show off. He looked as sick as a dog when you came home on Saturday night. He thinks he's a real hard man. It's just talk."

That night Zane and Paul sat several seats away from Nairne on the bus. She read her book and steadfastly ignored them. She was angry with Zane for taking Paul's side over hers. That evening after supper Zane got ready to go next door to play computer games.

"Why don't you ask Nairne to join in?" Daniel asked. "She seems a bit down." She had hardly spoken since arriving home.

"Oh, dad," Zane whined. "Paul only asked me. He didn't invite us both."

"I can't imagine he'll mind. Go on, ask her." Reluctantly, Zane returned to the living room.

"Nairne, do you want to come round to Paul's?"

"No thanks." She didn't look up from her book.

"See. She doesn't want to go." Zane informed Daniel on his way out.

"So what's up?" Daniel wasn't going to let this slip by. "Why don't you want to go round?"

"I'm not interested in computer games."

"Come on Nairne, I know when you're sulking. What is it?"

"It's Paul. He's such a show off. You should hear him at school: *I've done this, I've done that*; he talks crap and Zane takes it all in. And to make things even worse he's started hanging round with Laura Howard."

"Who, Zane?" asked Daniel.

"No, Paul, I think they're going out with each other. I'm sure she's only doing it to annoy me."

"Paul's a handsome lad, maybe she likes him."

"Handsome? No way, he's… he's…."

"Me-thinks the lady doth protest too much!" Daniel grinned at her.

"What, you think I'm jealous?"

"Aren't you?"

"Not of Laura Howard. God, I wouldn't go out with Paul if he were the only boy in school; he's a creep."

"You sure you're not jealous? Or feeling left out since

he and Zane are such good friends?"

"Dad you just don't get it, I'm glad Zane's got a friend, I'm only sorry it's Paul. I don't trust him and I don't think Zane should either."

"But you know how important this is for Zane, he needs to get out and mix with kids his own age. Paul seems like a sensible lad, he'll look out for him and it doesn't mean Zane likes you less. Maybe you need to give Paul another chance.... What do you think?"

"Fine, if you say so, but only one more chance."

The victim turned out to be James Purves, a local man, twenty-eight years old, married with a four year old daughter. The local paper carried a front page story; a photograph of the grieving widow, clutching a picture of her dead husband took centre stage. The police issued an appeal for calm; there was no conclusive evidence that the perpetrator was an incomer. Although the street was busy at the time of the stabbing no one appeared to have seen the culprit clearly. Three men were being sought in connection with the incident; they were described as white, mid twenties to early thirties, casually dressed; one was wearing a black baseball cap and was unshaven. No new witnesses came forward.

NINE

The next two weeks passed peacefully in the Grear household. Nairne and Paul settled into a mutual truce, although they weren't exactly friendly. Nairne sat apart on the school bus and no longer sought out Zane at breaks. Instead, she took a good book to school and occupied herself at lunch break. Paul and Nairne spoke, but never engaged in any lengthy conversations. Meanwhile, Pamela was a regular visitor at weekends. Nairne had gone through some of the recipe books with her and they decided on a menu for Christmas day. Pamela persuaded Garrick to take her to Edinburgh to one of the large supermarkets and invited Nairne along.

"You should go, you might enjoy it," Daniel teased.

"Hmm, it's not my kind of thing, shopping."

"Yes, but it was kind of Pamela to invite you; she thinks it would be a treat."

"Okay, I'll go, if you stop going on about it. I'll go round and tell her... Happy?"

Daniel laughed. He thought deep down Nairne wanted to go, but it would be bad for her image to admit it.

With only five days left to Christmas, they set off early. Garrick had business in the city and agreed to drop them off at the shopping complex. Pamela, dressed in her smartest outfit, sat in the front. The Range Rover was smooth and silent in comparison to their pick-up truck and Nairne relaxed in the back. The window wipers swished back and forth, with little effect. The torrential rain appeared to have deterred some of the crowds, but as they neared the city bypass, the road began to clog. Garrick was impatient, beeping the horn at any unfortunate driver deemed to be causing delays.

"Garrick relax, we're not in a rush." Pamela caressed his hand as he gripped the steering wheel.

"Not in a rush? We're wasting precious shopping time. Just wait Nairne, you won't believe this young lady when she hits those shops. It's a vocation and one she is very good at," he laughed.

"I'm not that bad. Honestly, you'd think that was all I ever do, I haven't been shopping for ages; I've got a bit of catching up to do."

"Nairne, I'm relying on you to keep an eye on her. Don't let her buy more than we can fit in the car."

Nairne sat back, enjoying the banter, as the buildings and landscape began to change from urban sprawl to gentrified dock-lands. The wide, flat roads were lined with cafes and bars. The red brick and glass shopping centre stood at the end of a long straight road. Garrick parked in the lower level of the subterranean car park.

"Right, Tony's picking me up outside, so here are the spare keys so you can dump your shopping as you go. I'll be back at about four thirty; I'll call if I'm going to be late." He handed Pamela the keys and gave her a kiss.

"Now Nairne, keep an eye on her, I don't want to be bankrupted. Oh, and take this, treat yourself." He handed her three ten pound notes.

"I can't take this…" she held the money back out.

"Of course you can, call it an early Christmas present and a thank you for all those delicious meals." He strode towards the exit, the phone pressed to his ear.

"Yes, Tony, okay, ten minutes…. See you then."

Pamela and Nairne took the lift to the top floor. The doors glided open revealing a throng of Christmas shoppers and an array of bright neon Christmas decorations. There was a wide mezzanine with glass balustrades; they walked to the railing and looked down. Exquisite reindeers and sleighs constructed from thousands of lights flew through the air. At the end of the building, a curtain of glass formed the gable. The view across the water was spectacular; rain lashed against the glass while small yachts bobbed like toys on the choppy water.

"What will it be first, pleasure or pain?"

"Pain, let's get the food," Nairne replied.

"Okay, pain it is. You take the list, I'll take the trolley."

The food hall was vast. They set off down the cramped aisle full of bad tempered shoppers with overflowing trolleys. Nairne read the list, and gathering some plastic bags from the roll, she set off to get the fruit and vegetables. Pamela guided the trolley through any gaps in the traffic and eventually reached the end of the aisle. Nairne was close behind with an armful of items ready to deposit. Nairne couldn't believe how much people were buying. The shelves were crammed with luxury produce from around the globe. It was amazing, and so were the prices.

The next aisle was slightly quieter; the lull before the storm as the fresh and frozen meat aisle was the busiest yet. Nairne squeezed between people to reach the food. Impatient women, with sullen children in tow, blocked the way while men barged about shouting questions to their partners.

The checkouts were mobbed and after queuing for ages they finally wheeled their full trolley to the lift, went down and unloaded the bags into the car.

"I can't believe how much people buy. How can they possibly get through all that in a few days?"

"I'm sure most of it goes in the bin," Pamela replied, as she lifted the last of their bags into the car. "People always over indulge, that's what Christmas is all about isn't it? You know we make a good team; I would have still been in the first aisle if I'd been on my own. I think we've earned some lunch."

Pamela selected a coffee shop on the top floor; it was quieter and more expensive than the main café area. Nairne took out her purse when the bill arrived.

"Put that away, this is Garrick's treat," Pamela chided, as she paid with one of her numerous plastic cards. "Anyway, this is a thank you for all my cookery lessons and for all the help you'll be giving me with the Christmas dinner. The boys will be amazed if I pull this off; they'll never believe I could do it."

"I don't see why not, it just takes practice, you'll see."

"You are sweet, darling, but they never expect me to be able to do anything other than shop. Then I don't suppose Garrick chose me for my cooking skills," she laughed. "He always says I'm a luxury item, chosen for my decorative value, but it would be nice if he credited me with some sense."

Nairne was horrified; Pamela spoke about herself as if Garrick had bought her in a shop like a piece of jewellery and she seemed flattered at that thought.

Next, it was time to start shopping for Christmas presents. Garrick had not been exaggerating, Pamela shopped as if it was a military campaign and she took no prisoners. She entered each shop and detected the most expensive items, as if she had some sort of price radar. After an hour or so of trying things on and asking Nairne for her opinion Pamela sensed Nairne was losing interest.

"Why don't you take the money Garrick gave you and find something for yourself. What would you like to get?"

"A book. I saw a bookshop along at the end of this row," said Nairne, perking up at the prospect.

"Well, if that's what you want. I'll keep browsing. I'll wait for you here."

Nairne rushed to the bookshop and located the Natural History section; she rummaged through the books until she located a large volume on insects of the Amazon. Nairne loved wildlife books and her favourites were insects and sea life. Her chosen purchase was packed full of photographs of the most unlikely looking creatures. While she queued at the counter an announcement interrupted the classical in-store music.

"Would all shoppers who are parked in the lower basement car park, please make their way to the nearest information point." Nairne paid for the book and hurried back to Pamela.

"Pamela, did you hear the announcement? I think there's an information point along there at the end." She pointed to the glass curtain wall.

The concourse was crowded and by the time they reached the desk a small crowd of shoppers was being addressed by a security guard.

"I'm sorry to inform you that the lower car parking area is flooding so please make your way back to your vehicles and move them to the front of the shopping centre. Security staff will guide you to a suitable parking location. Please accept our apologies for this inconvenience." Disgruntled shoppers rushed towards the exit signs as Pamela approached the desk.

"Excuse me, my boyfriend's Range Rover is parked in the lower basement but he's gone into the city for a business meeting. I have the keys, but I can't drive."

Nairne watched Pamela in action, the smile and the helpless look. The young man was charmed.

"Don't worry, madam, I'll radio down and get one of the security men to move it for you. He'll meet you at the bottom of the stairs. He flicked on his radio and called for one of his colleagues. Minutes later Pamela and Nairne met the burly security guard who carried their bags over to the car, popped them in the back and drove the vehicle out of the car park. A few moments later, he returned with the keys, his jacket soaked from the torrential rain.

"I've parked it to the left of the main entrance. Word of advice, I'd not wait too long before taking your daughter home especially if you have any distance to travel. This water is coming back up the drains so it won't be long before the roads start to flood."

"Okay thanks." Pamela took the keys from him and smiled. She took out her mobile and called Garrick.

"So what's been going on?" Garrick asked, shaking the rain off his coat.

"The car park flooded; they moved the car outside for us. The guard who moved it said he thinks the roads will soon be closed, so I thought we'd better get home."

"The roads were pretty bad on the way back here; the taxi had to take a detour." The three of them dashed to the car and minutes later they were driving down the quayside. The guard had been right, water was bubbling up from the drains. Garrick headed away from the docks, but the roads were worse.

"The ground must slope down," he said, ploughing through some deep puddles. "Good job we've got this thing, at least we'll be able to get through." He patted the steering wheel affectionately. They turned another corner and found a small car sitting in the road surrounded by water, stalled. A young man was pushing the vehicle while a girl was steering. Garrick edged round the side of them mounting the pavement and sending a giant wave towards them.

"Aren't we going to stop and help?" Nairne asked, looking back at the trapped car.

"Not our problem Nairne, we'd get soaked, and anyway they should have thought about it when they bought such a tiny car," Garrick laughed and Pamela smiled in agreement. Nairne sat back in silence. Another fifteen minutes and they were back at the bypass; the roads were treacherous. Nairne was relieved when they finally reached their destination. She got out the car and thanked Garrick again for the money.

"What did you get yourself then, something nice to wear?"

"No, I got this," said Nairne, pulling the book out the bag. Garrick looked puzzled.

"Oh, if that's what you wanted."

"Yes, it was, and it was very kind of you. Thanks."

Daniel was cooking when Nairne came in.

"So did you have fun?"

"Yeah, it was fine…"

"You don't sound too sure."

"Garrick gave me some money to get myself something." She put the book down on the table. "And Pamela and I got on really well, although I can't believe all the rubbish she bought. It was just…."

"It was very kind of Garrick."

"I know, he said it was a thank you for all the meals. Oh and the car park and the roads were flooded, and on the way home, we passed this poor couple with their car stuck in a giant puddle and Garrick drove round them. He said it was nothing to do with us and that it was their own fault. I thought we should have helped them…. You wouldn't have driven round them, would you?"

"No probably not," said Daniel. "But it's different in the countryside; people are used to helping each other out. I suppose in the city, especially in places like London, people are frightened to get involved with strangers."

Nairne wasn't convinced. Garrick certainly hadn't looked scared. In fact, he had seemed to think it was funny.

"Insects, a book on bloody insects!" Garrick laughed as he poured himself a drink.

"Oh, don't make fun of her, she's a lovely kid, just a bit different," Pamela scolded him. "Anyway, I couldn't have managed without her. So how did you get on?"

"Interesting, very interesting, I think Tony and I can do some serious business, so it shouldn't be long before we can expand our operation."

"So will we be able to move into town? Or maybe to Edinburgh, a nice apartment?" she replied excitedly.

"Let's not be too hasty, Tony thinks a rural location could be useful and I think we've landed on our feet here, especially since the old boy next door has agreed to take in the boys. Okay, so the house leaves a lot to be desired but think about it Pam, if things get worse we have our own water supply, power supply and enough land to produce food. This place could work out to be perfect."

TEN

It was the twenty-third of December, the last day of term and Nairne couldn't wait for three o'clock. Two weeks without Laura Howard; it was fantastic.

The atmosphere was buzzing; it was difficult to tell who was more excited the pupils or the staff. It had been a difficult term with all the new pupils. The school was like a war zone and the teachers were under-resourced peace keepers.

Nairne sat at her desk before the first lesson and watched as girls exchanged cards and gifts. Cries of delight greeted each useless trinket. As Laura handed over her beautifully wrapped gift to Tamara, now her closest friend, the contents of the small shiny parcel drew gasps of adoration.

Nairne didn't get any cards, but then she didn't give any out. She couldn't grasp it; they saw each other almost every day, so why exchange cards with cute pictures of robins and snowmen, take them home for a week then put them in the bin. Why didn't everyone agree not to give each other a card and save a whole lot of time and trees?

It didn't take long for Laura to notice.

"Oh look, what a shame, Nairne didn't get anything. That must mean she doesn't have any friends, poor Nairne. Do you want me to be your friend?" Her doll face contorted into a sad expression and she pretended to cry.

"Gypsies don't do Christmas, do they?" Tamara joined in, sniggering. Her comment elicited a squeal of excitement from Laura.

"Of course. You're right. Gypsies can't afford Christmas!"

"Why don't you come over here and I'll give you a

present you'll never forget," said Nairne.

"What, like I'm going to come over there so you can hit me. I'm not stupid you know," Laura fired back.

"Who said I was going to hit you? Come over and be my friend. Isn't that what you suggested?" said Nairne blowing Laura a kiss.

Laura's face turned scarlet as other kids in the room began to laugh. Everyone knew she was still mortified about Nairne kissing her, especially since Nairne had delighted in pointing out that Laura was a lousy kisser.

At two thirty, there was a full assembly with the obligatory Christmas carols. The hall was packed; if new pupils joined next year, they would need to have assemblies in two sittings, thought Nairne. As it was there was only standing room and the pupils were pressed in tightly. It took Mr Watson's loudest bellow to subdue the chattering.

"Okay, settle down. The quicker we start the quicker you'll be going home. Firstly, let me take this opportunity to thank you for your co-operation over the last few months. I know it has been difficult, but I am proud of the warm welcome you have shown to our new students. However, when we return there are a couple of items I need to raise. School is only going to be open four days a week, Monday to Thursday."

A shout from the back of the hall interrupted him.

"No-one will forget that sir!" Laughter broke out from pupils and staff.

"Thank you for that Darren, I'm sure I can rely on all of you to remember the extra time off. However, with only four days a week at school you need to work hard, make best use of the time and get some studying done at home. Secondly, the staff and the education authority will be using those days when you are not here, to work on some planning and property issues to cope with the ever increasing school role. We are expecting more pupils in the new term so your continued co-operation is vital. Now have a good break and I will see you all in two weeks time."

The bell rang and the pupils flooded through the door of the hall and out into the playground. Parents waited to pick up their offspring while groups of teenagers bade farewell to their friends and hurried to the school buses. Nairne pushed through the throng of kids and queued next to the appropriate bus. The doors were closed as the driver stood finishing his cigarette. She could see Zane's tall hair bobbing towards her. She waved and he signalled back, then she noticed Paul and Laura close behind, arm in arm.

"Hiya," she greeted Zane as he reached the queue. "Thank God that's over."

"Yeah, two weeks, it's going to be great," he responded. The driver returned to his seat and the doors of the bus opened; they piled on board. Paul lingered outside, his arms round Laura, he gave her a long kiss on the lips. Kids on the bus banged on the windows and whooped at them. Reluctantly, he let go and climbed aboard the bus, while she stood and waved, her face set in a perfect smile.

"Oh Paul, please don't leave me," Zane sniggered as he imitated the lovely Laura, pretending to wipe a tear from his eye. Not a bad imitation, thought Nairne.

"Piss off you spastic," Paul retorted, shoving into Zane as he sat down next to him. "You're just jealous because Laura wouldn't give some dumb bastard like you a second look." Zane stopped laughing immediately. Nairne could see the colour rising in his cheeks. She picked up from where Zane had finished.

"Two whole weeks. How are you going to cope, lover boy?" she goaded.

"It won't be two weeks. Laura's coming to visit on Boxing Day; it's all arranged so the two of you can piss off. You're pathetic."

"Pathetic. Us? We're not the ones snogging Laura, 'I'm so pretty but dumb', Howard."

"God, you're worse than him. You're just jealous."

"What of? Remember, I've snogged her. It wasn't that good." Nairne sat back in her seat. Paul fumed and Zane looked out of the window in silence.

When they reached the bus stop at the bottom of the drive the three of them alighted, but Nairne and Zane walked together as Paul strode ahead.

"He's really angry, I shouldn't have laughed at him," said Zane.

"For God's sake Zane, don't be such a wimp. You were kidding around. He had no right to say that. He's a bully and we don't need him." She spoke with feeling, but Zane didn't look convinced and deep down Nairne knew Zane did need him. Paul's approval and friendship were more important to Zane than anything she could say or do.

ELEVEN

The drumming of the rain woke her. It was dark. She glanced at her watch, half past six. Pulling the covers up around her head, Nairne listened to the thundering downpour. Christmas Day: they were too old to get up early and rush down to unwrap their presents as if every passing minute risked some disgruntled Santa Claus returning to snatch them back. When their mum was still here they always had a tree covered in decorations, with a stocking for each of them. After she left it became a more subdued affair; dad tried to make it feel special, but it wasn't the same. This year she wasn't sure what to expect; she imagined Christmas would be one giant party for Garrick and Pamela, judging by the amount of money Pamela had spent on drinks and presents.

As she rolled over and drifted back to sleep Dog arrived at the bedroom door, whining to be let in. The house was bitterly cold and Nairne obliged. Dog jumped onto the bed and ensconced himself under the top blanket. He wasn't supposed to come in here, but he looked chilled. Nairne pushed the curtains back. Rain lashed against the glass and the wind tore at the bare tree branches, bending the heavy limbs. She shivered and returned to bed, snuggling down under the covers; Dog snored peacefully. She didn't sleep; her mind was racing. Pamela was coming over at eleven thirty to start dinner; they had started preparing last night after persuading her father and Garrick to take the boys out for a couple of hours into town.

Pamela had selected some rather complicated recipes, but most of the work was done. Today they had to roast the turkey. Nairne had suggested goose, as Mr Cranshaw reared some, but Pamela was horrified at the thought of plucking and preparing it; she thought they looked like swans and it would be wrong to eat them. Nairne heard her father in the kitchen making breakfast; she sneaked into the bathroom before Zane. He took ages in there doing his hair, which he'd had cut a bit like Paul's and the rest of his mob at school. Nairne had poked fun, but dad had told her not to. He said it was good that Zane was taking an interest in what the other lads did; he said it would be good for his confidence to feel that he fitted in. Nairne never felt like she fitted in, but dad didn't seem worried about her self confidence.

Daniel and Zane stayed out of the way for the rest of the morning, while the kitchen became a hub of activity. It took several hours of work before the four course Christmas special was ready. As Nairne cleared up Pamela disappeared through to the dining room and set the table. She had brought two large bags with her. Nairne was intrigued, but Pamela had insisted that she didn't look until it was finished.

"Right, that's us nearly ready," said Pamela, drying her hands. Her face was flushed, as despite the dreadful weather, the kitchen was positively warm. "I'll pop home and get my face on and I'll be back over to start serving in twenty minutes. That will give the boys time to get ready."

"Okay," said Nairne. "I'll let them know the feast is imminent."

Pamela went through to the utility room and returned a moment later with a brightly wrapped present. She handed it to Nairne.

"This, darling, is for you, as a special thank you for all your help."

"Thank you. I'll save it for after dinner when we all open our presents."

"No, open it now," she replied excitedly. "I got it for you for the dinner; have a look."

Nairne carefully undid the ribbon, then folded back the

Christmas paper to reveal tissue paper beneath. She opened this to find an emerald green top covered in exquisite beadwork down the front. The body was short and fitted, the sleeves, tight with a flared cuff at the end. The second article was a long skirt of the same fabric. She held the top against her body.

"Perfect," said Pamela beaming. "I knew it. The moment I saw them I thought that is the outfit that will get Nairne out of those shapeless clothes. It's so you."

Nairne was speechless; the clothes were beautiful, simple and classy. Not what she would ever have expected Pamela to choose.

"Do tell me you like them!"

"They're beautiful; I don't know what to say."

"I can see it on your face. You're surprised I could choose something so right for you." She laughed. "Right, go and tell them dinner will be served and get yourself upstairs and get changed. I'll see you back here at half past. And Nairne, let your hair out."

Pamela and Nairne ferried the food through to the dining room, which had been transformed; it was adorned with sparkling new decorations. The best china and cutlery lay there and an exquisite Christmas themed floral display with red napkins covered in reindeer completed the settings.

"Oh, it looks like something from the television," said Nairne, as she laid the last plate on the table. "It looks fabulous!"

"And so do we, sweetheart," said Pamela, squeezing her arm. "I knew that outfit would be perfect for you." Nairne felt self conscious. The new clothes fitted perfectly and she wasn't used to wearing anything fitted.

"Right, dinner's ready." Pamela opened the door and called through. Garrick and Daniel were having a pre meal drink while Zane and Paul were sprawled on the sofa. They piled into the dining room.

"Pamela, this looks amazing," said Daniel. "It's been

years since the house has witnessed this kind of feast."

"Oh, she's always been a dab hand at the decorating," said Garrick. "Quite the little artist, but look at the food. You and Nairne have done us proud," said Garrick, looking at Daniel.

"I haven't helped at all" Daniel replied. "In fact I was banned from the kitchen. I think you have Pamela and Nairne to thank for this."

"You mean you helped Nairne cook all this?" said Paul, looking at Pamela as if he saw her in a new light.

"No," said Nairne, as she entered the room carrying the perfectly roasted turkey on a large silver platter. "I helped Pamela. It was her choices and she did almost all the cooking. She's been learning for weeks."

"Oh, come here," said Garrick, grabbing Pamela by the waist and giving her a kiss. "Now you are the perfect partner, beautiful and talented. And you're not the only one," he said looking at Nairne as she placed the tray on the table. "Nairne, you look fantastic." The others stared at her in amazement.

"Yes," said Daniel, obviously taken aback. The outfit clung to her and he realised his skinny little tom boy had grown into a graceful young woman.

"Don't you know it's rude to stare," said Zane, jabbing Paul in the ribs. He didn't respond, but his expression said it all.

Paul looked away. There was an awkward pause; Nairne just wanted to be somewhere else, she hated everyone looking at her.

"Right, we'd better sit down before this gets cold," she said firmly. "I'll get the wine." She fled into the kitchen with Pamela behind her.

"Don't be shy," said Pamela. "They all thought you looked great. Did you see Paul? He couldn't keep his eyes off you. If you play your cards right Laura Howard will be history."

Nairne was appalled. Her and Paul? He was a mean

spirited bully; she wouldn't look at him if he was the last boy in Scotland.

"But… I'm not... I mean, Paul and me …" she stuttered, but Pamela was already whisking her towards the door.

It was after five by the time they sat down to open their presents. Garrick and Pamela certainly knew how to spend money. Paul had new clothes, computer games, money, films, the list was endless. Daniel could see Zane was amazed at the volume of things. However, Garrick was also generous; he had bought a new computer game for Zane and some more wildlife books for Nairne.

"I don't know what you see in all these animal books," he said, as she unwrapped them. "But your dad tells me they're your favourites." She thanked them and sat pouring over the photographs.

Daniel's gifts were more limited; he didn't have that kind of money to spend, but he'd chosen things he thought they would like. For Zane, he had traded in his old air rifle and got him a newer one with much better sights. Zane was anxious to go out and try it.

"You can go out tomorrow if the weather improves," said Daniel. "And no messing around with it in the house."

"Is it safe?" said Pamela. "It looks quite real."

"Yes, both the kids know how to handle rifles. And they know they're not toys. They'd not do you any serious harm unless it was an unlucky shot, but they'll kill a rabbit at fifty metres or so." For Nairne he had made a toolbox. She loved helping him fix things and had already inherited most of his older tools. Now she had a beautiful handmade wooden box with her name on it.

"Thanks dad." She leaned over and kissed him on the cheek. "It's lovely."

Pamela and Garrick were amazed.

"I can't see my Pammy being impressed with a tool

box," Garrick laughed. "I've got to hand it to you Daniel, you know how to impress the ladies."

"No, but I know my daughter," said Daniel, winking at Nairne.

It was exactly as Nairne had expected. Pamela and Garrick knocked back wine, then brandy and by the time they were ready to leave, they were positively effusive. The gifts were bundled into bags. Garrick shook hands with Daniel and Zane and thanked them for their hospitality. Pamela gave them both a kiss on the cheek. The kids hung about awkwardly.

"Let me give a special thank you to that lovely young lady for teaching my Pamela how to cook." Garrick grabbed Nairne's arm, pulled her over, and gave her a kiss on the cheek. "You should be a proud man, Daniel; she's clever, talented and is turning into a beautiful young woman." Nairne was red with embarrassment; she didn't like people in her space, especially drunk men.

"Right, we'll see you soon and thanks again; it's been a great day." With this, the visitors returned to the house next door.

The three of them went back through to the living room and Daniel cleared away the glasses and mugs.

"We'll wash these up in the morning. Let's see if there are any good films on that we can watch."

"Okay, I'll just go and change," said Nairne.

"Don't you like your new outfit? You do look lovely," said Daniel

"Yes, you look like a proper girl," said Zane. "It's weird to think the boys at school will fancy my little sister."

"Yeah, like I'm ever going to be seen outside dressed like this," said Nairne. "I do have an image to maintain!"

"There's nothing wrong with dressing up," said Daniel. "You are allowed to."

"What, so Paul can ogle at her?" Zane laughed.

"Never mind Paul," said Nairne. "It was Garrick, he

was positively creepy." With that, she rushed up the stairs, and minutes later she was back down in tracksuit trousers and a sweatshirt.

"Oh, that's it, the sister we know and love," said Zane.

TWELVE

The weather changed on Boxing Day. The morning was dry, but colder and the previous day's downpour had frozen on the ground. Nairne rose early and tended to the animals; her father and Zane were still dead to the world.

Breakfast was a light affair as no one had much of an appetite.

"So what are you doing today?" Daniel asked them.

"I thought I'd have a look at my new books," said Nairne. "And if it stays dry maybe we could go for a walk later on; give the ice out there a chance to melt."

"Yes, okay, after lunch, that would be good; Zane, what about you?"

"Paul's invited me round this afternoon to try out that new game. You could come too Nairne, he said I should ask you."

"What, come round and spend time with that stuck up cow."

"Nairne, that's no way to speak about Pamela!" Daniel's tone was sharp.

"I'm not talking about Pamela. I'm talking about Laura Howard. Paul's invited her to visit. I wouldn't go round there for anything, no way. I can't believe we've got to let her anywhere near our house."

"Fair enough. Maybe not such a good idea," said Daniel.

Nairne and Daniel, with Dog in tow, set off for their walk shortly after one thirty. Pamela opened her kitchen window and called after them as they passed.

"Nairne, we're having afternoon tea when Laura arrives. Zane says you don't want to come round. Are you sure? You'd be very welcome."

"No honestly, I can't," said Nairne. She felt frustrated, she wanted to shout out to Pamela, 'don't let that awful girl in your house', but she knew she couldn't.

"Wait here a minute," Daniel walked over to Pamela.

"Pamela, thanks, it's very kind of you to ask both the kids round, but Nairne and Laura, there's some history there, probably better if she doesn't."

"Hmm, that doesn't surprise me," said Pamela. "I don't know what Paul sees in her, but what can you do?"

Daniel returned to Nairne and they set off down the drive.

"What did you say?" Nairne demanded.

"I simply told her you and Laura didn't get on. From her response I don't think Pamela is too keen on her either."

They headed along the road to Brigham Woods. The cold air made Nairne's cheeks glow and she pulled her hat down over her ears. The sky was heavy with thick clouds waiting to disgorge their contents. The woods were dark and silent, with a soft carpet of needles underfoot. They had walked about two miles when the soft white covering began to descend. Dog charged back and forwards barking and trying to catch the flakes that had made it past the tree canopy.

"I suppose we should turn round. The wind seems to be picking up and this looks like it's set in for the day."

"Okay," said Nairne. She called on Dog who had run on ahead. He stopped, cocked his head to one side in a quizzical manner, then after a moment's pause bounded back along the path. By the time they left the woods, the wind was howling along the road and the tarmac was hidden by snow. It stung as it blew into their faces and they walked in silence, heads bowed. It was a relief to reach the driveway; at least the wind was behind them. The cars had lost all definition, just giant white shapes with wheels. They entered the hallway, stamping their feet to release piles of wet crystals on the floor.

"That was certainly bracing. I think Laura's visit may be cut short if this keeps up," said Daniel. "I wouldn't want to drive into town once the light goes."

"Oh, that is a shame. Paul will be heartbroken," said Nairne sarcastically.

Daniel's prediction was correct. Next door, Garrick peered from the kitchen window.

"No, I don't like the look of this at all; maybe we should give them a shout and I'll drive Laura back."

"Give them another half hour. She's just arrived. We don't want her to think we're trying to get rid of her," said Pamela.

"You've changed your tune; I didn't think you were very keen."

"I'm not, I still think the lad should ask Nairne out. She's got spirit and it wouldn't do us any harm if the two of them became a bit closer?"

"Spirit is one way of putting it, but at Paul's age I'd have run a mile from a girl like Nairne, although, I must say she did look stunning in that outfit."

"Yes, I noticed. You couldn't keep your eyes off her."

"You're not jealous, are you?" Garrick laughed and grabbed her round the waist. "You've nothing to be jealous of. You know me. I like my women with something to grab hold of."

The snow fell and it kept on falling; three days of it. It drifted; thick white layers gathered on the sides of the road until the channel of the roadway disappeared. Still it fell. The house and yard became silent; the snow muffled the sounds. Pamela had never seen anything like it. She spent most of the time wrapped up in front of the fire. Garrick wasn't too keen on stirring from the warmth either, but he and Paul went out to see if they could help.

"Snow this deep is unusual but not unheard of," Daniel said. "But this is the worst I've seen in a long time." He was outside the front of the house clearing the doorway.

"What can we do?" Garrick asked, his voice raised against the wind.

"There are a couple of extra shovels in the shed. Nairne's over there, she'll show you. You could make a start and clear round the doors of your place and then we'll clear the driveway."

Paul trudged across the yard towards the shed. Nairne saw him approach, his feet sunk into the snow and the wind covered him in a fine layer of white dust.

"Your dad said you had a couple of extra shovels."

"I'll get them." She clambered over their carelessly abandoned bikes and pulled out two shovels from the back of the shed. Conscious of Paul watching her, she thrust the handles towards him.

"Zane's around the corner clearing the snow from the door of the chicken coup, he could give you a hand. I can finish off here on my own."

"Okay, thanks," Paul mumbled as he took the shovels from her and went outside. She heard him speaking to Zane and the two of them trudged back towards the house, joking and laughing.

Clearing the snow was exhilarating to begin with; their muscles glowed with warmth from the exertion while their exposed flesh felt numb with the cold. Nairne finished clearing round the chicken coup. She pushed the door open and went in with a bucket full of corn for the chickens. She spread it close to the doorway. Reluctantly they came out, clucking and complaining, and ate as quickly as they could manage; the snow banked up on each side of the door provided them with some shelter.

Next she began clearing the doorway to the stone outbuilding; she could hear Mona and Lisa trundling around inside restlessly, and Goat bleating gently.

Nairne put some food into a bucket for the pigs, fed the goat and laid down some more straw for them. The pigs were keen to get outside until they saw the thick white swirling mass that awaited them. She stopped and spoke to them, rubbed Goat's head and then closed the door back over. The others were about two thirds of the way down the driveway. The snow had to be scooped up and thrown high enough to get over the snow banks that edged the driveway.

"We need to keep it clear enough to get the pick-up through, in case we need to get into town in an emergency," said Daniel. "Once we've finished here we should go over to Mr Cranshaw's next door and make sure he's okay. He's getting on and I doubt his farm hand will have made it to work in this weather. He might need help with the animals."

"I'll come with you," said Zane. "Paul, what about you?"

"Yeah okay," said Paul.

"Why don't you head off now?" asked Nairne. "We could finish off here," she said, looking at Garrick.

"Yes, Nairne and I will soon get this finished; then we'll get back in and ask Pamela to put some lunch together."

"Right, come on boys," said Daniel. They trudged back up the driveway and climbed into the truck.

Mr Cranshaw was nearly seventy. He owned the small farm, and barely scraped a living. He'd always thought his son would take over the business, but catastrophe struck when Terry, his only child, perished in Australia several years earlier in one of the worst bush fires the country had ever seen. It burned for eighteen days. Millions of acres of land were destroyed, and towns, farms and settlements were wiped from the map. Daniel remembered the fire; he'd watched it on the news, the ineffectual fire barriers, the failed attempts to drop the scarce water resources on it. He hadn't known Cranshaw then. It happened about a year before they had moved there, a couple of months before Zane's accident. Mrs Cranshaw died a few months after they'd arrived; her heart just stopped one day. Her husband had found her lying in the kitchen, stone cold.

He remembered the funeral; the old boy was desolate. He and Angela had attended, although they didn't know the Cranshaws very well, but since Mrs Cranshaw's death and Angela's departure, the two men had developed a mutual trust. They didn't see each other often, but Daniel would drop by and ask for advice about the animals and Cranshaw would put work his way. More importantly, he recommended him to some of the other farmers in the area. For an incomer a recommendation from a real local was always helpful

The turn off to the farm was only about five hundred metres along the road. The driveway was thick with snow but the pick-up managed.

"It's not like Mr Cranshaw to let the snow get this thick," said Daniel.

"No, it's not," said Zane. They parked outside the front door and got out; there was a light on in the cattle shed. They walked over to it.

The snow was heaped in front of the doors so he could barely open them enough to squeeze through.

"I'll go and have a word; you two make a start and clear this away."

The boys, shovels in hand, began clearing the doorway to the shed. Daniel went inside. The shed was old, and the roof had seen so many repairs that Daniel doubted whether any of the original structure remained.

"Morning," he hailed Mr Cranshaw who turned and greeted him. He looked tired, exhausted in fact. He was putting out feed for the animals.

"Daniel, good of you to drop by and I see you brought some helpers." He glanced over at the frantic activity outside the doors.

"Yes, Zane and the lad who's staying with us, Paul Unwin. Remember I told you about him? Garrick's son."

"Oh yes, you volunteered didn't you. Those two friends of your lodgers arrived a few days ago."

"So where are they?"

"They're probably still in bed, sit up until all hours; you know what young people today are like."

"They should be out here giving you a hand," said Daniel. He couldn't believe that people staying here could lie in while Mr Cranshaw was out here trying to do all this work on his own. "I hope I've not landed you with trouble."

"No, no, if it hadn't been those two the council would have forced me to take someone else in soon enough, and anyway, I'm sure they'll work out fine."

"Let me help with that. I'll get some fresh water for the beasts and then if you want I'll get the boys to clear some of the snow from the driveway and the front of the house. It'll make getting back over here tomorrow a bit easier."

"Thanks Daniel, much appreciated. You're a good neighbour."

For the next hour they helped with the animals and cleared the snow from round the house. They also dug round Mr Cranshaw's truck in case he needed to go out. By the end of it, they were exhausted.

"Come on in for a drink before you go back."

"Thanks, but we should really get back. Do you need anything else?"

"No, that's me; I'll just fetch some wood in for the fire and try to get a bit of heat into the old place."

"Pass the log baskets out. The boys will fetch it, I'll just go and put the shovels back in the pick-up." The boys handed Daniel their shovels and followed Mr Cranshaw over to the house. The kitchen was dim; the lights were out and the room was cold. The fire had burned down to almost nothing. Mr Cranshaw removed his wet boots, went over, and passed the baskets to the two boys.

"Thank you lads. It's very good of you."

Paul and Zane went back outside. The wood shelter was built onto the gable of the house. They tossed the logs into the baskets and carried them back. The kitchen lights were on now and they could hear voices. The inner doorway opened and Mr Cranshaw appeared. Paul was first to hand over his basket. Two men were sitting at the kitchen table. They were scruffy with tousled hair and both needed a shave; they looked as though they had just woken up.

"Come on in and I'll introduce you to my guests," said Mr Cranshaw, his voice tinged with sarcasm.

Paul leaned forward into the room; the man sitting facing the door looked up.

"Hey Paul, how are you doing? How's that old man of yours?"

"He's fine Stevie; I'll tell him you were asking for him."

"Yeah, when this God awful Scottish weather stops we'll come round for few drinks." The other man nodded his head in agreement.

Zane put down his basket of logs and as he did so he caught a glimpse of the two men through the gap in the door. He froze. His heart began to pound; the sound in his ears was overwhelming. Next thing he realised they were all looking at him.

"Yeah, this is Zane; it's his house we're staying at, just up the road. Zane this is Stevie and Ed. They're friends of my dad's."

Zane stared at them.

"Shy, is he?" said Ed, laughing.

"Yeah, he is, anyway we'd better get going. Zane's dad's waiting for us. Goodbye Mr Cranshaw."

"Goodbye boys, and thanks again. And Zane, pass on my best to that lovely sister of yours." Zane nodded. The boys left and went round to the pickup.

"So did you meet the new lodgers?" Daniel asked.

"Yes, although I've met them before," said Paul.

Zane said nothing; in fact, he said nothing the rest of the way home.

THIRTEEN

They sat together for lunch. Pamela, still keen to cook, had rustled up some vegetable soup followed by sandwiches. Garrick looked exhausted from the morning's activities; he wasn't used to physical exercise. The three teenagers glowed from the exertion. Nairne loved that feeling, when you came in from the cold and your fingers and feet felt like they were burning as they heated up. The snow had stopped, but the clouds still hung, heavy and expectant so it was most likely a short respite.

"How was Mr Cranshaw?" Nairne asked as they sat at the table.

"Fine," said Daniel. "He was looking tired; the place is getting to be a bit much for him especially in weather like this. Callum, he's part time on the farm, hasn't made it in since Tuesday," Daniel explained to Garrick and Pamela.

"I could go round tomorrow and give him a hand with the cattle," said Nairne.

"That would be kind; I know he loves it when you visit. Zane, what about you?"

"Hmm, I suppose," said Zane

"Don't sound too keen. Two days hard work too much?" said Nairne jabbing him in the ribs.

"I thought you liked going round," said Daniel.

"I do it's … Oh, it doesn't matter…"

"Anyway, maybe by tomorrow Cranshaw's house guests might pull their weight."

"Oh, have Steven and Ed moved in?" asked Pamela.

"Yes, they arrived a couple of days ago."

"That's great," said Garrick. "I really appreciate you helping me find them somewhere."

"So do you know them well?" Daniel asked.

"Yes, we go way back. Stevie's worked for me on and off over the years. They're good lads."

"I hope so; Cranshaw's a good man, and I wouldn't like to see him taken advantage of." There was an edge to Daniel's voice that Garrick did not appreciate, but he let it go.

"I'm sure once they settle in they'll help round the place. Probably still feeling a bit like strangers in someone else's home. It does take a bit of getting used to."

The snow began to fall at half past five. An hour later the wind picked up as the temperature dropped. It continued like that for most of the night. They had a blazing fire in the living room and Nairne sat with one of her books while Daniel and Zane watched a film. The first news flash came at eight fifty. Nairne put down her book to watch.

The news broadcaster announced that gale force winds had swept across the south east of England. They had already experienced significant snowfall and with gusts of over eighty miles per hour in some places, power cables had been damaged and many roads, including two motorways were blocked.

"Police are warning the public not to travel unless they have to ….." Pictures of cars on a motorway, nose to tail, surrounded by swirling snow were followed by images of a derailed train outside York. There were no details of casualties, but rescue efforts were being hampered by the extreme weather conditions.

The next interruption was at ten fifteen. This time there was more information. Snow continued to fall and high winds were still wreaking havoc along the east coast. Massive waves had struck two sections of coast line causing floodwaters to surge into a number of towns. The army was trying to reach stranded householders. There were reports of several people being swept away and the temperature was falling. The report said tens of thousands of people needed emergency accommodation.

Neither Daniel nor Zane could concentrate on the end of the film. It all seemed so unimportant after the pictures of such devastation.

When morning came Nairne was woken by the cold. Even with an extra two blankets a hot water bottle and Dog snuggled at her feet she was frozen. Reluctantly, she slid out of bed and into the bathroom. After dressing, with extra layers of clothing she went down to breakfast. Her father had made a start; there was no work today, one glance outside showed more snow was banked up on yesterday's frozen layer. The radio was on.

"So are there any more details about the stuff last night?" Nairne asked.

"Yes, it sounds pretty bad. Apparently, two hundred thousand homes are without power and one of the water pumping stations was contaminated with floodwater so lots of people are having to use bottled water. You know, we really are lucky here. I think things are going to get a lot worse before this winter is over. Give that brother of yours a shout will you? I'll do the clearing up out here this morning if you want to pop over to Mr Cranshaw's."

"Okay, it's not nearly as deep as yesterday; Zane and I can walk over."

Zane appeared at breakfast twenty minutes later, pale and unhappy.

"Get a move on, we're going over to the farm after breakfast. I'll get the boots and things ready while you finish your breakfast."

He grunted a non committal response. Ten minutes later Nairne was still waiting.

"What's up? You don't look very well."

"No, I feel awful," said Zane. "My stomach hurts and I feel cold."

Daniel placed his hand on Zane's forehead.

"You don't have a temperature, but you certainly don't look too good. Why don't you stay in this morning I'll go over with Nairne after we've finished here?"

"Okay, I think I'll go and have a lie down," said Zane, excusing himself from the table. Daniel and Nairne had been outside for about thirty minutes when Paul surfaced.

"Hiya," he shouted over to Daniel. "Do you want a hand? My dad's still exhausted from yesterday, but I quite enjoyed it."

"Thanks Paul. Here!" Daniel held out an extra shovel and Paul came over and took it.

"I take it Zane and Nairne have gone over to the farm?"

"No, Nairne's feeding the chickens and Zane's gone for a lie down. He wasn't looking too well. I'll go over to the farm with Nairne after we finish here."

"I could go with her, if you want," said Paul.

"If you wouldn't mind. I know Mr Cranshaw likes to get all the animals seen to as early as possible and he'll need help clearing the paths." Nairne emerged from the chicken shed and trudged across the yard to join them.

"Paul's offered to go over to Mr Cranshaw's."

"Oh, right," said Nairne awkwardly. "I'll get Dog; he can come with us."

She called for Dog, who came bounding out of the shed barking, and they set off down the drive. Neither of them spoke, but Nairne could sense that Paul wanted to talk, but didn't know what to say.

"So, is Zane really ill?" he asked eventually.

"No, I don't think so, just a bit under the weather. He probably wanted to get out of clearing more snow."

"I enjoyed it yesterday," said Paul. "You feel so good after all that exercise when you go back in the house and it's all warm."

"Yes, I love that," said Nairne relaxing a little. "When your fingers and toes all tingle when they start to heat up and your head feels all clear."

They chatted all the way along the road about nothing in particular. It was strange, although they spent lots of time in each other's company, it was never just the two of them and most of their conversations were like guerrilla warfare. Each would rush in with their attack trying to pre-empt the other. In addition, each was always desperate to have the last word.

Mr Cranshaw was shovelling the snow away from the barn doors as Dog rushed to him demanding attention.

"Ah, Nairne, how good to see you," he smiled warmly. Nairne could see what her father meant; he looked tired and a bit frayed round the edges.

"We came to give you a hand," she said brightly.

"No Zane today? It's not often I see one without the other. Helping your dad is he?"

"No he wasn't feeling very well so Paul said he'd help."

"Much appreciated. Why don't you give me a hand with this, lad? And Nairne, you could check on the beasts. You have a way with them and they've been unsettled this morning."

Mr Cranshaw handed Paul another shovel and they continued to dig. Nairne slipped into the barn, leaving Dog outside sniffing his way round the yard. There were thirty-five cattle in the shed plus one large bull; he lay on his own while the others huddled together for warmth. Their breath formed clouds as they snorted and bellowed, excited at the prospect of fresh food.

After giving them some food and water, she went back outside. Paul and Mr Cranshaw were over at the side of the house clearing snow from the back door to the wood shelter. She went over.

"Do you want me to take some logs in for you?"

"Yes lass, that would be grand. There are a couple of baskets in the porch."

Nairne fetched the baskets, loaded both of them and carried the first one round to the house. She stepped inside the back porch and kicked off her boots. Then she padded through to the kitchen and began to unload the wood into a neat pile next to the stove.

Suddenly, she became aware of someone right behind

her. A young man stood there, his face unshaven. He grinned. Nairne stared at him.

"Sorry luv, did I scare you?" Although it was an apology, it sounded more like a threat.

"No, you startled me. I didn't hear you come in," said Nairne.

"I didn't want you to; I wanted to watch you work. So who might you be, lurking in Mr Cranshaw's kitchen?" he laughed.

"I might ask the same question," she retorted.

"Well, whoever you are it brightens my day to see a pretty girl. Why don't I give you a hand with that wood."

"If you want to be useful why don't you give Mr Cranshaw a hand shovelling the snow? I can manage the log basket myself thanks, if you'll let me past." She picked up the empty basket and moved forward. The man stood his ground.

"But I'm not finished chatting to you yet."

"I'm finished chatting to you, so let me past."

"Only if you ask nicely."

Nairne could feel her temper rising. She moved the kitchen chair to her left and went to go round the other side of the table. The second man was a couple of years older, just as scruffy but thicker set, with a beer belly already established. He moved round blocking the only other exit.

"Just say please and we might let you past."

"Piss off," said Nairne. She was furious. "Let me past." She moved forward to push past and he grabbed her; he laughed while they struggled. He spun her round and pinned her arms to her side.

"Calm down, I'm not going to hurt you, just one pretty please and I'll let you go."

Nairne's legs thrashed wildly, kicking at his shins. He held her tighter; her feet lifted off the floor.

They didn't hear Dog enter the room; he'd been hovering outside waiting for Nairne and eventually the cold got the better of him. He barked and the first man turned.

"I take it he's with you, stupid looking mutt." Dog barked excitedly as Nairne continued to thrash, then she stopped. Her limbs became completely still.

"Dog!" she exclaimed. Dog began to growl, a guttural sound from the depth of his chest, as his lips curled showing his teeth.

"Ed, deal with the bloody dog." Ed lumbered towards Dog. Dog moved towards Ed.

"I wouldn't do that," said Nairne. "He's a hunting dog. He'll bite and if you ever had any intentions of being a father…."

Ed paused. Dog looked wild; he was slavering, ready to pounce.

"She's winding you up, it's a stupid mongrel; give it a kick."

Ed dithered and Dog could smell the fear and performed his part exquisitely. It was a standoff. The stalemate was broken as Paul entered the room.

"Nairne I've brought the other basket….." He stopped dead in his tracks taking in the scene that lay before him. Dog poised in the middle of the room like one of the hounds of Baskerville, while Ed stood statue still, his fear of canines emblazoned across his face. Meanwhile, Stevie had his arms around Nairne, her hands pinned to her sides and her face red from anger.

"Stevie, what the hell's going on?" Paul demanded.

"Oh, we were just having some fun, weren't we Ed?" He released his grip on Nairne, who pulled herself free and turned to face her captor.

"See, no harm done; we were just messing about weren't we? Nairne? Just having a few laughs."

"I'm not laughing," said Nairne

"Oh, don't be like that, no hard feelings, eh?" He held out his hand.

Nairne looked at it, then without a moment's pause, she

swung her arm back and punched him, catching his jaw with a cracking sound. She rubbed her bruised knuckles.

She had caught him off guard and he recoiled from the force of the blow.

"Shit! That little bitch hit me."

Ed laughed.

"What the fuck did you do that for? You ugly little dyke."

"What so now I'm an ugly dyke. You know lesbianism hadn't crossed my mind, but having spent five minutes with you two so called men, the idea is becoming more appealing all the time. Oh, and Stevie, no hard feelings, I was just having a bit of fun." With that, she turned and walked out, Dog followed in her tracks.

"What the hell were you doing?" said Paul.

"What's it to you? You got your eye on her?"

"No, of course not! But if her dad finds out what you did he'll do more than punch you. She's only fourteen. And we've got to live over there; dad's not going to be happy about this."

"Yeah yeah, big deal," said Stevie. "Go on Paul. Run after your little girlfriend."

Paul found Nairne outside saying farewell to Mr Cranshaw.

"I'm fine Nairne. The lads aren't bad but they're not used to hard work; they breed them soft in the city."

"As long as you're sure," she responded. "Because if they give you any problems you let my dad know he'll sort it out. I'll come round again tomorrow if the snow's still here, but phone us if you need anything." Nairne wasn't happy leaving Mr Cranshaw with the two Neanderthals. She hadn't told him what had happened as he would only get upset. Anyway, she didn't imagine Stevie would try that again. She set off down the driveway Dog at her side. Paul shouted goodbye to Mr Cranshaw and ran after her.

"Nairne wait up….."

"Oh, you're coming with me; I thought you might be

hanging around with your dad's friends?"

"Look those guys were out of order. I told them so."

She was silent; Paul could feel the frostiness emanating from her even in the sub zero temperatures that surrounded them.

"Honestly Nairne, he was totally wrong grabbing you like that. I'm just glad I came in when I did."

"Why? You think I couldn't have handled them?" She said it with feeling, but she had been scared. She knew if Paul hadn't come in things could have got completely out of hand and although Dog would have attacked, she knew what happened to dogs if they bit people.

"Anyway, I thought your dad said they were okay. They didn't seem it to me."

"No, they didn't," said Paul. "But they were only messing around. Stevie wouldn't have hurt you...." He started to laugh.

"What's so funny?" she bristled. Her heart was still thumping from the adrenaline and she didn't like to be made fun of.

"No, I know it's not funny, but when you punched him. Pow..." he imitated the right hook. "The look on his face! He couldn't believe it. Neither could I."

"Should I have slapped him like a proper little lady? I tell you if he ever touches me again I'll hurt him properly." Her expression convinced Paul that it was no idle threat.

"So are you going to tell your dad about what happened?"

"Nothing happened," said Nairne. "We were just messing around and if I did he'd go round there and hurt Stevie and I know how this works. My dad would end up in trouble."

They walked the rest of the way home in silence, but it was a comfortable silence. Nairne could sense the respect from Paul and she had to admit he had stepped in when it mattered.

Nairne felt she had done enough socialising for one day and retreated to the living room with one of her new books. Dog stretched out on the floor and slept

"How was Mr Cranshaw?" Daniel asked coming through from the kitchen

"Fine, but you were right, he did look tired. I'll go round tomorrow if the snow is still lying."

"You could take Paul again, he seemed keen to help."

"Yeah, or Zane could come round since he's made such a speedy recovery. He's gone next door."

"Hmm, I merely thought you might have enjoyed working together. You certainly looked more relaxed with him when you got back." He winked mischievously.

"Dad!" she exclaimed throwing one of the cushions at him. "You're worse than Pamela. I've already said I don't like him, not one little bit!"

Paul and Zane sat at the computer screen; Paul loaded one of his new games.

"Wait until you see this, the fight scenes are unreal! Mind you, they could learn a thing or two from your sister."

"You didn't get into a fight with her did you?" Zane asked.

"No, not me, but when we were round at the farm she got into a bit of a disagreement with Stevie; you should have seen her."

"What happened?" Zane could feel his voice shaking, and his heart beat rising as Paul filled him in with all the glorious details.

FOURTEEN

Nairne opened the Raeburn in the kitchen and piled on several logs. Then she opened the shutters, revealing window panes covered in the most exquisite ice patterns. Outside was like a fairy tale world, dry and sparkling. The sun was rising and everything glittered. The snow was still falling, but it was gentle.

"Looks like another day for shovelling snow," she remarked to Dog, who sat pressed against the stove sucking in all the heat. She made a start on breakfast and shouted upstairs to wake the others. Zane was first to emerge; he peered outside.

"Not more snow!"

"Yes, looks like it. Are you coming with me to Mr Cranshaw's?"

"Do we have to?"

"Yes, there's no way Callum will make it in and anyway I thought you liked going round."

"I don't think you should go. I'll go with Paul, you can stay here," he said authoritatively.

"And why not?"

"Because… because you went yesterday so you should have a day off."

"So did Paul, maybe he should have a day off or are you only worried about me?"

"Yes, you should have a day off."

"Oh, come off it, I'm not falling for that. Why don't you want me to go? Paul can come too if that's the problem."

"I just don't think you should."

"Why, has Paul said something?"

Zane looked confused; he was hopeless at lying,

especially to Nairne.

"He told me what happened...., with that Stevie bloke."

"And?"

"You shouldn't have done it Nairne, he'll be really angry."

"So what? I'm not scared of him." This was not strictly true, but she wasn't going to admit that. "Anyway, he started it, pawing at me like that. What a creep!"

"Please don't go round, please. For me." There was panic in his voice.

"Okay, if you tell me why and I mean the real reason."

Zane paused, he looked at the floor; she could see he was struggling, trying to find the words.

"Zane, it can't be that bad."

"But it is.... it was him that stabbed that man in town. I saw him. When I was at the farm and Mr Cranshaw introduced him I knew it." He was shaking.

"Are you sure, absolutely sure?"

"I think so... oh I don't know; I only saw him for a moment."

"What about Paul? He was with you that night. Did he see him?"

"No, I had run on ahead.... Paul didn't get there until after."

"You need to tell dad, he'll know what to do."

"I can't, I gave a statement to the police; they'll know I lied. I told them I didn't see anything; I told them I couldn't help. And what if I'm wrong?"

"Why did you do that if you saw him?"

"Because Garrick told me not to tell. He said he would handle it. Every time they asked, he would answer before I could speak. He kept telling them I didn't see anything and saying, isn't that right Zane. I was scared so I went along with it. He said I would end up having to go to court and there would be questions about why I was out in town on my own at night. He said they would drag us into this big police investigation and that it was better to keep out of it.

He said he was looking out for my best interests."

"I don't understand. Why would Garrick do that…." she paused. "Do you think he knew who did it? Do you think he was trying to protect them?"

FIFTEEN

Nairne still thought Zane should tell their father, but she couldn't force him and it was his word against Stevie's. She could see it now; Garrick would have some completely convincing story to explain why he told Zane to lie. The boy had been through a terrible experience, he was muddled and confused, it was crowded, he could easily have been mistaken. Zane had only glimpsed the killer and with his mental capacities who would take him seriously.

She kept her promise to Zane. She didn't go round to the farm that day or the next and then the snow melted. Slowly at first, then faster. You could hear the drip, drip, dripping; the yard turned from an ice rink into a swimming pool.

Nairne was dreading going back to school even though it would only be four days a week. Pamela had offered to make sure the three of them were doing school work on their non school day, much to Daniel's relief and their combined horror. When Monday morning finally arrived, Garrick drove them in. Nairne and Zane would have preferred to take the bus, but they couldn't think of a reason to turn him down. Reluctantly, they climbed into the back of the Range Rover while Paul sat in the front.

"You're all very quiet this morning," said Garrick. Paul grunted while the other two remained silent. "Oh, school isn't that bad is it? I thought it was supposed to be the best time of your life, isn't that what they say? Nairne, I thought you were a bit of a brain box, you should be keen to get back in there. And Paul, you've got the lovely Laura to look forward to." He winked and prodded his son's arm.

Paul grunted again.

Laura was waiting, sporting a new coat and a stylish hair cut with Tamara standing loyally by her side. She spotted Paul as soon as he got out of the car and abandoned Tamara, mid sentence. Paul headed towards her.

"See you both later," he shouted to them.

"He didn't look too keen," said Zane.

"No, he didn't," said Nairne.

The top half of the school attended assembly at nine thirty. The mood was subdued. It was obvious when they arrived at their registration classes that something was wrong. The tension was palpable when Mr Watson walked onto the stage; silence fell immediately. His tone was sombre and no one cracked any jokes.

"Welcome back. I have important news for you and you will be given letters for your parents. Over the Christmas break, we have been working with the education department to solve the overcrowding issue and running costs for the school. We are expecting another two hundred new pupils over the next month and I am sure you are all aware there is insufficient room. Other secondary schools in the region are already full to capacity and the education authority is under immense pressure.

We are also faced with rising costs. The only workable solution in the short term until the Easter break is to reduce school hours and teach some classes on a rota basis. This will affect years three to six. We realise these years are vital in terms of preparing you for your exams. However, we must take into account that you are old enough to stay at home on your own and to understand the need to study on your days off. We had already agreed to a four day week for this next term, but in order to allow us to offer some level of support to all, this will be reduced to three days per week. You will each be given timetables to show the days you are to attend."

There was a murmur round the hall; the initial excitement of a four day week was replaced with a feeling of unease. The pupils appreciated that the authorities would never have come up with such a drastic plan unless things were bad.

"I can't believe this," Daniel snorted after reading the letter. "But I thought you would be more than happy with a three day week," he suggested to Nairne, as they washed up the dishes after supper.

"Hmm, I'm pleased in one way but Mr Watson seemed genuinely disturbed about what was going on. He looked exhausted; all the teachers did. Although I hate school there's no way they would do this unless it was a crisis. I suppose it's a sign of things to come."

"Yes, I know what you mean," said Daniel. "When I went to the petrol station the price had gone up by fourteen pence a litre since last week and there's a limit on what you can buy. Apparently they're having some supply problems and they don't want to run out."

"So, if they run out how would you do your job?" Nairne asked.

"I don't know, that's what's worrying me, but it might only be a temporary problem. Let's see what happens. But with price rises like this I can see why the council are having problems affording the school buses and the heating costs."

They finished tidying the kitchen and went through to join Zane; he was slumped in front of the television watching the news channel.

"No good films on?" Daniel asked.

"Yes, there was a western, but it got interrupted by a news flash so I switched to the news channel to see what was happening."

"So what was the news flash?" Daniel asked, sitting down next to him on the sofa.

"Oh, there's been a massive storm off the coast of America; a huge wave hit New York." The pictures on the screen bore more resemblance to a disaster movie than to proper news footage. "The reporter said thousands of people have been drowned."

The three of them sat watching footage of the Empire State building surrounded by flood water; Times Square was a deserted lake. There was a knock on the door. Nairne answered it. It was Garrick.

"Just saw the news, wondered if you had all heard."

"Yes, come through. We're watching it now." Garrick followed her to the living room.

"So Daniel, what do you think? Is it a freak storm or is there more to this?"

"I don't think this is a one off. It reminds me of the Tsunami in two thousand and five, but this one hasn't been caused by an earth quake."

"Pamela said there were weather warnings earlier today. They saw it coming but it gathered force as it hit the coastline. Apparently, the weather has been unusually cold there over the last few weeks so that won't help."

"No, it makes our floods seem small in comparison," Daniel replied. The four of them watched for some time in silence until the news shots became a repeat of what they had already seen.

"I'd better get back. I was interested on your views on this and this business with the school," said Garrick as he headed for the hallway. Daniel followed him.

"The school has got me worried. It's like Nairne said earlier on, there is no way they would do this unless things were really bad. It makes me wonder what will happen next. The council don't have the funds and still more people keep arriving."

"Like us," said Garrick, a touch of concern in his voice.

"No, you know I don't mean that. It's just that before this started the Government gave assurances that the number of people would be managed, but that seems to have fallen by the wayside. A bloke in town was telling me last week they reckon over thirty thousand people have moved into the area over the last six months. We were told ten thousand in total would be coming."

"Yes, I see your point, but how does the Government stop people getting here under their own steam. They can hardly put up a barrier at the border."

"You're right, but there are an increasing number of people who think that's not such a bad idea. My worry is they decide to do something about it."

"You mean take action?"

"Yes, people can be pretty ruthless when it comes to protecting their own."

SIXTEEN

January was a cruel month; temperatures plummeted and the weather swung from snow to ice to heavy rain. Even on their school days, they didn't always make it in; sometimes the roads were too treacherous for the bus or staff members were unable to get in and they had to sit in with other classes. Nairne had never liked school, but she longed for it to get back to normal.

They had looked forward to the days at home but it was a long day to sit working and it was too cold to go outside.

True to her word, Pamela checked on them to make sure their school work was completed. They would congregate in the main house as it was easier to keep it warm and there was some sense of comfort in being together. Daniel was at work during the day. He left early in darkness and returned in darkness. Garrick also went out frequently, but if he was at home, he would stay in his own house and visitors would stop by. Nairne rarely saw who visited, but she heard cars arriving and leaving. Daniel said Garrick could use one of the outbuildings for storage and sometimes she would see him going in or out with boxes, or see the men who visited him taking items away.

She was glad he did not come round. Since the incident with the two men at Mr Cranshaw's and Zane's confession, the less they saw of Garrick the better, she thought. However, she was curious about him; he always seemed to have money, but he certainly didn't do a proper job, not like her father or the other adults she knew. His work seemed to involve going to the pub and having 'business meetings'.

It was Friday, the third week of term, a non school day and

Nairne awoke to the sound of her father's pickup heading down the drive. She was cold, even with the extra bedclothes and pyjamas. Reluctantly she rose, washed, dressed and went downstairs. Zane appeared as she was preparing breakfast; he opened the shutters.

"Oh God! Not more snow." Thick sleet was falling; large wet globules ran down the windows and the ground was covered in a mushy mixture of ice and water.

"Your turn to do the chickens," said Nairne, smiling wickedly.

"Oh, no way! I'm not going out in that - I'll wait and see if it goes off."

"There will be no breakfast until you see to them. It's not going to get any drier so you may as well get it over with."

With a great deal of sulking and sighing, he pulled on his boots and coat and set out across the yard. Nairne was glad she had done yesterday; it had been cold and frosty but dry. It was still dark outside. Nairne could see Zane's figure crossing back over to the house, his hood up and coat zipped to the top in a vain effort to keep dry. She was at the sink filling the kettle when the car came screaming up the drive and round the corner. It braked hard, swerving wildly to avoid Zane who stood rooted to the spot. The wing mirror clipped him. He fell backwards, his body smacking into the ground. Nairne dropped the kettle. It clattered in the stone sink. Her heart was pounding as she ran outside.

The car door swung open and Stevie emerged.

"Christ sake, didn't you hear us coming? What the hell were you doing standing in the middle of the road? I could have killed you." Stevie reached down to help Zane to his feet.

Zane just sat there, his clothes soaked and when he tried to stand his legs buckled uselessly.

"You're okay though, aren't you? I hardly touched you. No harm done, eh?"

Still Zane was silent. Stevie got a hold of his coat to pull him up.

"Christ, I forgot. It's the silent half wit," Stevie muttered as he turned to the car where Ed was emerging from the passenger door. As he turned back he came face to face with Nairne.

"Get your hands off him!" she yelled, knocking Stevie out of the way. She turned her attention to Zane.

"Zane are you okay, Zane?" He nodded. All the colour had drained from his face.

"God! All we need! It's the crazy little sister. Look, before you start it was an accident. No harm done, eh son?" he said again, looking at Zane. "He was just standing in the middle of the road. He could have moved out the way."

Nairne put her arm round her brother and led him back to the house ignoring Stevie's excuses. She propelled him indoors and marched back to Stevie.

"Oh, here we go. Remember darling, I'm ready for you this time." He put his fists up and pretended to box. Nairne walked up close to him.

"You were going far too fast, you could have killed him. This is our land and you're not welcome. Get in the car and get out of here now."

"Yeah, right," he laughed and turned away.

"I told you to leave," said Nairne.

"Look love, it was an accident and your brother's okay. Anyway, we're here to see Garrick so why don't you go back in the house and look after your brother like a good little girl." He put his hand on her arm to steer her back to the house. Nairne pulled away as if she had been scalded. They both heard the door open as Garrick emerged.

"What the hell is going on? Nairne you're soaking wet, what are doing out without a coat?"

"I was telling your visitors to leave."

"Why? What's this about?" Garrick sounded annoyed.

"They knocked my brother down. They came tearing up

our drive and knocked him down."

"Stevie?"

"Hey, it was an accident, the lad's fine. I clipped him with the wing mirror, gave him a fright. He was right in the middle of the road. I've said sorry and he is all right. It's her."

"Is Zane okay?" Garrick asked.

"What do you think?" Nairne spat the words at him. "You think he's going to be okay after what he's been through before?"

"Okay, I understand. I'll get Pamela to come round. It's a nasty shock for both of you. Why don't you get back in the house and warm up? What else can we do to help?" Garrick could sense Nairne was not going to be easily placated.

"You can tell them to leave."

"Now Nairne, Stevie and Ed are business associates. They came to have a chat with me, but if it makes you happier we'll go into town."

"Yes it does, and I don't want them on our land ever again."

"Now be reasonable. It was an accident and we live here too."

"Fine, if that's the way you feel, I'll speak to my dad when he gets home. I'll tell him what they've done."

"Okay that's fine, I'll come over this evening and speak to your dad, but he'll recognise it was an accident and Zane is all right."

"Yes, and I'll tell him about the other time."

Garrick looked from Nairne to Stevie and back again.

"What other time?"

"The day I went round to Mr Cranshaw's and your good friend Stevie assaulted me."

"You're the one who was throwing punches," said Stevie, looking to Ed for support.

"And you were the one who had my arms pinned to my sides and refused to let me go. Garrick, you know my dad, what do you think he'll do?"

Garrick was sure he could guess and he wouldn't want to be in Stevie's shoes when Daniel found out.

"Look, young lady," he spoke in his most serious tone. "That's a serious accusation you're making, so if this is a story to get back at them for what's just happened I want you to think long and hard about this. It's your word against theirs."

"My word and Paul's," said Nairne. "He was there. He saw what happened."

"Paul," Garrick called out and Paul appeared; he and Pamela had been standing in the doorway watching what was going on.

"Is this true? Did you see Stevie assault her?" Paul could see from his father's eyes what answer he should give, but he could also see the anger in Nairne's. She was glaring at him, willing him to speak out.

"I did walk in, they were having a bit of an argument...." his voice trailed off as he looked at his feet.

"An argument, is that what you call it?" There was rage in her eyes. "You're a bloody coward, Paul Unwin. A coward and a liar."

Zane watched from the doorway. He felt sick, both from the shock of the accident and fear as he witnessed Nairne arguing with everyone. He was scared. He knew what Stevie was capable of; he'd seen it in his eyes. He shouted over from the doorway.

"Nairne, come back in. It's okay, it was an accident, I should have been watching where I was going." Nairne turned and glared at him as Garrick smiled sympathetically.

"See, Zane's fine about it. I know you're upset Nairne, but you're getting this all out of proportion. Let's get back inside. Pamela will come round, make you both some breakfast, then we can talk about this properly." He took her arm; she yanked it away from him.

"No, I don't want any of you anywhere near us. You're not welcome in our house." She stormed back to the house, pushed Zane inside and slammed the door.

Nairne was in the kitchen when Daniel arrived home; the room was warm but the atmosphere was not. Startled by his arrival, she dropped the pan she had been holding and it hit the bottom of the sink with a loud clatter.

"Nairne, are you okay?" He could see she was far from okay; she had been crying, and her cheeks were stained with tears. He put his arms round her.

"It's all right now. I know it must have been a shock, but everything's all right now."

She pulled back from him.

"How do you know?"

"Garrick called me straight away."

"I bet he did, couldn't wait to tell you his side of the story!"

"I've been to speak to him. You must have got such a fright, but he said Zane was fine. Where is he?"

"In his room."

"And is he all right?

"Yes, but no thanks to Garrick or those men."

"Garrick said you were angry. He said Pamela offered to come round but you said no. They understand that you got a shock and that you shouted at them in anger so don't worry about it. It will all be forgotten."

"No it won't. I won't forget. I don't want anything to do with any of them. They're liars and cowards." Her voice was sharp, her temper rising at the unfairness of it all; it was as if she was in the wrong.

"Now Nairne, that's not very fair is it? It was an accident. Garrick's friend, who was driving the car, called me. He was so upset; he was really shaken."

"Dad! Surely, you didn't believe him; he was just scared of what you might do to him. He wasn't sorry about anything. You should have heard him, the way he spoke to Zane it was like last time at Mr Cranshaw's. He's a bully."

"What last time?"

"When I went round to help Mr Cranshaw with Paul that day Zane wasn't well, Stevie grabbed hold of me....

"Yes and you hit him. He told me all about it. He was joking around, said you over reacted. I understand Paul was there and he said it was a misunderstanding. You know Nairne, you need to learn to control your temper."

Nairne glared at him with a look of pure contempt. She stormed out of the kitchen, ran upstairs and slammed her bedroom door behind her. Daniel sighed; she was well intentioned but she was so hot headed. Moments later Zane appeared.

"I take it she's still in a mood?"

"Yes, I'm afraid so. What about you, are you all right?"

"Yes dad, I'm fine I don't know why everyone's making such a fuss, the car never touched me. I should have been paying more attention. Nairne was so angry. It was terrible. I don't think Paul will ever speak to us again."

"Of course he will. They understand she got a shock. It was the heat of the moment. She'll come round, and so will Paul."

When Nairne looked back on that day she realised it was a turning point in so many ways. It was as if the whole planet was angry; the weather, which had been treacherous, deteriorated further. It rained all the time. The only respite came at night when the temperature plummeted and everything froze. February brought gale force winds that swept across the country causing havoc. London flooded again, worse than last time and the mass migration of people became a common sight on the evening news. The Government issued warnings and asked for assistance and co-operation before declaring a state of emergency and bringing in the armed forces to keep control.

New laws, allowing local authorities to seize empty properties were introduced. Price rises were a daily occurrence although there were measures in place to limit increases in basic food supplies. The Government couldn't afford for panic to break out. The United Kingdom was having an easy time of it compared to some places. Sea level rises of over thirty centimetres had been recorded over the last twelve months, unprecedented in living memory and large swathes of Holland were lost forever as the sea reclaimed her land. Africa was in chaos as drought swept across the continent. Bangladesh, one of the lowest lying population centres, flooded again and millions fled in search of higher ground. Surrounding countries tried in vain to close their borders, but the sheer pressure of people surged through.

Although school was only open three days a week Nairne dreaded it now more than ever. She sat alone on the bus, while Zane sat with Paul. Paul had attempted to speak to her, but she ignored him completely. Zane had tried pleading his case but it fell on deaf ears.

Home wasn't much better. Daniel was wrong to think things would return to normal. He had to admit Garrick and Pamela tried their hardest to win Nairne over, but without success.

Eventually he told her that Pamela, Garrick and Paul were welcome in his house and that while she was living under his roof she would have to cope with it. Instead of shouting or remonstrating, she had calmly answered that if that was his wish then she would have no choice, but that she could not forgive them. It was going to be a long cold winter, thought Daniel.

Nairne appeared to have forgiven Zane; however, as soon as Paul appeared she would retreat to her room. Her forgiveness of Daniel and his stance on the matter was going to take a bit longer. He missed their relationship. He had always felt close to Nairne. He had relied on her perhaps too much, but he had always felt they were friends as well as father and daughter. Now it was like living in the house with a tolerant stranger.

Garrick was heading into town when he heard Daniel's truck approaching.

"Daniel, good to see you. Have you been working late?"

"Yes, I've got a couple of house renovations on the other side of Lauder, so it's a good thirty mile drive. I'm beginning to wonder if it's worth the effort. I must have spent half my pay on fuel to get there. If the prices keep going up like this I'll be better off staying at home." He looked weary. Garrick had never seen him like this before.

"I might be able to help. Let's say I could get some fuel, cheaper than the pump price and no limit on amounts, would that help?"

Daniel paused; he was always wary of a bargain, especially now.

"Where's it from? You know I can't get involved in anything illegal, I've got the kids to think about; I couldn't risk it."

Garrick looked hurt.

"Daniel, I know you're not into that kind of thing. My business dealings are sometimes a little bit on the creative side, but not illegal. I pulled off a big deal earlier this week; I'm on my way into town to celebrate and part of the deal means we've started buying our fuel in bulk. You get a better price that way, so if it would help you could fill up whenever you need to. You know how much I owe you and I know you won't take charity, but if you pay me a fair price, say seventy percent of the pump price, then we are all fair and square. What do you say?"

"Garrick, thanks. That would be great even for the next couple of weeks until I can get some work a bit closer to home."

"Great, I'll drop the details round tomorrow and I'll let the guys know to expect you. Oh, and Daniel, Zane also has some news for you."

Nairne heard the back door open as she was laying the table.

"Evening, that smells good." Daniel ruffled her hair on

the way past. "Where's your brother? I hear he has some news."

"Oh, he's in the living room. Dinner's ready. You could let him know."

Daniel called on Zane who joined them at the table.

"I hear you've got news."

"Yes dad, it's great! I've got a job, after school and on Saturday's. Ed, Stevie's friend, runs a warehouse and he spoke to Garrick and asked if Paul and I wanted jobs. It's on the industrial estate. He's looking for help unloading goods, so it'll be hard work, but the pay's good and he'll give us a lift home."

Daniel could see how excited Zane was and the money was good for unskilled work. Zane felt it was very grown up to have a paid job.

"So do you think you'll be able to fit in all your chores, your school work and your new job?"

"Yes, I promise I'll do my homework and Nairne could do some of my chores, couldn't you Nairne?"

"I'm sure she could," said Daniel. "But what would be in it for her?"

"She would be my favourite sister ever!" Zane smirked.

"Or you could split some of the money you earn. After all, that would be fair."

"I suppose," said Zane. "Nairne what do you say?"

"I'll do your chores on Saturdays if you do mine on Sundays and you can keep your money." Zane paused, weighing up the pros and cons of the suggestions. It meant no long lie on a Sunday, but it meant he kept his earnings.

"Hmm. Okay, it's a deal."

After dinner, Daniel and Nairne cleared away the dishes.

"That was good of you to swap the chores round and not to take any of his earnings; he is so excited about it."

"I didn't want the money," said Nairne. "Not if it is anything to do with Garrick or his friends."

"Nairne, hasn't this gone on long enough. I know you're angry with Garrick, but it was good of him to get

Zane the job and to help me out. I think they're quite upset that you're behaving like this."

"Well they should have thought about that before they sided with Stevie. I've done what you asked, I am perfectly polite to them, but I don't want to be friends with them."

"Okay, but you know you shouldn't be so hard on people. Life isn't just black and white. People make mistakes. It doesn't mean they're bad people, does it?"

Nairne didn't respond. She didn't want to argue with her dad. She hated the way things were, but she couldn't let it go; she knew that Garrick was no good, and the whole argument about life being shades of grey was an excuse adults rolled out when they had done something wrong and didn't want to face the consequences. As far as Nairne could see, things were either good or bad. And Garrick was bad.

SEVENTEEN

Zane loved work; it was tiring and the warehouse was cold, but once they started, they soon heated up. Large box vans would arrive and he helped to unload the contents into smaller transit vans for delivery. Ed ran the place. Zane had seen Stevie a couple of times but only in passing. This was Ed's show.

Paul wasn't keen; hard work didn't suit him and he felt they should be paid more. He had broached the subject with Ed at the end of their first week.

"There are plenty of grown men out there desperate for work," Ed remarked. "You pair should count yourselves lucky. And remember, you're here as a favour to Garrick, so no messing about." Paul was subdued when Ed was there, but boasted to Zane that Ed was merely one his dad's lackeys and wouldn't have the nerve to sack them. Zane just kept his head down and got on with the work. As far as he was concerned the money was great. They worked from four fifteen to seven thirty. Nairne usually kept some supper back for Zane, which was just as well as he was always hungry.

Daniel had noticed that Nairne was doing many of Zane's chores.

"You know he'll get soft if you keep doing everything for him," he joked with her.

"Get soft, he's always been soft. Don't worry, I'm keeping a note and Zane will be made to pay up sooner or later."

"Oh, I bet you'll make him pay. I just hope Zane's prepared."

"Dad, has he said what actually happens at the warehouse?"

"They move stock and load it into delivery vehicles. That's what he told me."

"Yes, but what do you think is in the boxes. Zane said most of them don't have any labels. It could be anything."

"Ye,s but Garrick knows these men, there is no way he would get Zane, or Paul for that matter, mixed up in anything illegal. Anyway, I've been up there to get some fuel for the pick-up and it looks like a legitimate operation."

"Okay, I was just wondering, that's all."

But Nairne was still curious. There was no way she believed that Ed ran a business, he wasn't smart enough. She was sure Garrick and Stevie were behind it. Plus, everyone was vague about exactly what this business actually delivered. She tried asking Zane, but he was completely disinterested in the contents of the boxes.

Daniel had a job on the other side of Greenlaw Moor, over forty miles away and the weather forecast was far from good so he set off early stopping at the industrial estate to fill the tank. The gates to the yard were open. Daniel had agreed with Garrick that he would take a note of the number of litres and pay at the end of each week. He drove round to the rear of the building. A stainless steel fuel tanker was parked up ahead and the driver was filling the underground tank; Daniel's arrival startled him.

"Morning, I've just come to fill up. Garrick said it was okay."

"Oh, right." The man was flustered; his eyes darted back from Daniel to the door of the warehouse.

"Is it all right if I use the pump while you're filling the tank?"

"No problem. I'm nearly finished then I can get rid of this thing." He indicated to the tanker.

Stevie emerged from the back of the warehouse.

"Daniel, you're a bit earlier than usual, caught us at it," he laughed. Daniel looked puzzled. "Topping up the system." He glanced towards the tanker.

"Yes, I suppose you must get through a fair bit of fuel with the number of vans you're operating."

"It all adds up. Say, how is Zane enjoying the new job? I've not seen him much since he started."

"He loves it," said Daniel. "He's exhausted when he gets home, but he thinks it's great, and it's been good for his confidence."

"Between us, from what I hear he's a hard worker, unlike Paul who obviously thinks he's made for a more managerial role if you know what I mean. Anyway, I had better not hold you back. See you later."

"Okay, see you."

It was a hard day's work when he reached his destination: there were roof repairs to be done to two farm cottages, which were to be occupied later that week. The buildings, which had been empty for years, were in a poor state. Two other men were on site, one was making repairs to the plumbing system and the other was replacing a couple of broken windows. Daniel had met the glazier before on a previous job.

"I wouldn't fancy spending a cold February night in this place," he said over their lunchtime break. "It'll be perishing."

"Yes, especially if you're not used to countryside living," Daniel replied. "But it's in better condition than some I've worked on."

"I suppose all the good ones have gone," said the third man. "And let's face it, beggars can't be choosers. They're damned lucky to get anything at all, though I must say I wouldn't fancy taking in strangers."

"I'd have said that too," said Daniel. "But we've had a family staying with us for few months now. We've had our moments, but I'd not deny them a place to stay. After all it could quite as easily have been us in that position." The other two men nodded.

"Makes you think," said the glazier. "It can't go on like this, what with the crime and the overcrowding. Hell, the shops are beginning to run out of the basics. My wife had to queue for two hours yesterday for bread and this morning it took me thirty minutes at the petrol station. No delivery this morning, the tanker got hijacked on the A1. Apparently the driver put up a fight. Poor sod, he's critical; looks like they gave him a good beating. No, you wouldn't get me driving one of those rigs. Not now. Too dangerous. If it's not fuel, it's food or fags or drink, anything you can sell on easily. It's turning into bloody bandit country."

On the way home, Daniel tuned into the local radio station to check the weather report. It was five o'clock and the news headlines were on.

"Lothian and Borders Police issued a statement earlier this afternoon in relation to the United Petroleum tanker which was hijacked last night on the A1. The driver, forty-three year old father of two Alan Craig, died from his injuries earlier this afternoon. This is now a murder enquiry and drivers who were on the A1 last night are being asked for their assistance. The tanker was reported on the hard shoulder seven miles north of Berwick-Upon-Tweed. A silver or grey van was seen parked in front of the tanker. Police stated he had resisted his attackers and had been beaten repeatedly with a heavy object, possibly a crow bar. The tanker was stainless steel with the following company marking UP Int. on the side."

Daniel clicked the radio off.

It was after seven when Daniel heard the car come up the driveway.

"I'm just going to have a word with Garrick." His tone was sharp.

"Is everything okay?" Nairne asked. He didn't answer. Nairne cleared the dishes from the table and filled the basin with hot water. She could see her father and Garrick standing outside.

The kitchen windows were wet with condensation, but

it was clear to Nairne from the body language that they were having a heated argument. Her dad looked angry while Garrick appeared to be trying to explain himself. Her father's voice was raised, but she couldn't make out the words. After a few moments, he came back in, shutting the door behind him, forcefully.

"Dad what is it? What's wrong?" She was scared. He looked furious.

"Nothing for you to worry about, just something I needed to clear up with Garrick. Sorry, I know I've been in a mood. Come on, let me help you with those." Nairne knew better than to press him. He would tell her when he was ready.

The next morning Daniel was waiting for them in the kitchen.

"Won't you be late?" Nairne asked, looking at her watch.

"It's okay; I wanted to speak with Zane before I leave." Zane appeared a few moments later, hair uncombed and school shirt hanging down below his sweatshirt.

"Zane, I take it you're working tonight."

"Yes, why?"

"I want you to tell Ed that this will be your last night. I think it's too much, all these evenings and Saturday's. I'm worried it's affecting your school work." Zane glanced at Nairne with a bewildered expression.

"But dad, I've kept on top of my homework just like I promised! And I've done Nairne's Sunday chores, haven't I Nairne?" She nodded in agreement.

"I know son, but you look tired and you've got exams coming up. I just think it would be better if you were to stop."

"But that's not fair. What if I stopped doing evenings and only did Saturdays. Would that be okay?"

"No, I want you to tell him you can't work for him anymore. I know you think I'm being hard on you, but it is for the best." Zane began to plead, promising he'd work harder, let his dad check his homework, but Daniel would not budge. He left them to their breakfast. Zane was despondent.

"It's not fair, I didn't do anything wrong. I don't understand, he seemed pleased when I got the job."

"I know, but something's going on. Last night I saw him arguing with Garrick. He wouldn't tell me what it was about, tried to make out it was nothing, but he was furious."

"But my job isn't anything to do with Garrick, I work for Ed."

"Yes, but I think Garrick has got more to do with this than he's letting on," Nairne replied.

EIGHTEEN

At the end of the school day Zane and Paul set off to the warehouse as usual while Nairne travelled home alone. The house was chilled when she got in and next door was in darkness.

Heavy rain lashed against the windows as gusts of wind howled through the yard. She stoked the range, piling on large dry logs, then through to the living room where she lit the fire. Next homework, English and maths, nothing too taxing and by six o'clock she was finished.

Daniel arrived home at six forty-five. A north-easterly wind gave the air a bitter feeling as the branches of the trees swayed against the dark, cloudy sky. Dog was asleep, his breaths long and slow. Daniel parked at the side of the house, he could see a light on in the kitchen; there was no sign of Garrick's car. Daniel sighed. He felt despondent. He wanted to believe Garrick, but deep down he knew there was something wrong at the warehouse. Daniel unclipped his seatbelt, and rubbed Dog affectionately on the head.

"Come on, time to go in." Dog raised his head, pricked up his ears and stretched. They got out of the car and Dog dashed across the yard barking.

Daniel strode after him. Then he saw the goat standing in the yard, outside the enclosure; the gate of the pen was banging open and closed in the wind. Goat and Dog looked at each other. Dog knew better than to bark. He sidled up until he was on the other side of her and then edged forward. She backed away, Daniel opened the door of the pen and let her back in.

"Good Dog. Let's check the girls haven't got out." However, it was too much to hope for. Mona and Lisa were gone. Daniel walked back to the truck and retrieved a torch and they set off into the woods. Dog had previous experience of rounding up the girls, as this was not their first escape bid. The ground underfoot was slippery and Daniel was glad of the torch. He could hear Dog panting and snuffling along the ground looking for a scent.

Fat chance of finding them in this weather, he thought, but the last thing he needed was for one of them to attempt to cross the river. The rain had been falling for days and the river was in spate. By the time he reached the water's edge he was regretting his decision to look for the pigs; the river was thundering along, brown and swirling, there was no way they would have ventured into that. He could hear Dog further along the bank, forcing his way through the undergrowth and then to his right something large moved, branches snapped.

"Dog, over here boy, over here," he whistled. Daniel was reasonably sure it was Mona; she was by far the larger of the two animals and the noise sounded like something heavy. Dog rushed past him out of sight, but he could hear barking, then a deep throaty growl followed by a yelp. Daniel shone the torch in the direction of the noise.

"Dog, here boy, Dog here....."

Dog stopped, ears up and listened as he heard the sound of something hitting the ground and then a groan; Dog charged back to Daniel.

The man was standing next to the water's edge bending down, rolling something into the fast flowing water. He turned as Dog leapt. Dog gripped the sleeve of his coat; his teeth ripped through the fabric, finding flesh, then muscle. He clung to the man. The man fell to the ground with Dog clamped to his forearm. They struggled.

The man could feel the teeth tearing at his flesh as his free hand searched the ground for the club he had dropped moments earlier. He grasped it and swung it down, hard.

Nairne checked the clock, it was nearly seven and she was beginning to get worried. Dad had said he would be home by six thirty; she glanced out the window, but her view was obscured by the rain. She removed the soup from the heat and slipped on her shoes and coat. Opening the door, she peered out as Dog came bounding across the yard, barking, his eyes wild and his jaws slavering.

"Dog, what is it?" She bent down as he rushed to her. He was soaking, his matted fur was dark and as she pulled him into the porch; she saw the blood on his coat. He was whimpering. Nairne could feel her heart racing. How had Dog got here? Where was dad?

Taking a torch from the kitchen drawer, she put Dog onto his lead and went outside. She saw the pick-up truck parked next to the house.

"Dad, dad," she called, but her voice was lost hopelessly on the wind. Dog was straining on the lead so she followed him, across the yard, down past the animal pens; she noticed Goat was standing at the fence. There was no sign of the pigs.

They went through the garden and into the woods. Nairne continued to call. The wetness of the undergrowth soaked into her trousers; underfoot the ground was uneven and treacherous. Rain lashed against her face as Dog pulled impatiently. She could hear the rushing sound of the river. When they reached the riverbank the once sedate stream was a raging torrent; water pressed at the banks, surging into a swirling darkness. Dog charged from left to right, whining and distressed. Nairne shouted as loudly as she could as she swung the torch backwards and forwards. Then she saw it.

There was a shape about twenty meters downstream near the edge. It bobbed up and down with the current. She ran towards it. His body was wedged beneath a large branch that had fallen into the raging water.

"Dad!" Nairne reached out and caught hold of his clothing. She pulled and his head lolled back. He was barely conscious. His hair stuck to his forehead. His eyes fluttered, trying to focus.

"Dad, let me help you." She tugged uselessly at his jacket. Placing the torch on the bank, she slid into the waist deep water and felt the warmth of her blood seeping away. Within seconds, her legs were numb. Reaching under his shoulders she heaved. The water pulled back, yanking him in the opposite direction, forcing him under the branch, willing him to slip down. Nairne was crying with the effort. She pulled and pulled. Her feet slipped forward as if hands were grasping at her, dragging her down. Daniel looked up at her. She pulled his arm up and over the top of the branch. She raised his head out of the water. The broken arm lay motionless.

"I'll get help. Hold on, I'll get help!" She reached for the bank and dragged herself out of the water. Her sodden clothes and boots pulled her back. Dog barked, willing her to move. She scrambled onto the solid ground and struggled to her feet, her limbs dull from the cold. Picking up the torch, she raced through the trees. There was no time to look for a path; branches tore at her clothes and scratched her face, Dog ran ahead barking madly. She fell, her ankle twisted violently and as she pushed herself up pain shot through her leg. She hobbled towards the lights of the house.

Nairne's fists pounded on the door as Pamela opened it.

"Nairne, what's wrong? Oh my God, what is it?" The girl stood on the doorstep drenched; cuts and scratches covered her face. She was crying. Words poured out through sobs.

"Garrick, quickly! Something's wrong." Garrick appeared in the hallway. He put his arm round Nairne and propelled her inside.

"No, no, you have to come with me!" She pulled against him.

"Nairne calm down. What is it?"

"It's dad! He's fallen in the river. He's trapped. You've

got to help me!" She tugged on Garrick's arm.

"Okay." Garrick lifted his coat from the peg in the hallway and took the torch from her hand.

"Exactly where is he?" Nairne described the spot. "Right Pamela, call an ambulance and look after Nairne. I'll get a rope out the car and I'll go down and get Daniel out of the water. The dog can show me the way."

"No, I need to come and help!" said Nairne, panic in her eyes.

"Nairne, it's okay," said Pamela. "You're not in a fit state to go anywhere, you can hardly walk! Garrick will deal with this. Come on, let's get you into the warm." Pamela supported her weight and helped her to the sofa while Garrick and Dog set out into the darkness.

It didn't take long for Garrick to find the spot; Dog led him straight there. The water had forced Daniel's body under the tree limb; the only thing holding him was his broken arm draped uselessly over the branch. With each surge of water his head vanished beneath the surface.

Garrick cast around for a sturdy tree and tied one end of the rope to it and the other around his waist. Cautiously, he lowered himself into the icy depths. He took hold of Daniel and pulled his body free.

Daniel it's me, Garrick." The head lolled back, eyes fluttering. "I'm here to help you." He held the body in his arms as the water surged round them, engulfing Daniel, covering his head, pulling him down. The legs kicked weakly for a few moments, and then went limp. It took ten minutes and all his strength to make it back onto the bank, Garrick fell back exhausted. Daniel's head lay against his legs, the lifeless eyes gazed at him, unseeing: Garrick placed his hand over them and closed the lids.

"Why did you have to be so god dam righteous? Why couldn't you just turn a blind eye like everyone else?" he whispered.

The lights from the ambulance crew were visible at the

top of the hill and he heard their voices drifting in the wind as he shouted and waved the torch.

Pamela and Nairne stood in the door of the house. Wrapped in a blanket, Nairne was shaking although she no longer felt cold; she no longer felt anything. She could see Pamela's lips moving and hear sounds, but the words did not register. It seemed like an eternity passed. Dog was first to appear; he limped across the yard, whining, his bloody fur glistened in the light. He pushed himself against Nairne's legs as she placed her hand on his head. Next, two ambulance men emerged from the trees; their yellow coats shone magically in the darkness. The stretcher held between them was weighed down by the body covered in a white blanket. Garrick followed, muddy and wet. His hair clung in strands to his forehead; water ran down his face.

They reached their vehicle and opened the door to place the body inside. Nairne dashed forward. She could hear screaming; it was relentless. She could hear it, but she could not understand it was her voice; the sound tore through the air. Pamela squeezed her eyes shut, her hands cupped over her face. Nairne clutched at the blanket, at her father's body. The ambulance man prised her fingers free; he put his arm round her and she wept. Garrick came forward to comfort her.

"Nairne!" He took her into his arms, "I'm sorry I was too late...."

She pushed herself back, arms flailing wildly and stared into his eyes.

"You said you would save him, you promised ....." She spun away from him. Her legs crumpled uselessly under her.

PC Thompson was on her way back to the station when the call came in. She recognised the address, contacted base and said she would go. The lights of the ambulance illuminated the yard: the scene was distressing. The girl was on the ground weeping, not the tears of an upset teenager, this was a deep primal cry. The dog was howling; its eyes were wild, one side of its fur was bloody. A man and woman stood huddled together; they looked oddly out of place with the rundown buildings, the mud and the incessant rain. The woman looked like she had slipped from the pages of a woman's magazine. Although soaking wet, the man had a city softness about him. As she got out of the car, one of the ambulance crew was trying to get the girl to her feet.

The other one filled her in. PC Thompson nodded.

"Do you want me to try and calm her down? I've met her before, back in the summer, when her mum died, God, two parents in less than a year."

"What happened to the dog?" she asked. The driver glanced over at Dog and shrugged. PC Thompson introduced herself to Garrick and Pamela.

"I've met Nairne before. I'll try to calm her down. Do you know where her brother is?"

"Yes, he's out with my son, Paul. They should be back soon," Garrick responded.

"I'm sorry to ask you this, but I'll need to take Nairne to the hospital and I don't think she should go in the back with her father's body. Can you speak with Zane when he gets back? I know it's a lot to ask, but we are under pressure. I doubt I can get another officer out here before he gets home. I'll bring Nairne back after the doctors have had a look."

"Yes, yes of course...." Garrick's voice was barely more than a whisper. Pamela was sobbing. She wiped her eyes and mascara smudged across her cheeks.

The ambulance men climbed into the front of the vehicle and started the engine. PC Thompson took Nairne by the shoulder and helped her to her feet. She moved as if in a trance. Garrick opened the door of the police car and they helped her inside. Dog stood whining at the car door. PC Thompson opened the back door and Dog jumped in.

"I'll see if I can get one of the lads at the station to get the dog looked after. Looks like a nasty injury."

"Yes, must have got caught on something in the woods," said Garrick vaguely, as PC Thompson climbed into the car and drove away.

Garrick walked back to the house.

"Oh Garrick," Pamela wailed. "What are we going to do? Those poor children....."

"It's all right." He put his arm round her shoulder and comforted her. "We can look after them. After all, Daniel was so good to us; it's only right we should stay here and look after them...."

NINETEEN

Paul had never been close to death; he had never witnessed what grief does to people; Zane was a different person, a lost soul set adrift and Paul was the one who was there, who was closest and should have been able to help. But Paul couldn't help; he couldn't even grasp what this might feel like. He felt awkward, he wanted Zane to pull himself together like they did in the films, be sad for a few minutes, but then get on with it. It had been three days and still Zane went from one person to another looking for an explanation, looking for some sort of comfort: he cried all the time, like a child, tears ran down his face; it appeared to Paul that they were endless.

Paul knew when they got home that night that something was wrong. They had passed the police car and ambulance and Ed had made some comment, but they were too busy arguing over which CD they should play. Ed dropped them off and said goodbye to Zane. He was sorry it was his last day.

Garrick was waiting for them at the door and told Zane to come into their house. One look at Pamela was enough. The glamour was gone. She was pale, her eyes red. She had attempted to wash off the mascara stains, but the black inkiness was ingrained in the lines round her eyes. She clutched a crumpled handkerchief which she plucked at nervously; she couldn't look at Zane. Zane's face went from a huge smile to a look of confusion; he looked from Garrick to Pamela and back.

"What is it?" his voice was shaky, his confidence melted away.

Garrick told him, his tone steady, calm, rehearsed. Paul

could hear the blood rushing to his head, he felt almost giddy and the image of the ambulance and the police car flashed into his mind. He couldn't imagine what Zane must have felt. Once Garrick finished, Zane just stood there looking at him, his expression puzzled as though he had spoken in a different language. He didn't say anything. Pamela broke the silence. Her sobbing dragged Zane into the here and now. He began jabbering, a string of questions, disbelief and incredulity, his voice rose in pitch and volume. Within seconds, he was bordering on hysterical. Garrick took hold of the boy by the shoulders, looked him straight in the eye and told him it was true. Daniel was gone.

Nairne returned home late that night with the policewoman. They had been to the hospital and her ankle was badly sprained. Her appearance shocked Paul. It was as if she had aged years in a matter of hours. PC Thompson spoke to Garrick, her tone hushed. She wanted to find out if they could look after the teenagers; otherwise, social services would step in.

"Of course we can," Garrick responded magnanimously. "They're like family. Daniel was a great man and a close friend. We'd talked of staying permanently, of setting up business together, it's the least we can do." Pamela looked troubled, but she kept her counsel and it was agreed that they would act as contact until proper arrangements could be made.

The post mortem results arrived four days later and it showed death by drowning. Daniel had sustained a severe injury to the back of his skull, consistent with a fall. PC Thompson let them know the body had been released.

"At least now we can have the funeral. I'll get the date confirmed at the church. St Andrews is it? I had a chat with the minister there and he said they could make the necessary arrangements," said Garrick.

"There won't be a church service." It was the first

words Nairne had spoken in days. "My father was an atheist; he would never have wanted that. I thought you would have known that, since you were such close friends." She directed the words at Garrick like bullets from a gun.

"Okay, Nairne, I'm only trying to help. We'll make whatever arrangements you think are best." He cast a look at PC Thompson, a mixture of dismay and apology.

"My dad would have wanted people to gather and spend a short time thinking about him. We'll have some readings from one of his favourite books and then people can come back here for refreshments."

"We can book somewhere in town, darling," said Pamela. "They can organise it all for us."

"It's not for us, it's for my father. He would have wanted his friends to come to his home, to drink to him. We're not having some crappy buffet in some grotty hotel in town."

"But what about all the arrangements?" Pamela sounded stressed already.

"I'll do it."

So it was agreed. There would be no flowers, no gravestone. Pamela and Garrick were horrified, but Nairne was adamant and Zane just went along with it.

PC Thompson was glad to get out of the house. The atmosphere was terrible. Nairne emanated hatred, the boy looked broken beyond repair and the poor neighbours were trying, but the more they tried the more Nairne pushed against them.

The turnout for the service was high. Daniel, although an intensely private man, had been popular. There was a respect for the views he held. That, combined with the tragic circumstances of his death, increased people's need to pay their respects. After the cremation a sizeable crowd returned to the house for drinks and refreshments, and true to her word, Nairne organised the food with Pamela's help. It had the feel of a military operation as Nairne worked tirelessly in the kitchen for hours the night before. Zane meanwhile, moped around unable to settle to anything. Garrick assumed the role of host, shaking each person by the hand, accepting their condolences as if this was his house, as if the loss had been his loss. Adults smiled sympathetically at the two teenagers and whispered about how sad it was, how well they were bearing up. Nairne instructed Pamela to hand round the food, top up the glasses, make sure everyone had everything they needed. At three o'clock, Nairne and Zane put on their coats. Garrick spotted them and made his way across the room.

"Where are you going?"

"We're going to scatter our father's ashes," said Nairne.

"What, now? Where? Where are you going?" A hush began to descend on the room as people noticed the two of them with their coats buttoned and Zane clasping the urn.

"The river," Nairne replied, her tone flat.

"But Nairne, you don't need to worry about any of that, not today. We can decide later what to do with... the ashes." Garrick voice rose in pitch, he felt as if the guilt was written across his face and the girl was doing this to get a reaction.

"We're not worried. It's what we want to do. He was our father and it's our decision. It was the river that made him choose this place and it was the river that killed him and that is where he should go back to. It's what he would have wanted."

"Let us come with you at least," he implored, all eyes were upon him, this magnanimous neighbour, the Good Samaritan, the man who had taken charge.

"No thank you, I think you've done more than enough." The words cut him. He was sure everyone could sense the hatred in them. Pamela appeared at his side.

"Garrick." She placed her hand on his arm. "Let them

go. Nairne's right, this is a private moment for them to share." She led him away. The mourners looked embarrassed as if they were intruding. The conversation picked up as Nairne and Zane left. Dog, who had been lying in the porch out of the way of the noise and people, followed them silently. He still limped and the line of stitches was still visible.

As darkness fell Pamela was worried. Paul reluctantly offered to go and check on them, but there was no need. As he set off across the yard the two of them emerged from the woods.

"I was coming to make sure you were all right." The words sounded dumb as he said them. How could they be all right?

"We're fine thanks," said Nairne in the same emotionless tone. Paul couldn't understand how she could be so controlled. The three of them went back into the house. People were still eating, drinking, and talking. Voices were raised, as people reminisced. The reappearance of the poor children quietened the noise, but Nairne put on her best face and circulated thanking people for their kind words and cards. She was speaking to Mr Elliot, a local farmer when she saw him standing in the doorway of the kitchen, a bottle of beer in his hand; their eyes met and Stevie winked. Nairne felt the rage surge through her body like a jolt of electricity; the facade she had been presenting all day was gone. She strode across the room and shoved him into the kitchen; the force of her actions caught him off balance, the beer bottle slipped from his hand smashing on the kitchen floor.

"Get out of our house," she screamed. Silence fell on the gathering. Garrick rushed towards them. Dog stood next to her growling. Open mouthed, Stevie raised his arms to defend his face as Nairne rained blows at him. He flinched as she hit his right arm, pulling it up out of reach.

"Hey. Hey. Okay, I'm leaving. Garrick said it would be

okay; I only wanted to pay my respects."

"Respect!" Nairne yelled. "You don't know what it means! Get out of this house. Don't you ever come back; Garrick had no right to invite you. This is our house, not his and don't you ever forget it."

TWENTY

Two days after the funeral PC Thompson visited. She sat with Nairne and Zane, while Garrick and Pamela busied themselves in the kitchen.

"How are you both?" She reached over and squeezed Zane's hand.

"We're fine," said Nairne solemnly.

"I know this is hard but we need to discuss what happens next."

"We stay here," said Nairne defensively. "Dad left us the house and the insurance will pay off the mortgage so we'll be fine. We can look after ourselves."

"I'm sure you can, but..."

"But what?" Nairne replied.

"I'm afraid it's not allowed. You're only fourteen and Zane is only sixteen, not old enough to be your guardian so there are some options.... do you want me to go through them?"

Zane nodded in response while Nairne stared straight ahead.

"Okay, option one. Nairne, you go into care. There's a kid's residential home over in Galashiels, or possibly foster care and Zane you stay here. Option two, you both stay here and we apply to the court to accept Garrick as your legal guardian until your sixteenth birthday."

"No way!" Nairne snapped. "I don't want Garrick making any decisions for me, absolutely no way."

"Ssshhh," said Zane. "He'll hear you."

"I don't care if he does. It's okay for you; you're sixteen so you can do what you want."

"Nairne, I don't know why you don't like Mr Unwin, but he risked his life to try and save your father and he has offered to do this for you so you can stay here, together; he's trying to help."

"Trying to help himself more like," Nairne replied.

"All right, if you'd rather go into care I'll contact social services and we'll get the paperwork underway," PC Thompson sighed. "But I warn you now, the system is close to breaking point. You need to think about this, please."

"Nairne... please Nairne... I don't want to stay here on my own." Zane started to cry, silently. Tears welled up and rolled slowly down his cheeks. He wiped them away, embarrassed.

"Okay, fine, I'll stay, but it's not fair."

"I know, I know it seems that way.... I'll let Mr Unwin know and we'll get the paperwork organised." And so it was agreed. The formal hearing took place the following week and Nairne returned home in the company of her new guardian.

It was two weeks since Daniel's death and Nairne knew they had to go back to school. There had been no pressure, but the longer they left it the harder it would be. Zane was reluctant. He thought, as head of the family, he should get a job; they'd need the money, but Nairne was adamant that dad would have wanted Zane to sit his exams and there was only three months to go. Besides, they had enough savings to last if they were careful. So, after some persuasion and a promise to help with his homework, Zane agreed.

The next morning they boarded the school bus with Paul and took their usual seats as a hush fell.

"What are you lot staring at?" Paul snorted; heads turned and conversations revived. It was the same when Nairne entered her class for registration, sympathetic glances, whispers, pitying looks. Mrs Walsh took registration and as the pupils fled to their first lesson, she called Nairne back.

"It's good to see you back at school, Nairne. We were all very upset. Your father was a good man and he'll be missed." Nairne bit her lip, as a lump formed in her chest. She was not going to cry. "Now I better not hold you back." Mrs Walsh leaned over and squeezed Nairne's hand, for just a second.

"Thanks Mrs Walsh."

By lunchtime she was feeling a bit more relaxed. The other kids were still subdued and awkward but she realised they didn't know what to say. There was no sign of Zane or Paul, but she caught up with them on the bus that evening. Zane was sullen while Paul made a big effort to chat; Nairne joined in for Zane's sake.

The house felt so silent and cold when they got home even though Pamela had been round to light the stove. She'd invited them for dinner, but they declined; after all, they couldn't go round every night, they had to get used to the place.

Dog, who was used to going out with Daniel every day, was overjoyed at their arrival. He leapt about excitedly until Zane snapped at him.

"That's not very fair, he's been waiting for us all day. Why don't you take him out with you when you check on the animals and I'll get us some dinner organised," Nairne said in her most authoritative tone. It worked. Zane changed clothes then set off across the yard with Dog in tow. They ate in silence. After dinner Nairne helped Zane with his homework, but he was distracted.

"Was everything okay today?" Nairne asked. Tears ran down his cheeks. "I'm sorry, I didn't mean to upset you...." He shoved his chair back and rushed from the room; she heard his bedroom door slam shut.

On Wednesday morning Zane was still silent and needed some serious prodding to get up and then not a word was spoken on the way to school. By the evening Nairne was worried: he wouldn't tell her what was wrong, he hardly ate any of his dinner and his homework was left undone. Thursday was a bitter day as the wind howled through the house. Zane did not appear for breakfast despite several reminders. Eventually, Nairne went upstairs; he was still huddled under the duvet.

"Zane the bus will be here in ten minutes, if you don't get up now you'll miss it."

"I'm not going, I don't feel well." The disembodied voice emanated from beneath the covers.

"I'll go without you." Nairne knew Zane hated being left in on his own, but even this threat didn't work so she left him and went next door. Pamela appeared.

"Paul, that's Nairne here, are you ready?" Pamela called through. "Where's your brother?" she enquired, looking past Nairne.

"He says he's not feeling well and won't get up, but I don't think he wants to go to school. Could you check on him later?"

"Of course I will, don't worry." Paul appeared and they set off down the drive.

"So what's wrong with him?" Paul asked.

"I don't know, something at school I think. You hang around together, has something happened?"

"No, nothing," said Paul, but the colour rose in his cheeks. Nairne was sure he knew more than he was saying.

Tamara was unhappy and she didn't like it. Life had been good since she moved here, a new best friend, Laura, and boyfriends who were also friends. Tamara and Craigie, Laura and Paul; just the way it should be, only now it was ruined. Therefore, Tamara felt justified in taking out her anger on one of those responsible, Nairne Grear; the girl was trouble, her and her brother. Tamara wasted no time when Nairne arrived that morning. She shoved past her and as Nairne challenged her, she let her have it.

"I hope your brother's pleased with himself. Just because he's a loser he has to ruin things for everyone else." She flounced past.

"What are you talking about? What has he ruined?" Nairne responded.

"Like you don't know, sitting there gloating."

"If you have something to say Tamara, then say it."

"All right then, your brother broke up Laura and Paul. We've all said it; Paul shouldn't waste his time hanging about with that loser."

Nairne stormed past her, along the corridor to the class next door. She spotted Paul perched on one of the desks surrounded by his friends. She butted in.

"Are you going to tell me what's been going on?"

"I don't know what you mean." Paul looked to the group for support.

"Then I'll tell you. Zane won't come to school and Tamara tells me that he broke up you and Laura, so have you been picking on him?"

"Of course not, we're mates. Just ignore her, she's trying to wind you up."

"Well it's working, so tell me what happened."

"Look Nairne, it doesn't matter. She's pissed off because I dumped Laura...."

"Because of Zane apparently, so explain it."

Craigie interrupted; Nairne wasn't going to be satisfied with some half-baked story.

"Tell her Paul, if you don't someone else will." The rest of the group shifted uncomfortably. Paul stayed silent.

"Right then Craigie, you tell me or I'll go next door and make Tamara tell me." This was no idle threat and Craigie and Tamara were still an item so he didn't want that to happen.

"Okay, Laura made a comment about your dad and Zane overheard her, then she laughed at him for crying. She was being a bitch; you know what she's like. Zane should just ignore her."

"What did she say?" This time when Paul answered his face was red and he couldn't look Nairne in the eye.

"She said your father fell in the river because he was drunk. She said that time your dad and her mum were called to the school that he was drunk then; her mum could smell it. So I dumped her because she was totally out of line."

Laura was later than usual for school; she needed extra time to get ready; to get her hair and makeup just right. She was still smarting from being dumped and she was going to make sure she looked even better than usual; she'd show Paul Unwin what a mistake he'd made. There were only a few minutes to registration when she entered the classroom, she waved at Tamara and sidled between the desks. Nairne stood up, blocking her path.

"Excuse me!" said Laura, belligerently. "I want to get past."

"So?" said Nairne.

"Nairne, get out of my way."

"No."

"So what can I do for poor little orphan Annie?" A hush descended on the class and all eyes turned to watch the unfolding situation.

"I heard what you said about my father."

Laura looked round and caught Tamara's eye.

"I only said what everyone else was thinking, so if you're waiting for an apology you'll have a long wait."

"I don't want an apology, what would be the point. We both know you wouldn't mean it."

"Then what do you want?" Laura sneered.

"I want you to feel the way my brother is feeling. The way you feel when you lose something so precious, you don't think you will ever cope. And since the only thing you seem to treasure is that vacant, smug, pretty little face of yours....."

Nairne hit her before the sentence was finished. The girl toppled backwards, blood gushed from her broken nose as she hit the floor. Nairne was on top of her pummelling her head. This was not a fight: it takes two people to fight and Laura had no chance to join in.

TWENTY ONE

The down side of not going to school was spending more time with Garrick. He went to the school to plead her case with support from Mrs Walsh. She had stopped the altercation and elicited a confession from a tearful Tamara, but Mr Watson explained that the local authority took a strong line on violence in school; he could not overlook the severity of the incident. Laura's mother wanted Nairne and the school prosecuted. Laura's injuries were significant, a broken nose, a badly bruised eye and two broken teeth. The only reason Mrs Howard backed down was the realisation that if the police got involved Laura's previous behaviour would become public knowledge. That, combined with the fact that three other pupils, Paul Unwin, Stuart Craig and Tamara Potter-Smith had confirmed that Laura had been spreading rumours about Nairne's father, which she claimed originated from her mother, made her see sense. So Nairne was suspended until the end of the academic year. Mrs Walsh was horrified; Nairne was a bright girl with an academic future, while in Mrs Walsh's opinion, Laura Howard was about as much use to the world as a poodle at a foxhunt. At least she ensured that the school provided books and homework schedules for Nairne to allow her to continue her studies.

Nairne was not alone at home. Although everyone had tried to persuade him, Zane would not return to school. Ed offered him a job, three days plus two evening shifts at the warehouse.

On her second week off school Nairne accompanied Pamela into town. The supermarket shelves were bare and what little remained was expensive. Vegetables were unaffordable and Nairne was pleased they still had a small supply, although this was dwindling rapidly. Nairne withdrew some cash from the bank as she needed to get supplies for the garden from Henderson's, which was situated on the edge of the industrial estate.

It was a traditional family business, selling tools, overalls, boots, animal feed and horticultural supplies. The red brick Victorian building had seen better days, but the staff were friendly and knowledgeable. Nairne pushed the door open and a bell tinkled deep within the shop. Pamela gazed in astonishment at the vast array of items as Nairne went to the counter and pulled out her list.

"Hi, I wondered if you had all these items in stock?" She handed the neatly written list to the elderly man behind the counter. He pulled his glasses down his nose and he peered over them.

"Ah, young Nairne isn't it, yes; yes I think we have most of these. We don't have any of the Primo carrot seed left, but we have another early. Oh and the potatoes, no earlies left, but I can give you second earlies, Maxine. Would that be all right?"

"Thanks Mr Henderson, that would be fine." Mr Henderson went through to the back of the shop and collected the various packets and packages.

"I've also got these which might interest you." He placed two trays of young strawberry plants on the counter. "They got the order wrong, sent me far more than I asked for, so why don't you take a couple of trays."

Nairne knew he was lying, but it was very generous of him to give her the plants.

"They're great. Zane will be pleased. He loves strawberries." Mr Henderson put all the goods into two strong carrier bags.

"Now I can put that onto the account for you?"

"No, I'll pay cash," said Nairne, taking the notes out of her wallet. "Can you let me know how much we owe you?"

Mr Henderson paused. Daniel Grear had been a careful man who settled his account at the end of every month so when he died there had only been a small amount outstanding.

"It's all right young lady; your father had settled up with us, there's nothing else to pay. He did have a regular order for the animal feed; do you want to continue with that?"

"Yes thanks. Zane could pick it up; he's working on the estate."

"Oh, that would be fine; we'll have the order made up for the first Monday of every month."

They left the shop and started to walk towards the town centre.

"So how did you know what to get?" Pamela asked. "There seemed to be hundreds of seeds to choose from."

"Dad kept a record of what we planted so I went back through his notebook. Now all I need to do is get started, because looking at the prices in the shops Zane and I are going to have grow as much food as possible."

As they reached the end of the road, a car pulled up. It was Stevie. He wound down the window and Pamela stepped forward to speak with him.

"Nairne, Stevie's offered us a lift home. Come on, get in." Pamela opened the door and climbed in. Nairne stood on the pavement. Stevie leaned over.

"Oh come on, no hard feelings. Let me give you both a lift home. Looks like it's going to rain." Reluctantly, she got in the back.

"See, it's not that hard is it?" Stevie smiled, she could see his smug expression in the rear view mirror.

"So Pam, what brings you out here?"

"Nairne wanted to get some seeds from Henderson's."

"What, flowers for the garden?" Stevie chuckled.

"No, vegetable seeds," said Nairne pointedly. "They grow in the ground, you can eat them." Stevie's smile disappeared.

"No school today, Nairne?" From his tone, it was obvious he knew what had happened. "Sorry I forgot, you don't go to school, do you? Is it true you hit Paul's girlfriend? Jealous were you?"

"Stevie!" Pamela's voice was full of disapproval while Nairne steadfastly ignored him. He dropped them outside the front door, Pamela invited him in for a coffee.

"If you don't mind, that would be great Pam." He turned off the ignition.

"Nairne, aren't you coming in for something?" Pamela asked, as Nairne unlocked the door to her part of the house.

"No thanks, I've got quite a lot to do. See you later." She went inside and shut the door, grateful to get away from Stevie.

"It looks like it's just you and me," said Pamela. He grinned in response and followed her into the house.

"So how's it working out, looking after those two? I thought you would have moved in with them – it's a more comfortable house," he asked, as Pamela poured the coffee into a mug for him.

"Garrick suggested it to me, but I think they need a bit of space. We don't want them to think we're trying to steal the place from under them. Teenage years can be a difficult time and they've been through so much already. It's Zane I worry about; he's such a sweet boy. Whereas Nairne's a headstrong girl, she knows her own mind and isn't afraid to show it."

"Hmm, you're right there, she needs taking in hand if you ask me; she needs a woman like you Pam, to take her under her wing, get her to realise her full potential, if you know what I mean."

Pamela was flattered; she smiled and refilled his coffee cup.

Nairne unpacked the seeds and plants and changed into her gardening clothes. The rain had not come to anything so it was a good day to make a start. She'd already drawn up a planting plan. She and her father had done this together every year since they moved here, even before Angela's departure. She helped him lay out the vegetable beds that first year, dig in the manure they bought from one of the neighbouring farms, and then together they planted the seeds. Nairne had been so excited when things started to appear. Every morning before school, she checked on the delicate seeds in the greenhouse, and then she would wander up and down between the vegetable beds, getting her school shoes muddy, much to Angela's distress, before running back to the house to give a report on progress.

This year she would do it alone; it was a daunting task. At the end of last season, they had covered the empty beds with large sheets of black polythene to protect the ground from the worst of the winter weather. Her target for today was to dig over one of the eight beds and get the greenhouse tidied up.

The air was cold, but she soon heated up. Removing the sheet of plastic on her own was hard work, but at least it wasn't windy. Carefully, she folded and stored it away at the back of the shed for next year. Dog sniffed round the garden barking at her encouragingly every few moments. The spade sliced through the soft, dark earth. Progress was swift. She heard the door open; Dog came bounding across to her and stood, growling.

"What is it boy?" she ruffled his ears. Stevie emerged from the house, pausing to watch her. She turned away and continued to dig, ignoring him. After a few minutes, she heard the car door close and the engine start. Nairne did not lift her head as he drove past.

Pamela came out to see if she wanted lunch, but Nairne declined. She didn't want to offend Pamela, but she didn't want to end up dependent on her or Garrick. They were only her guardians until she was sixteen in fifteen months time, and even now she was sure they could manage on their own, only the rules didn't allow it. By the end of the week, with some help from Zane on his days off, all the beds were ready. The greenhouse was washed inside and out and seed trays were ready to be filled. Mr Cranshaw took her into town to pick up four large bags of compost and the seed planting began.

Pamela was amazed by Nairne; within a couple of weeks the greenhouse was full of tiny seedlings, Pamela had never seen seedlings growing. She was a city girl; she'd never had a garden. Nairne had matured since Daniel's death. There had been no more scenes. She was still not particularly friendly towards Garrick, but her attitude to Pamela had mellowed. She even seemed willing to spend time with Paul. At the weekend he had helped with the digging; there was obviously a technique to digging that Paul hadn't quite mastered. His back ached for days afterwards, although he wouldn't admit it.

Nairne was always busy. If she wasn't in the garden she was in the woods collecting fallen branches, which Zane sawed into lengths for burning next year. If the weather was bad she did her schoolwork. Nairne completed all her course work for Paul to deliver. She was determined she wasn't going to fall behind.

"You have to hand it to her," Garrick remarked after Nairne had brought round her English homework. "She is one determined young lady; you could learn a thing or two from her, son." Paul grunted in response. He was also surprised by Nairne's energy. On Saturday she had serviced the motor for the wind turbine. He wouldn't have had any idea where to start even with instructions, but she had taken the engine apart, cleaned it and re assembled it in a matter of hours.

Keeping busy was the only way to get by. She had to keep going, being organised and responsible, making sure Zane got up in time for work, making sure he had clean clothes to wear, that there was food on the table, that the bills were paid, that the garden was looked after; they'd be relying on the food she was growing. Zane's wages wouldn't keep them both and without the rent from Garrick and Pamela they would not be able to manage. Nairne had already dipped into the savings at the bank. It was hard work being responsible. Zane still cried at the slightest provocation, but he went to work and on his days off he did his chores. Nairne had to remind him what to do, but he rarely moaned about it, as he used to. He felt guilty; it was his fault that Nairne was suspended from school. He also felt ashamed; he should have been looking after Nairne, not the other way round; but he would make it up to her, he knew he would.

TWENTY TWO

The warehouse was freezing, but Zane knew he'd soon heat up once he began unloading the pallets. Zane enjoyed the job. He still felt sad, especially if he thought about his father. If only he had been home that night, he would have been able to pull him out of the water. He was strong, he would have been able to save him. Zane spent a lot of time thinking about that. They usually finished early on Wednesdays, but there was a late load that night so they had stayed on, then Ed had to make a detour into town to drop off some paperwork.

The other men at the warehouse were all right. They teased him, but he didn't mind. Ed had been great about giving him the job back. After the funeral Ed had called and said the job was there for him if he wanted it. Zane missed school, not the work, but the other lads. Nairne wanted him to stay on at school and he knew his father would have wanted that too, but he knew he would never pass his exams and the offer of a real job was a good opportunity. Plus, there was Laura Howard; Paul had been great, as soon as she'd said that stuff about dad Paul had called her an evil little bitch and told her it was over. Zane was amazed. Laura was so pretty; all the boys in the class fancied her, but Paul had dumped her just like that.

Paul usually worked on Wednesday evenings, but it was Garrick's fifty- third birthday so they were going out to dinner. Zane and Nairne had been invited, but said no: Zane because he had work and Nairne because, well because she was Nairne. He didn't understand why she disliked Garrick so much, he had been good to them since dad died and he said dad had talked about setting up in business with him. They'd argued about it earlier that day, she said he could go if he wanted to, but she didn't want to spend an evening with Garrick, not even if it was his birthday. Zane wanted to go, but not on his own; he'd never been somewhere like that where you got lots of courses and sets of cutlery, and the menu would be in French.

The warehouse was quiet, with only him, Ed and Jason. Gunny should have been working, but he hadn't shown up. Zane didn't know Gunny well. He was in his late thirties with tattoos covering both his forearms, his long fair hair was usually tied back in a pony tail and his angular face sported a droopy moustache and long sideburns. He seldom spoke, but when he did the other men paid attention; they treated him with respect.

"Where the hell is he?" Ed snapped, chucking the mobile on the desk. His tone was hostile, a tone he would not have used if Gunny had been present; for although Ed was in charge he was wary of Gunny.

"If he doesn't show up soon we'll have to call the whole thing off."

"Mr U won't be happy with that. Try Stevie, maybe he's seen him," said Jason. Ed picked up the phone.

"Stevie yeah, about ten minutes, Okay yeah, a bit of a problem, Gunny's not shown..... Of course I've tried the mobile.... Yeah, could you go...right."

"So?" said Jason.

"Stevie's on his way, he's going to Gunny's place to see if he's there."

Zane continued to unload boxes as the other two men greeted a solitary Stevie.

"No sign of him. The place was in darkness, no sign of his motor or Leanne." Leanne, Gunny's girlfriend; sometimes picked him up from work. She fascinated Zane: she was excruciatingly thin; in fact, she was so thin he could have picked her up and snapped her in two. She was also the palest person he had ever seen. She always dressed in black and her short hair was dyed black and spiked. She rarely spoke, but laughed nervously if anyone so much as looked at her.

"That's that then – we need to leave here in the next ten minutes if we're going to make it and we can't do it with the three of us. Shit, when I get my hands on....."

"What, what'll you do?" Stevie laughed. "Gunny would rip your throat out soon as look at you."

"Right, well you can explain it. Gunny's your guy, so this is your cock up," Ed replied.

Stevie looked thoughtful.

"Okay so we need four guys and we have four guys." He gestured towards Zane, at the far end of the warehouse unloading a pallet.

"Oh, you're taking the piss," said Jason. "He's a kid and not a very bright one at that."

"Yeah, but with the gear on they're not going to know. He's a big lad, all he has to do is stand there and look the part, he doesn't have to say anything."

"But can we trust him?" asked Ed, nervously. "Don't you think you should check it out with Mr U?"

"Yeah, I'm going to run to him every time we have a problem. Who's he going to tell? Anyway, we'll make it worth his while, he needs the money and it pays better than stacking boxes. Just let me handle it."

Stevie sauntered over to Zane.

"How's it going Zane? Are those lazy bastards leaving you to do all the hard work?"

"No, it's good, I like working here," said Zane in response.

"Afraid Ed can't give you a lift home tonight. We've got a bit of work on, deals to do, you know how it is. We'll drop you off in town, if you like."

"Okay, thanks."

"Right, ten minutes, we'll get our stuff together." Zane

finished unloading the pallet then picked up his jacket. The other three men were waiting for him at the front door, Stevie had his phone clasped to his ear; he was agitated.

"What do you mean you can't make it? God's sake, you know we're relying on you. I suppose that's that then, we'll have to cancel the whole thing. Yeah it's cost me, but if you can't do it...." He clicked the phone to off.

"Looks like you can get a lift after all; my bad luck's turned out to be your good luck, eh."

"Why? What's wrong?" Zane asked. The three men looked despondent.

"Nothing for you to worry about, only a business deal, but I need four guys at this end to help with the work and now I've been let down..... It doesn't matter; you win some you lose some."

"Maybe I could help," said Zane, looking round the three faces.

"You wouldn't get home until late, what would your little sister think? I don't want to get on the wrong side of her again I can tell you." The others sniggered.

"She's not in charge," said Zane. "I can go home whenever I want, plus if it helps you and Ed out."

"What do you think lads?" The other two considered the offer for a moment.

"It would help us out, so it's only fair we make it worthwhile," said Ed

"You're right there," said Stevie, taking out his wallet. "What would you say to two hundred, would that be fair?" Zane's eyes widened at the sight of the bundle of twenty-pound notes; Nairne would be amazed.

Zane took the cash and placed it in his inside pocket. They climbed into Stevie's new people carrier, a sleek black number with tinted windows. Stevie and Ed sat in the front with Zane in the back. They set off towards town. Jason followed in a transit van.

"So what do you need me to do exactly?" said Zane, he wanted to get it all clear to make sure he did a good job.

Maybe they would ask him again.

"Don't worry son, there's nothing to it," Stevie laughed.

TWENTY THREE

Nairne was sulking, it was after ten and Zane was late. She knew he was only doing this to get back at her because she wouldn't go to the birthday dinner, but she couldn't. It would have been hypocritical. Garrick had been trying hard, but that didn't make everything all right, all that stuff about dad setting up business with him; it was rubbish. Dad would have spoken to them; he would never have invited the Unwin's to stay without discussing it. Plus, Nairne hadn't missed the comments from Garrick about the two of them rattling around in the house on their own. She knew he was angling to move in; they might be her guardians, but the house belonged to her and Zane.

At quarter past eleven she heard the taxi bring the revellers home. Reluctantly, she went and knocked on the door. Paul opened it.

"Hi Nairne, is everything all right?"

"No, can I come in?"

"Sure." He let her in. Garrick was slumped in the armchair, drunk, with Pamela sitting giggling on his knee.

"Sorry about them," said Paul, looking embarrassed. "Too much champagne." Garrick looked up.

"Oh Pamela, we have company. What can we do for you this evening Nairne?"

"I'm sorry to come round so late ...it's Zane, he hasn't come home. He should have been back by eight. I'm worried."

"Sit down," Paul cleared a space for Nairne. "Right, let me get my phone." Garrick fumbled in his trouser pocket causing Pamela to squirm and giggle even more. "Okay, I'll ring Ed." He pressed the buttons and moved forward in the seat, tipping Pamela onto her feet. He stood up, swaying slightly.

"Ed, yes Garrick here, have you seen Zane this evening..... And what time was that? Okay, thanks."

"What did he say?" Nairne asked eagerly.

"He said he dropped Zane off in town at seven thirty as he was going out so he couldn't give him a lift home. He hasn't seen him since."

"But that was hours ago." There was panic in her voice; Pamela and Garrick were too far gone to concentrate, but Paul was concerned.

"Maybe he met up with friends and lost track of the time," said Pamela.

"Yes, but he would have phoned by now."

"Why don't I call some of the guys from school? Maybe they've seen him," Paul volunteered.

"Okay, thanks." Nairne replied. She felt cold and clammy; maybe she was overreacting, Zane was sixteen, she wasn't his mum and he could stay out late if he wanted.

Paul took out his phone and called up the first number.

"Hi Spud, sorry, I know. Have you seen Zane this evening?. No, okay, see you." He called the next number and the next, but there had been no sign of Zane.

"Maybe the lad's got himself a girlfriend," said Garrick, smiling slyly. "After all that might not be something you want to discuss with your little sister."

"Dad," Paul's tone was sharp. "You're not helping. I'll go and make you both coffee then we can decide what to do."

"I know what to do," said Nairne. "We need to call the police and go into town and look for him."

"How can we go into town?" said Paul. "Dad's in no state to drive."

"I'll go round and get Mr Cranshaw. He'll take me in."

"Nairne, it's very late to disturb Mr Cranshaw," said Garrick. He could see she was not going to be deterred. "I'll ring Ed back, I'm sure he'll take us."

"Okay, I suppose," said Nairne.

"Right, go and get your coat."

By the time Nairne returned, Garrick and Pamela had finished their coffee and were beginning to sober up. They agreed it wasn't like Zane, but there was probably an innocent explanation. Moments later the car pulled up outside.

"Pamela, you go next door in case he calls. I'll take Nairne in," said Garrick.

"I'll come with you," said Paul. "If that's okay."

"Thanks, that would be good," Nairne replied.

They stepped outside to find Stevie at the wheel of the car. Garrick got in the front and Paul and Nairne got in the rear.

"So what happened to Ed?" Garrick asked.

"Oh, he told me what had happened, but he'd had a few drinks. I didn't think he should drive so I said I'd come over. Hope that's okay with everyone."

The drive into town was silent. No one knew what to say. Nairne was emanating such a feeling of worry it was palpable.

"Where do you want to start?" asked Stevie as they pulled into the main square.

"The police station," said Nairne. "Drop me off there."

"Don't you want to have a look round first?" asked Garrick.

"No, take me to the police station; they'll know if there have been any accidents or anything. The rest of you could have a look round."

"Okay," said Garrick. "Stevie, you and Paul have a look round the pubs, see if anyone has seen him."

Garrick rang the bell and the duty officer came out and opened the front door for them.

"How can I help?" said the chubby faced police officer.

"It's my brother," said Nairne. "He hasn't come home; he should have been back at eight." They explained the whole story. However, as PC Roper politely explained, Zane was over the age of sixteen and was only a few hours late. He couldn't be recorded as a missing person yet.

"Could he have a new girlfriend perhaps?" the PC enquired. "Maybe visiting with her?"

"No, he would have said."

"And when he left for work what sort of mood was he in?"

"He's been down about everything that's happened and we did have an argument, but nothing serious...."

"So could he be angry with you maybe?"

"I suppose, but he's almost four hours late. Where would he go?"

"I'll phone and check with the hospital and I'll check the incident record to make sure there haven't been any accidents or fights then, if it makes you feel better, I'll put a call out to the officers on duty to keep their eye out for him. If you still haven't heard from him in forty-eight hours come back in and we'll make it official."

Nairne was disappointed. Garrick gave the officer their home and mobile numbers and thanked him for his help.

Paul and Stevie searched all the pubs and the centre of town. Reluctantly, at twelve thirty they drove back home in silence. Nairne thanked them and went into her own house. Pamela was still sitting up waiting by the phone.

"Oh, Nairne," she could see from the expression on her face that the trip had been fruitless. "Come on, you get upstairs to bed, I'll stay here tonight. I can sleep on the sofa in case he calls. You look worn out." Nairne began to cry and tears streamed down her face.

"Pamela, what am I going to do? I know something has happened. Zane would have called, I know he would."

By Friday afternoon Garrick and Pamela accompanied Nairne to the police station.

"How can I help?" enquired the desk sergeant.

"We're here to report a missing person." As Garrick

spoke the internal door opened; PC Thompson appeared.

"Mr Unwin, what are you doing here?" she looked at the three of them. It was obvious by their expressions it was serious.

"It's Zane," said Nairne. "He's missing." PC Thompson turned to the desk sergeant.

"Dave I'll deal with this one if you like." She ushered them through to a small interview room. They went through the whole story while PC Thompson filled in the forms. Nairne gave her a recent photograph of Zane.

"So what happens now?" Garrick asked.

"We'll circulate Zane's description to other stations and see what comes up."

"But what if something has happened to him, what if someone's harmed him or taken him or ...." Nairne was agitated.

"I know you're worried Nairne, but most people who disappear come back. Normally they need to get away, if they're unhappy or depressed. I don't think you should think the worst. Let's see if we get anything back from this. You could get some posters made, put them round the local area and see if it jogs anyone's memory. You said that Zane's boss, Ed Lafferty, dropped him in town, do you know where? We'll check our CCTV and see if we have him on camera. Perhaps you could get Mr Lafferty to give me a call." She handed Garrick a card and gave one to Nairne. "Just in case you think of anything else." As PC Thompson showed them out Garrick hung back to speak with her.

"So what do you think, will we find him?"

"Only if he wants to be found, to be honest, Mr Unwin. I didn't want to say this in front of Nairne, but the service is so stretched, a missing sixteen year old isn't going to get priority treatment. We're so busy dealing with the gun crime, hijackings, and fuel wars that, unless we think someone has harmed Zane, there's nothing for us to investigate. The lad has the right to leave home if he wants; although I must say, I am surprised."

"Yes, so are we."

The mood was sombre when they arrived home. Garrick asked Paul to make up a poster on the computer. The sooner they did that the more chance someone would remember something.

"I'll go and see Ed, get him to speak to the police. Maybe the CCTV will find something." Nairne was grateful. Garrick and Pamela seemed genuinely concerned, and so did Paul, who immediately set to work on the posters.

Garrick drove over to Mr Cranshaw's. The old man was out in the yard.

"If it's Stevie you're after he's not in. Any word yet on young Zane?"

"No" Garrick shouted back. "We've been to the police station and they've made it official now. I wanted to catch up with Ed – they want to speak to him. I called the warehouse and they said he was sick."

"Yes, not looking himself these last few days. He's in the kitchen. Go on in."

Garrick went round to the back door. Mr Cranshaw was right, Ed looked terrible. He had bags under his eyes, and his complexion was waxen. He sat hunched at the kitchen table, a mug of tea in his hands and his dressing gown wrapped tightly round him.

"Something you ate?" Garrick asked.

"You could say that," said Ed. "What brings you out here Mr U?"

"We've been to the police station with Nairne. They've listed Zane as a missing person, but they want to speak to you."

"Why, what's it got to do with me?" his voice was panicky. Garrick could see it in his eyes. Ed was scared.

"Calm down, I told them you dropped him in town. They want to check the CCTV, to see if they can see what happened to him. She wants to know when and where. I don't know why you're getting in such a state."

"Why did you have to drag me into it?"

"Into what? You told me you dropped him off so why wouldn't I tell them that? And it's better if you go and see them. We don't want them turning up at the warehouse, do we?"

"Shit, I knew this would happen."

"What is the problem? Just tell them where you left him."

"I didn't, I didn't drive him into town."

"Then why the hell did you say you did?"

"Cause... I don't know, because you knew he'd been at the warehouse so you knew I must have seen him....." his voice trailed off, he could see a thunder cloud gathering around Garrick.

"Ed, what is it? What's been going on?"

"Look I'm not saying another word Mr U; you need to speak to Stevie."

It was late that afternoon when Stevie turned up; Pamela let him into the house. He was as cock sure of himself as ever until he saw Garrick's face.

"Pamela, Stevie and I are going out for a while. I'll see you later." With that Garrick man-handled him back out of the house and into the Range Rover.

"So where are we going? " Stevie asked.

"Somewhere private where we can discuss a few things." Ten minutes later, they pulled up outside the warehouse. Garrick unlocked the front door and they went in.

"Right, you had better start talking. Give me a good reason why I don't just leave you in the mess you've made."

TWENTY FOUR

It was four weeks since Zane had vanished. Nairne was like a ghost. She moved silently about the house, keeping to herself. Most of her days were spent in the garden.

Rows of tender young vegetables were sprouting and the greenhouse was bursting with seedlings. Nairne went to Mr Cranshaw's at least once a week and she'd help him on the farm and he'd help her with any queries or questions about the animals. She took eggs when she visited; he used quite a few, with Stevie and Ed in the house. It was also time to see about the pigs. A friend of Mr Cranshaw's had provided the boar to service Mona and Lisa in previous years so he made the arrangements.

"Are you sure you'll be able to manage the garden and the animals?" he asked.

"I'll be fine," said Nairne, "Pamela's started helping with the chickens now she's stopped being scared of them, and I need the income."

"If there is anything I can help with let me know."

Mr Cranshaw was extremely fond of Nairne; if he had been blessed with a daughter, Nairne would have been perfect. She loved to visit, but only when Ed and Stevie were out. They had both helped in the search for Zane. Garrick had sent them all over the area with posters and they'd been round all the pubs asking about him. In spite of this, she felt even less at ease with them. Stevie was as obnoxious as ever while Ed wouldn't look her in the eye, he avoided contact with her and seemed inexplicably upset by Zane's disappearance.

Ed wasn't the only one who was upset, Paul was very down. He had made an immense effort to befriend Nairne, helping in the garden and taking over some of Zane's chores. Nairne's attitude had mellowed; she couldn't say she liked him, but he was proving that he was a good friend to Zane. Every night when he got back from school he would come to ask if there was any news; he'd put posters all round school and he'd posted information on the internet. Garrick had even offered a reward, but none of it had brought results.

"It's daft us staying next door when you're rattling around in here on your own," Garrick announced, shovelling another fork full of Sunday dinner into his mouth. "Think how much cheaper it would be, only heating one house, plus you'd have company. I know we can't replace your family, but we are worried about you spending so much time on your own."

"Thanks," said Nairne. "But I'm fine." She didn't want to discuss it, she didn't want them living in her house.

"What if Social Services come round? We're your legal guardians. They would be horrified to find you were on your own. We don't want to get into trouble with the authorities. We'll still pay rent, just like now and it's your house, so once you reach sixteen if you feel you want to be on your own then we'll move out."

"If we move in what happens when Zane comes back? There won't be enough room," Paul asked. Garrick glared at him.

"Obviously, when Zane gets back we can move back next door. After all, this is only temporary to keep Nairne company."

Nairne was too tired to argue about it. Besides, she had no plausible reason to say no. Garrick was right, it would save money. Nairne suggested they wait until Friday when Paul would be home from school and that would give her time to pack her father's things and make space for them. Pamela offered to help.

"We'll get some big strong boxes and you can store everything in the attic," she volunteered.

"No, let's pack it and take everything to the charity shop. He's not coming back and at least someone else can get use from them. He would have wanted that. We could put some of Zane's stuff away in the attic."

On Friday, as planned they moved in. It was amazing how much stuff they had amassed in such a short space of time. They ferried boxes round for most of the morning. Pamela, although relieved at getting into a more comfortable house, felt like a trespasser and Paul just didn't want to do it. How would Zane feel when he got back to find this interloper sleeping in his room? It was wrong.

Nairne helped shift the boxes and then went out to the garden to give them time to unpack. The house felt like someone else's home now, not hers. She had kept a few items of her father's including his penknife, a leather belt he always wore, and his books. They now lined one side of her bedroom. The rest of the possessions were merely things, they weren't important and it was stupid to keep them.

Paul came sauntering out to speak to her.

"Nairne, about the boxes of Zane's things, I could leave them next to the wardrobe so when he gets back everything is waiting for him." She could tell he was uncomfortable with the whole thing.

"Okay, if you think there's enough space."

"Yes, it will be fine," he replied smiling.

TWENTY FIVE

The world had been a dark and inhospitable place for so long that Nairne had begun to doubt it would ever change, but by late May the temperature soared, four weeks with no rain and six consecutive days of bright summer sun.

Nairne filled the watering can from the water butt and opened the door of the greenhouse; the air was hot and dry. She poured the water onto the flagstone floor and then into the base of the seed trays. Reaching up she opened the roof vents letting a cool breeze flow through. It was four weeks since they had moved in with her and almost eight since Zane had vanished. The house no longer felt like home, but out here in the garden, this was definitely her domain. They all watched in awe as she managed the animals and tended to the vegetables. Sometimes Pamela would come out to the garden and ask questions about the various emerging seedlings, or she would sit with Garrick in the afternoon sun and drink wine. Paul would come out and help with the digging and weeding, but the notion of planting things seemed to scare him.

She felt excited. There was no way Zane would miss her birthday. He would send a card or phone, or maybe even turn up. She could see it now, he would stride up the drive, smiling and laughing and tell them all where he'd been, then he would move back into his room and the others would go back next door.

She suspected Pamela was planning a surprise birthday dinner; there had been furtive examinations of the recipe books and vague questions about her favourite meals.

Nairne knew Zane's disappearance had hit Paul hard. He was under pressure at school; it was exam time. Today, he was sitting his English exam. She had watched him set off for the bus looking far from confident. In two weeks he would be finished for the summer and potentially for good. New pupils now outnumbered the locals and unless you had resits the school was urging pupils to leave.

Nairne was relieved to escape from the oppressive heat of the greenhouse to the outdoors. She fetched the hoe from the shed and began work.

Garrick had slept late again; his head was pounding from last night's alcohol. He had stayed up late. He knew he wouldn't sleep. These days he never did, so he'd opened a new bottle of Scotch to help him relax.

Pamela was tidying the kitchen purposefully when he went in. He could tell from her body language she was in a mood.

"You missed Paul; it's his English exam today. I thought you might have wanted to drive him in." She switched the kettle on. "Coffee?"

"Yes, black and strong," Garrick replied gruffly.

"Breakfast? I can do some eggs." She opened the fridge.

"No, just coffee."

"It's no trouble."

"I said no, I don't want anything!"

Pamela did not respond. She poured the coffee into a cup, placed it in front of him, and slammed the door on her way out.

Garrick sighed. He drank the coffee, stepped out into the back garden and watched Nairne. His eyes followed her every movement, unable to tear his gaze away. After a few minutes she turned and saw him. He waved awkwardly; she nodded in response and went back to her work. At least she spent her days outside. It was the evenings he couldn't bear: the four of them, like a parody of the perfect nuclear family, trapped together in the house with her incessant chat about her father and what would happen when Zane got back. She was friendly with Pamela and Paul, but she tolerated him, like a bad smell you have to learn to live with. She was polite, reserved and unwilling to show him the slightest trust. It was difficult. She made him feel so angry. After all, Daniel had brought about his own downfall with his holier than thou attitude, an attitude inherited by his daughter and as for the boy, what could he do?

The fourth of June arrived. Nairne was woken by a knock at her bedroom door. Pamela entered with breakfast on a tray, Dog followed closely behind.

"Happy birthday darling." She placed the tray on the bedside table and gave Nairne a hug. No work for you today and that's an order." Dog barked in agreement. "After breakfast we're going to town so you can buy yourself some new clothes and before you start worrying buy whatever you want. Then, you're to have a lazy day doing whatever you want and this afternoon we will be having some food, and of course cake and I've invited a few people over."

With this, the whirlwind left the room and Nairne sat up and ate her breakfast. True to her word, Pamela made Garrick drop them in town then she let Nairne choose both the shops they visited and the clothes she bought. In the afternoon, Pamela laid on a spread with sandwiches and homemade lemonade, which tasted great. The guests included Mr Cranshaw and Callum from the farm and a couple of Zane and Paul's friends from school. Stevie and Ed attended, with instructions from Pamela to be on their best behaviour. They sat with Garrick and all three looked like they would rather be anywhere else on earth. PC Thompson arrived, in off duty clothes.

"Hi Nairne. Happy birthday." She gave her a hug and handed over a card and present. "Pamela told me the date so I thought I'd pop over and see how you are."

"Oh, fine I guess, and I'm hoping Zane might be in touch. He wouldn't miss my birthday, I know he wouldn't."

PC Thompson smiled sympathetically; she knew it was unlikely, but if Zane was going to get in touch today might just be the day. Nairne got her a drink and plate so she could help herself to some food. Pamela came over and greeted her.

"I see you have some news of your own," she looked PC Thompson up and down.

"Yes, I guess it's obvious since last time I saw you. I'm due in October. I'm going to be finishing work in three months. My husband thinks it's too risky to stay on the job now I'm expecting."

"Congratulations," said Nairne.

It was good that her guardians had organised a proper celebration for Nairne, thought PC Thompson. After chatting to Pamela and Nairne she went over to join Garrick, Ed and Stevie.

"Pamela has laid on quite a spread and Nairne seems to be enjoying herself."

"Hmm, yes," Garrick replied, his tone distracted.

"Nairne is very lucky to have all this support from you and your family, and all that help looking for Zane from the pair of you." She smiled at Stevie and Ed. Ed shifted uncomfortably in his seat, while Stevie gulped beer from the bottle clutched in his hand.

"We were..., sorry...., are fond of the lad. It's a pity we haven't managed to find him," Stevie responded.

"At least not yet anyway, but we mustn't lose hope. Nairne certainly hasn't. It's funny though, I would never have believed he would run away. They seemed like such a close family. Maybe Nairne's right, maybe he'll get in touch today," PC Thompson responded.

"I just hope she doesn't get her hopes up," Garrick stated.

"No, but then it's hard not to when it's all such a mystery, especially the CCTV," she replied.

"CCTV?" Ed asked, nervously.

"Yes, I've been over those tapes at least half a dozen times, from the night he went missing and there is not one image of him. It's as if you dropped him at the end of that bridge and he just vanished. Anyway, I must go and thank Pamela for the invitation. It was good to catch up with you again."

Nairne, Paul and the other two lads played football while Dog pursued the ball barking and leaping into the air. The telephone rang. Nairne dashed to answer it. The ball rolled slowly to a stop as everyone waited for her to emerge. A few seconds later she reappeared; her expression said it all.

"It was a wrong number." She picked up the ball and kicked it and the game continued, but the mood was subdued.

The last of the guests, Stevie and Ed, both worse for wear, left in the early evening. The cluster of empty beer bottles marked their attendance. Garrick and Pamela retreated indoors with the remains of the food and half a bottle of wine. Paul and Nairne sat together and watched as the sun began to dip in the sky. There had been no more telephone calls, no letter, nothing.

Eventually, they went indoors. Pamela and Garrick were arguing. The conversation stopped as soon as they entered the room. Pamela jollied everyone along as she was determined the day was going to be a success. Garrick sat down and topped up his glass from the open whisky bottle at his side.

"Pamela, thanks for everything. It was a great party but I'm tired. I think I'll call it a night," Nairne said, as she headed for the hallway. Pamela could see the sentiment was genuine, but Nairne did not look like a fifteen year old celebrating her birthday. She looked like a child with the weight of the world on her shoulders. Paul followed shortly afterwards as the atmosphere was toxic.

Pamela lay next to Garrick in bed.

"Garrick, why are you acting like this? I thought you wanted to move in here and look after Nairne. So what's wrong?"

"There's nothing wrong. You're imagining it," he snapped back, but Pamela was not going to give up that easily.

"Oh come on Garrick, it's me you're talking to and I know there's something wrong. There's the drinking for a start. Since when did you get through that much Scotch. Then the fact you're avoiding us, coming in late, all these so called business meetings; I've hardly seen you since we moved in here."

"Christ, you're never happy," he retorted. "All I got next door was bloody complaints about how cold it was, that we only had a shower and that the kitchen was too small, but now you don't like living here either."

"Keep your voice down," she hissed. "They'll hear us. I didn't say that. I said I didn't like the way you were behaving. You're avoiding us, it's bloody obvious, even Paul's commented on it." She paused. "Are you seeing someone else?"

The question was like a bolt.

"Of course not, I'm not avoiding you, it's oh, just drop it."

"No, what is it?" she persisted.

"It's her, Nairne, I, she.... it's the way she talks about Zane. When Zane gets back, all the stuff they'll do together and Paul's not much better.....it's bad enough when she sits there with her father's books, telling us about all the terrible things that are going to happen as the water and the temperature rises; she sounds just like him. I don't want a bloody lecture on how bad it's going to get and how well prepared he was. It didn't do him much good did it?"

"Garrick it's only natural, she misses them plus it's good that she and Paul still talk about Zane, they need to go on hoping that he'll come back. After all, you know what the police said, most runaways do come home." Pamela could see she had hit a nerve, as Garrick appeared to flinch from the words. "What is it Garrick? Tell me!"

"Drop it, you hear me, drop it now! Now can we just get some sleep?" He switched off the bedside lamp and turned over. She could hear him breathing, sharp, shallow breaths.

"Oh Garrick what have you done?"

There was no response.

TWENTY SIX

"I can't believe school is over for ever," said Paul as he walked into town with Nairne.

"So what now?" she asked.

"Ed says I can start at the warehouse, just three days a week and learn the business, and dad's promised to teach me to drive so then I'll be able to drive you into town."

"I like the walk; it gets us out of the house….."

"I know what you mean. I don't know what's got into dad; he's been in a foul mood for weeks. I've never seen him and Pam like this before; they've always been like really solid. It's probably just stress; I know things must be pretty tough with the business. You see it on the news all the time. I mean with over six million unemployed that's got to make it harder, right?"

"Hmmm," said Nairne noncommittally. She had also noticed Garrick's mood and the drinking. If he wasn't down at the pub having a business meeting he was nursing a bottle of whisky.

Garrick had promised to run them into town but by half past eleven he hadn't surfaced from his bed so they had decided to walk. The town was bustling with people and cars. The main square was at a standstill with traffic queuing in all directions. A line of new arrivals stood outside the town hall: bags, cases and bundles of possessions grasped in their hands.

"Let's get to the supermarket before it gets any busier," said Nairne. They entered the shop and swiftly found the sugar they were looking for. Nairne was going to make jam, as there were too many blackberry and raspberries to eat.

When they reached the town square, the queue outside the council offices had turned into a crowd.

"All those people… there can't be anywhere left for them to stay, the town is full," said Nairne. As she spoke, a scuffle broke out. Within seconds, it had escalated into a fight. Men pushed and shoved. People were jostled and knocked to the ground. A staff member came out and tried to restore order, but it was useless. Within minutes, the police arrived. Four officers wearing body armour and carrying truncheons arrested three men. Two others had bloody noses to show for their involvement and an elderly woman needed help onto her feet.

"What's wrong with them?" Paul asked, shaking his head. "They only need to wait in line."

"They're frightened there will be nothing left for them. My dad always said it doesn't take much for people to lose control. If they don't get what they need, they'll go out and take it."

The roads were quiet on the way home as most people could only afford fuel for essential journeys. It was a beautiful day with a clear blue sky. Pamela was concerned when they told her what they had seen in town.

"You should see it in the city," Garrick commented, refilling his coffee cup. "Last time I was in Edinburgh the police were out on the streets in full riot gear. "Look at this." He placed his newspaper onto the kitchen table and stabbed his finger at the photograph on the front page. It showed scenes of rioting in Birmingham. "Soldiers were sent in to regain control after gangs had taken over and raided a shopping complex. Three people were shot dead for looting; one of them was only fourteen years old. He'd stolen two boxes of tinned meat for Christ sake! I think we should all count our blessings because it's going to get a lot worse before this is over."

"How long do you think this heat will last?" Paul asked, as they walked along the road to Mr Cranshaw's later that afternoon. He waved his baseball cap backwards and forwards to keep the flies off his face.

"Oh, ages yet. The forecast is for it to get hotter," Nairne replied. "I can't wait to tell Mr Cranshaw about the healthy litter. Nine, that's two more than last year. If Mona is as lucky it'll be our biggest number ever!" They climbed the farm drive. Mr Cranshaw had said he would come check on the piglets. Nairne had phoned but there was no answer so they'd decided to go round. They were soaked with sweat by the time they reached the farm steading. Dog, who had been lagging behind, suffering from the heat ran passed them barking.

"What's up with him?" Paul asked. Nairne paused, touching Paul's arm she indicated to their right. A young heifer was standing next to one of the outbuildings; the animal raised her head and jumped with fright as Dog approached. Nairne whistled and Dog trotted back obediently. They walked on cautiously; not wanting to startle the animal.

"Look, there are more in the garden," Paul whispered.

Nairne indicated to Paul and they skirted round them. Up ahead the gate to the field lay open. Some of the herd were milling around near the entrance.

Nairne went right and Paul went left. By shouting at the cattle she forced them back into the field and shut the gate. The animals bellowed in response and shuffled backwards, snorting and banging into one another. The water trough at the edge of the field lay empty. The animals stood round it expectantly.

"Paul, can you fill the trough?" She indicated to the hose pipe and tap. "I'll see if I can find Mr Cranshaw."

Stevie and Ed must be at work, thought Nairne as she walked round to the house. Mr Cranshaw's truck sat alone, the back door was open and Dog, who had tired of looking for cattle, had gone inside. Nairne followed him in to the coolness of the empty kitchen.

"Mr Cranshaw!" she called, as she worked her way

round the downstairs rooms. There was silence. She climbed the stairs. Her skin felt hot and prickly; she felt anxious. Mr Cranshaw's bedroom was deserted, the bed neatly made, a picture of his wife and son occupied the small bedside table. The next two rooms were untidy, but empty. She left the house and began to work her way round the outbuildings, Dog at her side was sniffing and panting, but still there was silence. Finally, she entered the empty cattle shed. A couple of young cattle were lurking inside, seeking shelter from the heat. She startled them and they skittered on the concrete floor and headed for the nearest exit. It was dark except for the slivers of sunlight, which pierced through the old roofing panels. Nairne blinked as her eyes became accustomed to the gloom. She could hear a soft wheezing sound.

"Mr Cranshaw?" her voice echoed around the cavernous space. There was a cough and Dog rushed across the shed. Mr Cranshaw was propped against the far wall of the building, Nairne rushed to his side. His complexion was waxen and beads of sweat covered his forehead. His shotgun lay at his side. He tried to speak but it was barely a whisper. Dog nuzzled against him.

"Mr Cranshaw, are you all right?" Nairne gasped.

He nodded.

"I'll be fine, if you can just help me up."

"Hold on, I'll get Paul. He's outside."

Within minutes they had Mr Cranshaw back onto his feet and they helped him to the house. He sat down heavily at the kitchen table, his breathing laboured. Nairne fetched some water.

"Good job you decided to drop by." He tried to smile and lighten his tone.

"What happened?" Nairne asked. "All the cattle were out of the field."

Mr Cranshaw glanced over to the window.

"Don't worry, we herded them back in except for a couple of stragglers," said Paul reassuringly.

"Thanks, I don't know what to make of it. I was out working in the top field. I came back for a drink at about ten and while I was in the house, a cattle truck arrived. You wouldn't believe it, two men, bold as brass reversed the truck up the gate. I watched them from the window; they were going to steal the cattle, in broad bloody daylight!"

"What, like cattle rustlers?" Paul asked, bemused.

"Aye, if you like. So I went out into the yard and shouted, 'what the hell do you think you're doing?' One of them strides towards me with a stick in his hand and shouts, 'get inside old man and you won't get hurt.'" He shook his head as if in disbelief. "So I followed his advice, came in, got the shotgun and went back out. I fired the first shot through the windscreen of the truck. That got their attention and I told them the second shot was for the last man to get off my land. They leapt into the cab and drove off. Some of the cattle had bolted across the yard. I tried to get them back into the field, but they're too fast for me these days. I went into the barn to round up some others and once I got inside I felt a bit light headed so I sat down just for a minute....."

"It's shock," said Nairne.

"Will I call the police?" Paul asked, taking out his mobile.

"No need, I dinnae think they'll be back," Mr Cranshaw replied.

"No, but the next farmer might not be so lucky," said Nairne.

"I suppose you're right."

"Before I call," said Paul, "you do have a license for the gun, don't you?"

"Aye. Anyway, I only gave them a fright. They're damned lucky I didn't aim straight at them."

While they waited for the police to arrive, Nairne and Paul rounded up the last few cattle. The smell of the water in the trough had encouraged them to gather near the gate and they appeared relieved to get back in for their share. When the two police officers arrived, Mr Cranshaw related his story to them; they nodded and jotted down notes.

"With the damage you did to the windscreen we might pick them up," said the older of the two officers. "But if they come back let them take whatever they want, I assume you're insured and a few cattle aren't worth dying for."

"Are they likely to come back?" Nairne asked.

"This is the first report in this area of someone doing this in broad daylight, but there's a growing demand for meat on the black market and it must be coming from somewhere."

As the police officers finished their questions a car pulled up outside. Dog, who had been relishing the attention from the younger of the two officers, jumped up and rushed to the door. The low guttural growling signalled the arrival of Stevie who strode into the kitchen and stopped in his tracks at the sight of the uniforms.

"Ah, Steven. You won't believe what's been happening. This is Steven, one of my lodgers," said Mr Cranshaw. The two officers nodded.

"You startled me. I didn't realise we had visitors," said Stevie, trying to recover his cool. He glanced at Nairne who was holding Dog back.

"We'll be on our way Mr Cranshaw; we'll contact you if we make any progress and remember please, no heroics."

"Bloody cattle rustlers!" Stevie snorted, as Mr Cranshaw explained what had happened. "You were damned lucky, they could have been armed. Anyway, I thought you were going over to Berwick for that tractor part."

"Aye, that's right, but they called this morning. The supplier sent the wrong part. Just as well or I could have come back to find the animals gone and the place robbed."

"Yeah, I guess you had a lucky break," Stevie replied.

TWENTY SEVEN

"You must be delighted, and Lisa's turning out to be as good a mother as Mona." Mr Cranshaw leaned on the fence and watched as Lisa lay on her side with the tiny piglets nuzzling at her teats.

"So can you speak to Mr Roberts for me and see if he'll take them same as last year?"

"Aye, I'll call him, but I think we should ask for more than last time, feed prices have gone up and he'll be getting a premium price in the shops. Anyway, there's something else I need to speak to you about." His face grew sombre and Nairne could feel a sense of anxiety descending. "Ever since that bother with the cattle, I've been speaking with my nephew Hugh over in Langholm and he's asked me to go and stay with them."

"What, for a break?" Nairne asked hopefully.

"No, lass. They think I should l sell up and move. His place is a bit smaller than this, but if I sell I could give him some capital to invest, God knows he needs it; they have three young kids to take care of. He's a good lad, I'll be safe over there and at least my hard work over the years will help the family. Now Nairne, I'd like to take you with me, but Garrick has spoken to the authorities and they say it is unlikely I'd get permission, but if you want we'll take them on, see what we can do."

Nairne struggled to hold back the tears; Mr Cranshaw was like a grandfather to her. She would love to go with him, but that would mean leaving everything her father had worked for, and what would happen when Zane came back. What would he think?

"Thanks Mr Cranshaw, but I should stay here. Dad would have wanted me to look after the place, but you will keep in touch, won't you?"

"Aye lass of course I will. I'm sure Garrick would run you across and you can call anytime, for advice on the animals or just to have a chat." He patted her on the shoulder, and stared off across the yard, tears welling in his eyes. "Now I just have to break the news to the lads. I'm afraid they'll have to find new lodgings."

Mr Cranshaw's farm was sold at auction. The room was packed with representatives of the local estates. However, the winning bid came in by telephone from a farmer from Kent who was selling up and moving North. His farm in the south, although larger, had plummeted in value due to the water shortages while land further north was soaring. Nairne sat next to Mr Cranshaw watching the bids go up and up. The atmosphere in the room was electric. The final sale price was a fortune, larger than Nairne could imagine.

"To think your land is worth all that money," Nairne said excitedly.

"Aye, but it takes a lot of money to buy land anywhere else that's worth having as they aren't making any more of it," he replied.

It did give Nairne pause for thought. Although their place was only a couple of acres, it was worth more than houses in London. It was now too expensive for Garrick to buy!

The sale progressed swiftly and within two weeks, Nairne and Paul helped Mr Cranshaw pack his possessions. He was leaving the furniture and the herd were going as part of the sale along with the farm equipment, but there were still a few personal items to sort.

Nairne and Paul left with various gifts, which Mr Cranshaw felt they could use. Nairne got several books on animal welfare and a large Swiss army knife with multiple blades that had belonged to Mr Cranshaw's son. Paul got his air rifle. It was older than Zane's but in good condition. They walked back along the road in silence, clasping their gifts.

"You'll miss him, won't you?" Paul asked sympathetically, glancing at Nairne. This was the closest he had ever seen her to tears. Even when Daniel died and Zane went missing, he had never once seen her cry except in anger, but now she looked like all the separate losses were piled on top of one another weighing her down.

"Yes, I will. He's been like family to me especially since....."

"Langholm's not that far away. I'm sure dad would take us over." The sentence sounded hollow, Paul couldn't actually imagine Garrick ever having the time or the interest. He was always out at business meetings, or in the pub, as Pamela would say. His father seemed distant as if he was grappling with some dark demon.

That evening the four of them sat at the dining room table, Pamela had prepared a salad using only produce from the garden.

"It's so amazing that I can walk out the back door and pick everything we need to have dinner." She beamed as she set the salad bowl in the middle of the table.

"Yes, everything you need if you're a bloody rabbit," said Garrick, helping himself to a pile of lettuce leaves from the bowl. Pamela ignored him pointedly.

"So how did you two get on? Is Mr Cranshaw all packed up?"

"Just about," said Paul. "And you should see what he gave us." Paul went to the hall and brought back the air rifle. "Look, isn't it great. It was his son's."

"I didn't know he had a son," said Pamela.

"Yes, he was killed in Australia in one of those bush fires," Nairne replied.

"Oh dear, the poor man..." Pamela paused, mid sentence. "Sorry Nairne I didn't mean... to upset you."

"No, it's fine. I'm just sad to see him leaving."

"Show them what he gave you!" Paul exclaimed. Nairne pulled the knife from her pocket and opened out each of the six blades and tools.

"Oh my goodness, what a strange gift! I thought it would be something of his late wife's. A knife! Garrick would you look at that. It's a lethal weapon." Garrick grunted.

"Yes, but it's got lots of useful tools as well," said Nairne. "He also gave me books on how to look after the animals, but I can call him if we have any problems. He said the new people are moving in next week."

"Talking of next week," Garrick's tone was friendly for the first time in days. "I understand Stevie and Ed haven't been able to find anywhere. Apparently they no longer qualify for help with accommodation as they are single men and it's impossible to find anything... anyway, I said they could stay here, until they get sorted out. They can have the other part of the house."

Nairne's fork slipped from her hand and clattered against the edge of the plate. Pamela glared at Garrick.

"I think you might have spoken to all of us before you offered," said Pamela.

"Why? Would you have said no and seen them out on the streets?"

"I'm not saying that, but I do think it would have been polite to discuss it." Pamela glanced at Nairne as she spoke.

"It might have been better if you had asked me if it was okay," said Nairne, her voice harsh. "The answer is no. So you can go back and tell them, as last time I looked this was my house."

"Yes, we know that," said Garrick. "But while I am acting as your guardian I have to do what I think is best. Don't worry, I'll make them pay a fair rent and you'll get that money."

"I don't want their money," Nairne replied. "I don't want them in my house."

"Well, young lady, that's too bad because I've given them my word and I'm not going back on that so you had better just get used to the idea."

Nairne pushed her chair away from the table and left the room, Dog followed behind her.

"Garrick, you know how she feels about them," Pamela sighed.

"Pam, not another word. I've made my decision and that is it."

TWENTY EIGHT

The Government fell on the fifteenth of July. The news flash appeared on all channels.

"It's hardly a surprise," said Garrick. "I'm amazed they've lasted this long. I said when they formed the coalition, they needed to close the bloody borders, letting all these immigrants flood in, but they left it far too late... and as for all these ex pats. If you emigrated for the good life twenty years ago why the hell should you get back in now times are tough."

"But Australia is much worse than here. Whole communities have been destroyed by the droughts and the fires, and they are British citizens," said Nairne.

"Yes, well, they made their choice when they went to Australia; they have no right to be here now."

"That's what lots of people in Scotland think about the English," Nairne replied pointedly.

Garrick switched off the television and stormed out of the living room, Pamela sighed.

"He asked for that," said Paul supportively. "We hardly have a right to be here, do we?"

The forthcoming election dominated the news, but most people ignored it. With over a quarter of the population displaced many were no longer registered to vote or didn't care which party was in power; they were too busy worrying about the escalating prices and rising unemployment. Even though Nairne listened to the news, her mind was also on other things - Stevie and Ed. They were due to move in and the thought of it filled her with such rage that she wanted to lash out at Garrick and hurt him, that was why she had picked a fight with him.

The following Saturday she watched them arrive from her room. Ed and Stevie carried suitcases, badly packed bags and boxes into the other part of the house. Paul and Garrick helped and she could hear laughter as they worked. Pamela appeared from the kitchen with a tray of cold drinks and snacks and they all sat outside.

"Paul, ask Nairne if she wants to join us," said Pamela.

"Okay," Paul got up from the table, climbed the stairs and knocked on Nairne's bedroom door.

"Nairne, we're having lunch, do you want some?"

"No, I'm not hungry." She spoke without turning to look at him.

"Oh, come on, they're not as bad as all that are they? You can't hide up here in your room for ever." She spun round.

"I'm not hiding, and yes they are that bad, even if they helped look for Zane. Stevie is bad news, I know he is. I think you know it too."

"Okay, so he's no boy scout, but he is a friend of my dad's so he can't be that bad." Nairne didn't respond. Paul retreated, leaving her to her own thoughts.

It was too hot even for August. The soil was dry and Nairne spent time weeding. Weeds competed for moisture with the crops. She mulched round the precious plants with homemade compost and watered them in the early morning when the sun was not as strong. The greenhouse was bursting with produce: heavy blood red tomatoes hung in sets, bending the plants; cucumber tendrils wound their way up wires on the back wall of the greenhouse and the exotic yellow flowers faded as the fruits began to form. The shelf space was crowded with aubergines and peppers; fruits in green, purple and red jostled for space. For the last week there had been an abundance of raspberries, which they ate after most meals. The strawberry plants, given to Nairne by Mr Henderson bore rich red fruits. She had covered them in netting to save these gems from the greedy blackbirds, who attacked the under-ripe fruit given any opportunity.

Outside, the potatoes were in flower, a sign that they would soon be ready to lift. In the smallest of the vegetable beds, carrots, protected from carrot fly with a layer of fleece, were flourishing. Some crops had been less than effective, the cauliflowers and brussel sprouts had succumbed to the ravages of the massive slug population, which had been encouraged by the wet spring. However, overall, she was pleased with how the garden had performed.

This pleasure was marred by a growing concern. The plot had never been intended to feed six adults; since the arrival of the unwelcome house guests, true to his word Garrick made them pay rent. However, Nairne noticed that Pamela was constantly popping round with food. The rent hardly covered the costs of that food. Nairne had also noticed Stevie watching her when she worked in the garden; it made her flesh crawl so it was no surprise to find she was looking forward to going back to school.

Paul had received his exam results and, although they were worse than expected, after a chat with Garrick it was agreed he would not be going back. Garrick had shouted at him, but deep down Nairne thought Garrick was pleased. Paul would work four days a week at the warehouse, learn the business and work his way up. Paul was delighted, although Nairne sensed Stevie wasn't quite as taken with the idea. She guessed he had viewed himself as the natural successor to Garrick, but he could see that he would be training Paul for that particular role.

On the first day of term Nairne rose early, saw to the greenhouse plants and then got ready for school. She was filled with a mixture of excitement at going back and fear of what would be waiting for her.

An assembly was called for nine thirty. Mr Watson looked older; the stress of trying to fit too many pupils into an inadequate space was taking its toll. There were some new members of staff, but some of the regulars were absent. The assembly was grim. The top three years of the school were crammed into the airless hall, and were informed that, just as before, school would only be open three days per week; the rest of their work would be done at home. The school roll was traditionally between five to six hundred pupils; this had swelled to over nine hundred so the younger children were given priority.

Timetables were issued, as were lists of subjects available. Nairne noticed that the school was now offering a horticultural and agricultural course to equip pupils with basic knowledge in the care of plants. In the summer new laws had been introduced to encourage people to grow more of their own food. There were other new rules within the school, including the installation of a metal detector to prevent pupils bringing knives onto school premises. Although the school uniform had been abandoned there was guidance on dress codes, including a ban on gang and football colours. Pupils under fifteen were forbidden from leaving school premises during the day as there had been complaints of shop lifting and fighting in town.

Nairne saw Laura and Tamara at lunchtime, but instead of the usual jibes and taunts they avoided her. Later that afternoon Spud explained this miraculous change in behaviour; after Nairne's removal from school, Laura and Tamara had found a new victim, Nadia, from south east London. It had been the same old thing, name-calling and gossip. The girl was of Arabic descent and many of the comments suggested she was an illegal immigrant. Unfortunately for the conspirators, Nadia's father was a lawyer, or as Spud put it, 'a shit hot legal eagle,' and he threatened legal action against both girls. Tamara had foolishly put her views in writing on line, so both girls were on a final warning. Any more trouble and they would be out. Spud delighted in sharing the news and Nairne received an invitation to hang out with him and his mates, if she wanted; after all, she was one of the gang now. She'd been excluded from school. Nairne felt almost happy. Maybe this year at school wouldn't be quite so bad after all.

TWENTY NINE

August ended but the heat wave continued and water rationing was introduced across most of the England: Crops failed and more people headed north, to Scotland. There was no accommodation left and services were stretched to breaking point. However, not everyone was feeling the pinch, Garrick's business was booming.

"Dad, once I pass my driving test I could learn how to work the forklift at the warehouse," Paul announced over dinner.

"If you pass," Garrick laughed, reaching over for some more bread. Nairne sat in silence. Pamela appeared from the kitchen with the drinks.

"Of course he'll pass; he's got you for a teacher. Then you can teach me," Pamela commented as she sat down.

"Why the hell would you want to learn to drive. Bloody women drivers. No offence, but you're not exactly the practical type," he responded, stuffing food into his mouth. Ed and Paul sniggered in agreement.

"If you lot can do it, then it can't be that difficult," she retorted.

"But we've only got one car and once Paul learns, he'll want to use it. Anyway, I'm far too busy. Besides, if you want to go anywhere you just need to ask."

Pamela was annoyed.

"I might want to go somewhere without you, go and see friends, or go shopping. It would save you having to run me everywhere."

"God, that's not much of an argument, giving you an opportunity to go shopping whenever you fancy. Christ, I'd be bankrupt in days!" he chortled. "Never mind the cost of fixing the car every time you prang it."

"I think you should learn," said Nairne. "Statistics show that women are safer drivers than men. Maybe someone else could teach you."

"Yes, why not. Stevie, you wouldn't mind taking me for lessons, would you?" Pamela flashed one of her best smiles. The mood in the room changed from banter to a challenge. Garrick glared at Stevie. He had said no to Pamela and he was in charge.

"If Garrick doesn't mind it would be a pleasure." Stevie returned the smile.

"You go ahead if you want to waste your time, be my guest." The expression on Garrick's face betrayed his emotions; he was furious.

Nairne had anticipated what would happen when she made the suggestion. She had sensed the tension between Garrick and Pamela. Ever since Zane's disappearance, Garrick's mood had been black, as if a huge weight was pressing down on him. She also knew it was her. He could barely tolerate being in the same room as her. Every night he would sit and nurse a bottle of whisky, clasping the glass as if it held the answer to all his problems. She knew there was already tension between him and Stevie, maybe if he saw Stevie as a rival he'd ask them to move out.

Initially, Pamela despaired at Garrick's moods but gradually despair turned to intolerance. Nairne felt sorry for Paul. She watched him grow more anxious as his family began to implode. He tried to make excuses for them whenever they rowed.

His attitude to work had changed drastically; he wanted to impress Garrick desperately. He was also Nairne's only ally, with Mr Cranshaw gone and the boys, as Garrick called them, living next door she felt like a guest in her own house.

On the twelfth of September, everything changed: Nairne set off to school as usual, but half way through the afternoon, the power failed. A message circulated that the whole town was out. Classes ended early, but the school buses were not ready so Nairne set off on foot. She was more than half way home when a car passed. It slowed down and sat, engine revving, waiting for her to catch up. She approached cautiously; she didn't recognise it. As she drew level, the driver leaned out. He had a pony tail and his arm, which hung out of the window, beer bottle in hand, was a tapestry of tattoos.

"Can we give you a lift?" he grinned.

"No thanks."

"It's Nairne isn't it?"

"Yes," she hesitated and peered into the car. Next to him sat the palest girl Nairne had ever seen. She had a shock of black hair and the only colour on her face was her blood red lipstick.

"I'm Gunny and this is Leanne. We're heading to your place, for the party. Hop in."

"No, thanks anyway, but I'm enjoying the walk."

"Ok, love, see you later." With that he took a slug of the beer and stepped on the accelerator. As the car sped away, Nairne made the connection. Gunny worked at the warehouse, and she recognised the girl from Zane's description. He always said she looked like she had died and no one had told her. But what party?

When Nairne arrived home, cars littered the yard and she could hear laughter and shouting coming from the garden. She entered the house. An agitated Dog was waiting for her in the hallway.

"What's the matter," she rubbed his ears and he pressed himself against her legs. Nairne walked through into the empty living room then the kitchen; the back door was open and noise filtered through. She stepped outside. There were some fifteen people there, the only familiar faces were Pamela, Stevie, Ed and the couple from the car.

"Pamela, what's going on?" she demanded. Pamela turned and rose from her chair.

"Nairne darling, come and join us," Nairne could tell

from her tone and her inability to stand up straight that she was drunk.

"Why are you having a party?"

"Oh, we just thought, in light of the news..... Let me get you a drink." Pamela staggered towards her and they both entered the kitchen.

"Where are Garrick and Paul?"

"Oh, they were away in Edinburgh, but they'll be back soon."

"So who decided to have the party?"

"Stevie and I ... Stevie suggested it, he thought since we still have electricity it would be a nice gesture, for the lads at the warehouse in light of the news."

"What, because we have a power cut, Stevie's throwing a party?"

"Oh, you haven't heard, have you? I thought the school would have said."

"Said what?" Nairne was beginning to feel uneasy.

"This isn't a power cut because of some electrical fault; the power has been turned off. It's been on the news and the radio. It's the Russians: they've turned off the gas and oil supply to Europe." Pamela was rambling. "No more fuel! What will happen with food and things, and the police and the troops are out on the streets, that's what they said. Your dad was right Nairne, this is only the start....."

Nairne felt cold; it was so sudden. Everyone knew there were problems with fuel supplies; everyone knew that the Russians were difficult to deal with, but why now?

"I'm going watch the news." She went through to the living room and switched on the television. All the channels were showing the same news flash.

"At ten fifteen this morning, after seven months of negotiation, the Russian Government turned off the gas and oil supplies to Europe. This accounts for forty percent of the UK's requirements. Russia claims she can no longer afford to supply Europe as her reserves are declining. There is speculation that Russia has struck a deal with

China to divert supplies there. The UK along with its European partners is holding emergency talks with the USA, however, it is unlikely that sufficient supplies can be found in the short term so a programme of rationing will come into effect. There will be no electricity supplies for the next forty-eight hours. After that, there will be supplies for each region of the country for three hours in every twenty-four, until a resolution can be found. Travel should be restricted to essential journeys only. Schools will be closed until further notice. A state of national emergency has been declared."

Nairne switched it off. She went up to her room and changed clothes. Looking out of the bedroom window she watched as Pamela draped herself over the side of Stevie's chair. He was sitting back, feet on the table and a can of beer in one hand, the other was placed in the small of Pamela's back. Across the table, Gunny, a cigarette in his hand and Leanne on his knee, was regaling the others with one of his exploits. Nairne heard another car coming up the drive. She hoped it was Garrick; at least if he and Paul were here.... but it was another man she had never seen before. He parked outside the front door, lifted a couple of crates of beer from the boot and walked into the house. Tentatively, Nairne crept down the stairs. Dog ran on ahead and went out the back door. She hesitated in the kitchen, the place was a mess, dirty dishes filled the sink, she opened the refrigerator, it was almost empty except for beer. Outside she heard Dog barking excitedly. She stepped out into the garden in time to see Stevie lash out at Dog with his boot. He caught the animal on his left flank. Dog squealed in pain.

"Bloody dog, you see that it tried to bite me...."

"You shouldn't have teased him like that," said Pamela. "Here boy," she threw a piece of food to Dog, who ignored it and ran to Nairne for protection.

"Nairne," Stevie laughed. "Come to join the grown-ups?" He patted his knee in invitation.

"I would if I could find any," she replied. "And Stevie, don't touch my dog."

"Or what?"

"Stevie!" Pamela rebuked him. "You two play nicely; I don't want any unpleasantness at my party. Nairne, let me introduce you to everyone." Pamela reeled off the names of the people round the table ending with Gunny and Leanne.

"Oh, we met earlier. We passed Nairne on the way here, even offered her a lift. But she was reluctant to get into a car with a strange man," Gunny laughed, showing the gold caps on two of his teeth.

"And they don't get much stranger than him," said Ed, proud of himself for making the joke.

"Would anyone like something to eat?" Pamela asked, playing the hostess. There were murmurs of approval. "Nairne would you give me a hand?" They retreated to the kitchen. Pamela opened the refrigerator and took out another bottle of wine; she reached for the bottle opener.

"Pamela, I think you've had enough," said Nairne. "Especially if you want to start cooking." For a moment it looked like they were going to have an argument then Pamela simply shrugged and giggled. Nairne put the kettle on and made coffee.

"Right, so what are we making?" Nairne asked.

"Oh, whatever. What do we have?"

"Not much by the looks of the refrigerator, I suppose we could do some salad and things and you could defrost food from the freezer. I'll go and get some things from the greenhouse and garden."

The greenhouse was stifling, even with the windows and door open. Nairne picked some tomatoes and cucumber, relieved to be back outside she lifted some carrots and picked some lettuce. When she returned to the kitchen, Pamela had made little progress.

"The boys want a barbecue, and we don't have much left in the freezer. I told them the piglets haven't been taken for slaughter yet, but Gunny says that's not a problem."

"What do you mean?" Pamela's answer was interrupted by a commotion outside. Dog bolted from the room, barking. Nairne followed him into the yard.

The squeals emanating from Mona were painful to hear. Both pigs and a number of the piglets were loose in the yard; they trampled through the vegetables in panic, pursued by an assortment of drunken men. Leanne squealed in delight, tears running down her face as she shouted encouragement at Gunny. Stevie, Ed and Gunny were attempting to corner one of the piglets; trampling over the vegetables as they went.

"What the hell are you doing?" Nairne screamed at them.

"We're going to have a barbecue," Gunny replied, a knife held in his hand. "Don't worry love; I used to be a butcher."

"Pamela, stop them!" Pamela emerged from the kitchen.

"Nairne it's only one piglet. They're due to go for slaughter soon anyway."

"Look what they're doing to the vegetables! That's our food. Do something!"

"Nairne, it's all right, don't worry." Nairne stormed past shoving her out of the way, and ran upstairs into her room. Her heart was thumping. Adrenaline rushed through her body. She was shaking. The shouts and squeals continued from outside.

"You've got it!" Stevie whooped with delight as Gunny seized the struggling piglet.

"Put it back in the pen," Nairne shouted over to him.

"But we're going to eat it," said Gunny.

"Oh my God!" Leanne squealed as she turned and saw.

"I said put it back in the pen! And the rest of you can leave."

Silence fell. Nairne stood outside the back door of the house, the air rifle held up to her shoulder, pointing directly at Stevie's head.

"Nairne," Pamela whined. "What are you doing? Someone could get hurt."

"And that someone will be Stevie," she replied, calmly. "Go on; get the pigs back into their pen, and Stevie, I suggest you stay very still."

Gunny did not move; he looked to Stevie for guidance.

"It's only an air rifle....and she's bluffing," said Ed.

"Easy for you to say it's not pointing at your head," Stevie replied sarcastically. He gestured to Gunny to do what she said.

THIRTY

"That was Darren from the warehouse," said Paul, as they reached the single track road to the house.

"So it was," said Garrick. "They must have finished early if the power's been out. You know the way things are going we are lucky to have this place. At least we'll have running water and some electricity."

He parked outside the house. Gunny's car was there next to Stevie's. The place was quiet. Paul was first into the house.

"Pamela, we're back, I take it you've seen the news....."

He stepped out of the kitchen to find Leanne and Pamela sitting at the table on the patio. Leanne was crying. Nairne was standing to the left, Zane's air rifle aimed squarely at Stevie, who was only a few feet away. Gunny and Ed were making futile attempts to tempt Mona back into her enclosure. A mess of broken plants and footprints had replaced the vegetable garden.

"Pamela....what's going on?"

"Thank God. Where's your father?"

Garrick emerged from the kitchen and surveyed the scene.

"Garrick, she's gone mad, there's no reasoning with her....." Pamela sobbed.

"Nairne." He spoke to her sternly. "Put down the gun."

"No, not until they have put the pigs back, then they can leave."

"But Stevie and Ed live here."

"Not anymore."

"I don't know what's been going on, but whatever it is it's over. Paul, give Ed a hand with the pigs, Gunny take Leanne and go home, and Leanne make sure you drive, he's no use to me without a license. Steven and Nairne come on – inside."

Everyone did as they were told. Nairne lowered the rifle and put the safety catch on. She followed Pamela and Stevie inside.

Garrick's instinct would have been to believe that Nairne had flown into a tantrum. He knew she had a short fuse, but one look at the devastation outside told him that whatever had been happening, it had got totally out of hand.

"So, who's going to explain what happened?"

"It was just a misunderstanding, though I'll say this only once, you ever point a loaded gun at me again and...."

"And what?" said Nairne. "What will you do? Stab me? Isn't that your weapon of choice?"

Garrick and Stevie stared at her. Did she know, wondered Garrick. Or maybe only suspected. He ploughed on hoping to change the direction of the conversation.

"Nairne, whatever they did pointing a loaded gun at Steven it's not on, your dad..."

"Don't you talk about my father; you have no right to mention his name."

"Pamela, maybe you can explain?" Pamela glanced from Stevie to Nairne and back.

"Oh Garrick, we were just having a few drinks with the boys, a sort of thank you since work will be in short supply with no power and rationed fuel. I, we thought...." she glanced at Stevie, "that it would be a nice gesture. The boys wanted a barbecue so Gunny suggested we kill one of the piglets and one thing led to another...."

"So why didn't you tell them to stop?" He glared at her.

"Because she was too keen on trying to impress Steven," Nairne said, mimicking Pamela's voice. "And she was too drunk to do anything useful." Pamela tried to explain, but Garrick glared at her.

"None of you seem to realise how serious this is," said Nairne angrily. "That was our winter food supply they've just destroyed. And as for the pigs, they don't belong to Gunny, or Stevie, or you, or Garrick. The pigs, the house and everything else belongs to me and my brother."

"Oh Nairne, we're sorry, it was just a bit of fun. I guess we'll simply have to buy more of our food over the winter, won't we Garrick." Pamela looked to him for support.

"What if there isn't enough?" Nairne retorted.

"We have plenty of money haven't we?" Again she looked at Garrick.

"I'm not talking about the money, that's your answer to everything; Garrick will just spend more money. What if there isn't enough food to go around. Don't you see? This is only the start."

"Nairne's right, what's happened today changes everything." Garrick said. "This isn't a temporary power cut; this is a fundamental change to the way this country runs so we need to be a bit smarter than this. Right Stevie, let me make this clear. If I want to organise a party for my staff I'll do that. You and Ed get out of my sight; I'll see you in work tomorrow, sober understand? Pamela, get through there and sort out that mess. Nairne, let's go and see what the damage is." With that the two of them went back outside.

"I don't know who he thinks he's talking to," Stevie snarled. "Siding with that psychotic little bitch, 'this house is mine and my brother's'. Christ, does she still think he's coming back?"

"Steven, keep your voice down." Pamela rubbed her hand along his arm. "Just do as Garrick says. It'll blow over in a couple of days, you'll see."

The pigs were back behind their fence, and Paul, armed with the yard brush and spade was trying to undo some of the mess. Ed sidled past them and into the house. They heard the car screeching down the driveway.

Nairne stared in despair; all that work for nothing. She was seething with rage. She wanted to cry, but there was no way she could do that, not in front of them.

"Nairne, I'm not sure what to do with the plants," said Paul, standing next to what had been the carrots. The tops were broken and trampled. "I've cleared the soil off the paths and fixed the fleece over the cabbages but.... some of the plants are past repair."

"What should we do?" asked Garrick.

"I don't know," said Nairne. "There's nothing we can do, is there? Nothing we can do about any of it. Everything is wasted, everything, ever since you arrived.... it's all just turned to shit." She walked off across the yard and down the drive, Dog followed obediently.

"Nairne, where are you going?" Paul shouted after her but she didn't turn round. "Dad?" He looked expectantly.

"Let her go. She'll come back... she needs time to calm down. Come on I'll give you a hand," Garrick replied wearily.

THIRTY ONE

Night fell and there was no sign of Nairne. Paul paced up and down anxiously, while Garrick sat, whisky bottle at his side, and fumed. Pamela, who had cried to begin with tried to make up with him.

"What if she doesn't come back?" Paul asked. "What then?"

"She'll be back, and if not, then we'll go down to the police station and report it, and they'll find her," said Garrick unconvincingly.

"Like they found Zane," Paul retorted.

Pamela's face turned red and she threw Garrick a nervous glance. He glared back in return, a warning look, one that Paul knew.

"What's wrong?"

"Nothing," said Pamela. "Why?"

"The look on your faces when I mentioned Zane. What is it? You know something, don't you?"

"Of course not," said Garrick aggressively.

"Yes, you do. Did the police find something? Is it bad news? You wanted to keep it from Nairne, didn't you?"

"Paul, drop it," said Garrick.

"But dad, he's my friend..."

"I said drop it or else." With that, Garrick rose from his chair and stormed from the room, taking the whisky bottle with him. Paul looked at Pamela.

"Leave me out of this," she said. "Just do as your father asks. He's under a lot of strain. Please leave it. It's nothing."

Nairne returned late the following day. Garrick was about to go to the police station when she walked back into the house.

"Nairne, darling we were so worried, we haven't slept a wink. Where have you been?" Pamela rushed after her; the question remained unanswered.

After feeding Dog she went upstairs, showered and changed into clean clothes. When she returned downstairs and went into the kitchen to make herself some lunch Garrick took charge.

"Nairne, I know you were upset, but staying out all night was totally irresponsible!"

"Well, I'll fit in well here then, won't I," she replied.

"Okay, okay, so the boys were totally out of line, I've spoken to them, they're sorry, and as for Pamela, it was the wine, you know what she's like…"

Nairne took her lunch outside, ignoring his protestations as she turned her back on him.

After she had eaten, she began to clear up the mess from the day before. Paul came out to help.

"I know you're upset, but dad is trying. You know he would never have let yesterday get out of hand like that."

"Wouldn't he?" Nairne asked, accusingly. "He was pretty quick to get his feet under the table after my dad.... and he treats the place like he owns it. Letting Stevie move in, he didn't even discuss that one with me did he?"

Paul couldn't think of what to say. She was right, dad had known she would never agree, but he'd gone ahead anyway.

"Okay, so he was wrong, but he is worried about you."

"Maybe he should be more worried about himself," said Nairne.

"Why, what do you mean?" Paul's tone was hard. "What's dad got to worry about?"

"You saw her yesterday, making excuses for Steven."

"What are you saying? She'd had too much to drink; she's just a bit of a flirt."

"Whatever," said Nairne turning her back. She wished she hadn't said anything, Paul looked upset, but she knew what she'd seen. The way Stevie had touched Pamela yesterday, he wanted everyone to see, to make him look big in front of the other blokes, and Pamela had not exactly protested.

"If you've got something to say...."

"It's none of my business," said Nairne. "Forget I mentioned it. You're right. She was just flirting."

Nairne continued with the silent treatment for the next couple of days. Stevie and Ed returned and apologised, but Nairne couldn't bring herself to accept it. Pamela grovelled at every opportunity and Nairne, although angry, couldn't bear it any longer. They had enough electricity to keep the refrigerator, freezer and the lights going. The wind turbines, their blades motionless in the calm weather, were of little use. Garrick and Paul went into town on the fourth day. When they returned, they called everyone into the kitchen to report on what they had found.

"The town was busy, but the shops were bare, lots of them weren't even open. The supermarket shelves were empty and there was some trouble in the square," said Garrick. He looked shaken.

"What about the warehouse? Was everything okay?" Stevie asked.

"Yes, we checked. Darren and Gunny are taking turns to keep an eye on the place. Gunny said there were a couple of blokes hanging around yesterday, but he scared them off."

"So what are the authorities doing about all this?" said Pamela, her voice edgy and panicky.

"What can they do?" Paul replied. "I met a boy from school who said they had no water for most of yesterday. The council sent tankers, but only enough for drinking and cooking."

"So what's wrong with the water?" asked Ed.

"Some parts of the town get their water pumped to them and the pumping stations are down. When they contacted the council they were told the power supply couldn't cover everything."

"I'm sure it'll be all right, after all, the Government knows what it's doing," said Pamela. The others looked sceptical.

"What about the bigger towns, would it be worth trying one of those, or Edinburgh to see what it's like there?" Stevie asked.

"We could try it," said Garrick, "But I doubt it will be any different." It was agreed they would take a trip to Berwick. Garrick took Stevie and Ed with him, after the trouble he'd seen in town he felt it would be safer.

They were gone for a long time. Meanwhile, Nairne and Paul worked outside. Nairne had decided the best thing to do was to lift any damaged crops and use them first. Since the weather was dry she wanted to get some of the root crops like the potatoes out of the ground and let them dry off before putting them in the basement for storage. It would have been good to pickle and store some of the vegetables if Garrick could manage to buy vinegar. Nairne had never done this on her own before. Dad had always been in charge, but she knew what to do and they had a cookery book. There was also a surfeit of fruit from the plum trees and raspberry canes to be harvested and the greenhouse was bursting with tomatoes and cucumbers. The excess could be made into soups or preserves. Paul dug up the potatoes and laid them on wire racks to dry before storage. Nairne started lifting the rows of damaged carrots. The tops were broken and some of the crop was crushed, but she salvaged what she could.

"I'll take these in and get Pamela to wash them, then I can make some soup later on," she said, carrying the large bundle of orange vegetables. She found Pamela sitting at the kitchen table, a glass of wine in front of her.

"It's a bit early to be drinking," said Nairne.

"Yes, I know you're right," Pamela sighed. "I needed something to steady my nerves."

"Why? What's wrong?

"Steven just called, they're on their way back ...." she sobbed.

"What is it?"

"They got some supplies at the supermarket, apparently there were huge queues and there was no fresh food, even the freezers were bare....."

"Pamela!" Nairne said sternly. "What's happened?"

"They were run off the road a couple of miles from Berwick and two men tried to rob them. Just as well he took Stevie and Ed with him. Otherwise God knows what might have happened," she sobbed.

"Have they called the police?" Nairne asked.

"No, from what Stevie said the place was chaotic. I think the police have enough on their hands."

When they returned, Ed was sporting a bloody nose, Garrick was pale and badly shaken, but Stevie, even though he had a deep cut to his left arm, was revelling in it. Every detail of the fight, every blow struck was retold. His shirt and trousers were soaked in blood and even his shoes were covered.

"That'll teach the little bastards. Think they're hard. Got more than they bargained for, eh," he said grinning.

"Yes," said Garrick. "They certainly did."

Pamela poured each of them a drink. She got tissues for Ed's nose and then she examined Stevie's arm. Nairne could see the colour drain from her at the sight of the blood when he removed the strip of fabric he had wrapped round the wound. She thought Pamela was going to faint.

"I'll get something to put on that," she said vaguely.

"There's a first aid box in the bathroom," said Nairne.

Paul ran up the stairs and returned with it. Nairne washed her hands, undid the box and began to remove an assortment of items including disinfectant and bandages. She tipped some disinfectant onto a piece of clean lint.

"This will hurt," she said looking at Stevie, her face expressionless. She wiped the lint roughly across the bloody wound and heard the sharp intake of breath. "It's not too deep, but I think you'll need stitches, I could do that as well. I'm sure I have a needle and thread in here somewhere." She tried to keep a straight face as she rummaged in the box. Pamela and Stevie both looked shocked at the notion, while a smirk passed over Paul's face.

"No, just patch me up, I'll go over to the hospital," said Stevie. Nairne put a dressing on the wound.

Nairne and Paul unloaded the shopping from the car. There was no fresh produce, but they had managed to get tinned food and two dozen bottles of vinegar.

"The robbers would have been a bit disappointed with this," said Paul, setting down another crate of vinegar bottles.

"Yes," said Nairne. "I thought your dad would have had trouble getting this. You'd think more people would be starting to preserve their food for winter."

Paul looked at her as if she was from another planet.

"What?" said Nairne, a smile almost crossing her face. "What's so funny about that?"

"Do you actually believe most people have got any idea what's going to happen?" said Paul. "They're still sitting back thinking things will return to normal. That guy from school I met the other day said his dad was talking about not paying his water rates because the water had been turned off. Then he went on to tell me all the gossip at school, like this was merely a minor blip. School is closed; no-one's mentioned reopening it."

"So did he have any interesting gossip?" said Nairne, sarcastically.

"Actually he did have one piece that might cheer you up. Apparently, Laura's dad has lost the farm. They were only tenants but he's got into debt and the tenancy has been revoked. Looks like Laura will soon be without a posh house and her pony."

Nairne felt confused. It served Laura and her awful

mother right, but losing your house, especially at a time like this.... Where would they go?

Stevie and Ed left for the hospital as Pamela stood on the doorstep looking concerned. Garrick had been quiet since his return; he still looked pale, even after three glasses of whisky. Pamela returned to the kitchen.

"I hope Steven will be all right, that was a nasty cut. God, just think, if you had gone on your own....." Her words hung in the air.

"If I'd gone on my own, they'd have stolen twenty four bottles of vinegar and some tinned food," said Garrick. "Instead of....."

"Instead of what? You seem annoyed. Those boys were injured saving you. That was so brave tackling some yob with a knife."

"Christ's sake Pamela," Garrick responded, his tone angry. "They were just desperate kids, scared out of their wits; they didn't want the car, just the food. And it was Stevie's knife, God, you should have seen him, he's..."

"He's what?"

"A bloody animal that's what. One of them ran off and the other bloke, God what a mess....., how do you think Ed got that nosebleed? That was while we were pulling Stevie off the guy once he was on the ground. I tell you he is one sick individual."

THIRTY TWO

September ended and they plunged from summer to winter overnight. Rain fell, hard and constant. Most of the summer crops had been harvested safely and Nairne spent the next two weeks in the kitchen, cooking, pickling and freezing the produce. Paul helped out when he wasn't at work while Pamela moped around. It was a wet afternoon; Nairne was becoming increasingly annoyed at doing most of the work so eventually she came out with it.

"Pamela, what's wrong with you? Why don't you give me a hand?"

Pamela shrugged and sat down at the table.

"I'm sorry, darling," she said, her tone dejected. "I suppose you'll find out soon enough, but Garrick's told the boys to find somewhere else to stay. He says it was only a temporary measure, that it's not his house, and that you wanted them to leave. Nairne sweetheart, they don't have anywhere else to go.... I know you don't always get on with them, but they're good boys."

Nairne was taken aback. It seemed unlikely that Garrick was suddenly concerned about her feelings; perhaps he had noticed how attached Pamela was becoming.

"I think they should leave," said Nairne, staring directly at Pamela. "I think it would be best for me and you and Garrick in the long run, don't you?" There was no mistaking the tone of her statement. "And let's face it Pamela, there won't be enough food to go round or electricity to keep both parts of the house running, not once the days get shorter. So when are they going?"

The frankness of her response threw Pamela.

"I'm not sure, I think he gave them until the end of the month."

The end of October could not come soon enough for Nairne.

On the twenty third of October, Garrick was woken in the early hours of the morning. His mobile phone rang persistently.

"What the hell..." he muttered as he switched on the bedside light and answered it.

"What, what now.... what about the boys? Yes okay. I'm on my way. Okay."

Pamela stirred.

"What's wrong?"

"It's Gunny, he wants me to meet him at the warehouse, one of the security guys from the factory next door called. Someone's broken in. I need to get down there."

"What, now?"

"Yes. You go back to sleep, I'll not be long."

The phone rang at seven thirty. Nairne, who was the only one up answered on the second ring. It was Gunny; he was agitated and wanted to speak to Pamela. Nairne dashed upstairs and woke her. Pamela rushed downstairs and snatched the telephone from the table.

"Yes, what, oh my God.... yes, thanks Gunny, we understand... Okay." Pamela replaced the receiver and sat down heavily.

"Nairne, go and wake Paul."

"What is it?"

"Please get Paul and Steven, I need Steven."

Nairne did as she was asked and minutes later they were gathered in the living room.

"It's Garrick," said Pamela in her most melodramatic tone. "He's been arrested."

"What?" said Paul, incredulously. "When? Where is he?"

"Gunny called last night; he'd heard that someone was trying to break into the warehouse. Gunny arrived after

Garrick and the police were there, searching the place; they took Garrick away. He waited outside the police station, but Garrick never came out. The police are still at the warehouse going through paperwork."

Paul was stunned.

"Why would they arrest him? It's his warehouse," said Paul.

"Yes, but not his goods," said Stevie.

"What do you mean? My dad's bought everything in the place."

"Paul, don't be so naive, how do you think your dad manages to buy fags and booze and luxury goods when the bloody supermarket shelves are empty. The stuff is stolen," Stevie replied harshly. "Let's hope there's nothing that can link us to the place."

"So what now?" said Pamela, looking to Stevie for assistance.

"All we can do is hope the system is so stretched that the coppers don't have the resources to do more than charge him with receiving stolen goods, but it'll still mean time."

"You mean prison?" Nairne asked.

"Yes, that's right."

"I'll call Tony, he'll know what to do," said Paul. "He'll be able to get dad a good lawyer."

"Yes," Pamela concurred. "Tony will be able to help."

Paul was persistent, but Tony was unavailable; in fact, all of Garrick's trusted business associates were unavailable. They managed to secure a lawyer but it did not look promising. Forty-eight hours after his arrest, Garrick was refused bail. Although the prison system was at breaking point, as Garrick's lawyer explained, the charges were serious. The police had linked some of the impounded items to three violent robberies on transport companies. Garrick was charged with the hijackings and selling on the goods.

Paul was distraught. Initially, Pamela was shocked, but within a week Nairne came downstairs to find her drinking with Stevie.

She attempted to pull herself together as Nairne entered the room.

"Why don't you join us?" Stevie winked at Nairne.

"No thanks, I have work to do. Anyway, isn't it time you started packing since you'll be moving out in a couple of days?" said Nairne.

Pamela looked embarrassed; there had been no mention of Ed and Stevie moving.

"I don't know what you mean," said Stevie, smiling.

"Pamela said Garrick told you to find somewhere else by the end of October, which is tomorrow."

"Oh, right. But that was before all this trouble. Ed and I had found a great place, but we can't leave now. It wouldn't be right."

"We can manage. After all, what useful tasks do either of you do?"

"Oh, don't be like that," said Stevie. "You're always trying to start an argument with me, when all I want is to be friends."

"What, like you are with Garrick?" said Nairne. She left the kitchen and went through to the living room where Paul was slumped in front of the television. He was lost without Garrick. He glanced up and muttered 'hello'.

"Paul, why don't we go for a walk?" said Nairne.

"It's raining," he sighed, not tearing his gaze away from the screen.

"So we'll get wet. Come on," she nudged his legs. "Anyway, I want to talk to you."

"You can talk to me here," said Paul.

"I need to speak to you privately. It's important. Come on, we'll go down to Brigham woods; Dog needs a walk." Reluctantly, he got up and they got their coats and boots.

"I'll tell Pamela where we're going."

"Don't," said Nairne, putting her hand on his arm.

"Let's just go. She'll never miss us."

They strode down the driveway; the rain was falling straight down. Dog ran on ahead towards the woods. Once they were under the shelter of the trees, Paul couldn't wait any longer.

"What did you want to talk about?" he said, curiously.

"Did you know your dad had told Stevie and Ed to leave?"

"No, when did he do that?"

"Pamela told me a couple of days before he was arrested. He told them to move out by the end of October. Pamela said it was because I didn't want them here, but I don't think that was why."

"What, you mean Stevie and Pamela?" Paul replied sceptically.

"You have to admit, Pamela is coping very well and today Stevie tells me they're staying. And don't you think it's weird that Gunny phoned your dad, not Stevie, when he heard about the break in. Who would you call if you thought you were going to be faced with burglars?"

"Gunny told me he tried calling Stevie, but his mobile was switched off."

"What and Ed's was switched off as well?"

"Okay, so are you saying Stevie set my dad up?"

"Yes."

"What, so he could get it together with Pamela?" his tone was incredulous.

"No that's merely a perk," said Nairne. "It's not Pamela he wants, it's this place."

"But why?"

"It's got everything he needs: its own power, it's off the beaten track, out buildings to store his stuff once he takes over your dad's business, land for growing food, and its own water supply. My dad chose this place carefully; he knew things were going to get bad, he knew water and power would be essential. Ever since that day Stevie went to Berwick with your dad, it's been different; your dad seemed frightened of him."

"Stevie saved him. He got stabbed remember."

"It was only a cut," said Nairne. "Whose blood do you think Stevie was covered in?"

"What do you mean?" said Paul.

"The blood, his trousers and shoes were covered in it. There's no way all that came from his arm, or Ed's nose bleed. Whatever happened that day, your dad saw something that made him want Stevie to leave. Next thing your dad's out the picture plus, there's what Zane told me."

"What's Zane got to do with this?" said Paul, a sick feeling started to form in his guts. He knew Garrick and Pamela had been hiding something from him.

"Zane told me Stevie killed that man in town outside the pub."

"But he didn't see anything. I was there remember."

"Yes he did. He ran on ahead of you, didn't he?" Paul nodded.

"He said your dad told him it would be better to say that he hadn't seen anything, that no one would believe him. He didn't know Stevie then, not until he saw him at Mr Cranshaws. Zane said when Stevie stabbed that man he pulled out the knife and smiled, like he'd enjoyed it."

Paul stopped walking and stared at her.

"So Zane knew Stevie had killed someone." The colour had drained from his face. "What if Stevie found out?"

"What do you mean?" Nairne asked, although she thought she knew.

"What if Stevie found out what Zane had seen, maybe that's why he left; maybe he was frightened of what Stevie might do."

"What if Zane didn't leave....." Nairne's expression was one of complete horror.

"Nairne?" Paul held her arms and looked directly into her eyes. "What is it?"

Her legs buckled under her.

"What if Zane didn't leave? What if Stevie got rid of him.... and the only way Stevie could have found out was from your dad.... He knew what Zane had seen, he knew he could identify Stevie, he told Zane to lie to the police to protect Stevie."

Paul was rooted to the spot. It all made sense, the way Pamela and his father had reacted when he mentioned Zane.

"Zane's dead," she whispered. "Isn't he? Isn't he?" she screamed at him.

"I don't know... the other day when you ran away, I mentioned Zane's disappearance and my dad and Pamela were all shifty; they wouldn't look at me... but there's no way my dad would do that... no way… he liked Zane."

Nairne sat there on the ground weeping.

It took Paul some time to calm her down enough to walk home. If she was right, they had to be careful.

"We could go to the police…" said Paul. "But we don't have any proof." Nairne was silent. As they reached the bottom of the drive he had an idea.

"I'll ask Pamela, I'm sure she knows something. Maybe she'll help us."

Nairne's reaction was explosive.

"No, we can't trust her. Your dad told her he was going to ask Stevie to leave so he probably told her why, but she's in there getting drunk with him."

"Maybe she's scared of him, if she knows what he's capable of she knows we need to keep him sweet."

Nairne was not convinced, but it was possible that Pamela was simply acting.

The house was silent when they entered. Nairne took Dog through to the kitchen; there were two empty wine bottles on the table, a couple of dirty glasses and a saucer covered in cigarette butts; the room stank of smoke. Nairne opened the window and fed Dog. Paul came through.

"Do you want something to eat?" he asked.

"Yes thanks," said Nairne. She felt shaky from the long walk and the emotions and now there was a sense of relief that no one was here. Paul started to heat some soup.

"I'm going to get changed," she said, looking down at her muddy trousers. She went to her room, slipped her trousers off, pulled a clean pair from the wardrobe, and put them on. The bedroom door creaked; she jumped and turned to find Stevie standing in the doorway in his jeans, his chest bare and his hair wet. He had a towel in his hand.

"Sorry, did I frighten you?" he smiled. "Pam said it would be okay if I had a bath. No hot water next door, Ed let the fire go out." Nairne stared at him.

"Where is Pamela?" she asked, trying to hold her voice level and calm.

"Oh, she went for a lie down, bit of a headache, she's been a bit upset with Garrick away.... you know she needed a bit of comforting. Where did you and Paul get to, you were gone for ages?"

"Nairne, lunch is ready." Paul shouted up the stairs.

"Okay, I'll be right down," she shouted back, loud enough to wake the slumbering Pamela. "Excuse me." She tried to pass him. He put his arm out to bar the way and she saw the unmistakable mark of a dog bite on his forearm.

"Saved by the lunch bell," he laughed and moved out of her way. Nairne's legs were shaking as she hurried down the stairs.

Paul gave her a quizzical look. She held her finger to her lips. She closed the kitchen door and a moment later, they heard the front door slam shut.

"Who was that?"

"Stevie, he was upstairs when I was getting changed, he came into my room. He'd just had a bath."

"Where is Pamela?"

"Oh, she's having a lie down. Apparently, after

polishing off two bottles of wine, with Psycho Steve she was a bit upset, missing your dad and he said she needed comforting."

Paul scowled; Nairne could see the rage in his eyes. He stormed upstairs, pausing momentarily at the bedroom door, he knocked and went in.

"Pamela, are you all right? We're having some lunch."

Pamela's crumpled form lay under the covers, her hair untidy and her lipstick and mascara smudged.

"Oh, Paul darling," she attempted a smile. "I wasn't feeling too good...."

"Yes, Stevie said." His tone was accusatory and he could see the panic in Pamela's eyes. "Lunch is on the table if you're feeling better." He turned and went out of the room, leaving the door open.

THIRTY THREE

Pamela was good; Nairne watched as she tried to ingratiate her way back into Paul's affections by making his favourite dinner and asking his advice on financial matters, now he was the man of the house. However, if Pamela was good, Paul was even better. He moved from hostile, to wary, to indifferent and finally forgiving. The incident with Stevie was not alluded to directly, and Pamela's explanation that she'd had too much to drink and Stevie had acted like a gentleman, providing a shoulder to cry on, as Paul was nowhere to be found was accepted. The lawyer had been in touch to let them know it would be several months before Garrick's trial. Visitors were permitted once a week. The remand centre was on the other side of Edinburgh, so Stevie and Pamela went. She said Garrick had insisted that Paul should not see him in a place like that, plus he and Stevie had business to discuss. The warehouse was closed and the goods inside impounded so operations had to restart from scratch. Garrick had the contacts and the cash and Stevie could control the workforce.

"Dad said I would be taking over the business," said Paul, when Pamela explained what was going to happen. "Plus, now I've passed my driving test I can take you up there next week."

"Oh, I know darling and nothing's changed, but with all the police attention and with Garrick away, it would be safer to let Stevie handle things for now. But when your dad gets out.... well, you'll see."

So the new business began operating from two of the outbuildings next to the house. The workforce was reduced to Gunny, Ed and Paul. Nairne was unhappy about the new arrangement, but she had no say in the matter and her mind was focused on getting evidence of what Stevie had done to her brother rather than caring about stolen goods.

It was a wet, cold Tuesday evening. Paul and Ed were out working and Pamela and Stevie were not yet back from their weekly visit to see Garrick. There was a knock on the door and she opened it to find Gunny and Leanne on the doorstep. Although it was only half past five, darkness had descended.

"Nairne," Gunny greeted her as if they were old friends. "I've got some stuff to pick up and deliver. I'll not be back until after nine, so I wondered if Leanne could wait here with you?" Leanne looked suitably needy. "There's no power at ours and it's freezing." Nairne opened the door.

"No, that's fine. Leanne come on through."

"Thanks, see you later doll." He kissed Leanne on the cheek and strode off across the yard towards the outbuilding. Leanne stood in the hallway.

"Go on through," said Nairne, ushering her into the living room. Dog stood, stretched and came over to check out this new visitor. Leanne was nervous of him.

"Oh, don't worry, he won't bite, unless you're related to Stevie," said Nairne jokingly. "Give him a pat and then he'll go and lie down again."

Leanne laughed nervously and did as instructed. Dog wagged his tail in response, sniffed at her hands and legs and then went back to his place in front of the fire. Leanne perched on the edge of the sofa.

"Can I get you a drink? Tea, water or beer?"

"Beer would be great," said Leanne smiling. In the stark light Nairne could see how painfully thin she was. Her skin was almost translucent, the veins at her temples were clearly visible and even her lips were pale. Her eyes, which were unusually large and dark, were encased in a ring of coal black makeup. She took the bottle from Nairne with a hand of bone and sinew.

"Thanks. Sorry about this, but I hate being in on my own when there's no power, it's like so depressing. You're so lucky out here, with this place; what with your own power and water supply, everyone says so."

"Do they?"

"Oh yeah, the boys are always saying that, like what a great set up you have. It's like... a little fortress. Even when things get worse, you'll be okay out here." There was an edge of awe in her voice. "You look at what's happening and think how other people are going to manage? Soon there won't be any running water, that's what Gunny says..... I'll be okay, I've got Gunny, he'll look after me."

"So have you been together long?" asked Nairne. She guessed Leanne was only in her early twenties while Gunny was at least forty.

"Yeah, for like ages. I was sixteen when we met. I was always in trouble at home and then I met him at a party one night and we just split."

"You ran off with him when you were sixteen?" asked Nairne curiously.

"Yeah, but that's cool because Gunny has experience, like moving up here, he knew when it was time to get out; he could see what was coming in London and now all those people who want to leave can't find anywhere to go."

Silence descended. Leanne looked round the room and spotted a picture on the mantelpiece; she reached up and took it down.

"Was that your dad?" she enquired. The picture was of Zane and Daniel taken a couple of years ago.

"Yes."

"I never met your dad, he looks... dependable, but your brother Zane was lovely, what a sweetheart."

"Yes," said Nairne again, her voice almost a whisper. Leanne took another slug of beer. "It's so sad......him dying like that.... You must have been gutted."

Nairne had no idea what to say. She still missed her

father so much, even talking about it hurt.

"Gunny was like so upset; I've never seen him like that," Leanne volunteered, staring at the picture. Nairne was confused, as far as she knew Gunny had barely spoken to her dad.

"He blames himself. I told him there's nothing to be gained from that but....."

"But why does Gunny blame himself?" Nairne asked confused.

"Yeah. I know, but Gunny was very fond of Zane he thought he was a great lad, always keen to help, but I know you're right, he shouldn't blame himself. That's what I keep telling him, but it's like if he hadn't been off work that night, if he'd gone to the warehouse well.....who knows."

Nairne's heart was pounding, the adrenaline pumped through her veins. She had to stay calm and keep Leanne talking. She obviously thought Nairne knew what had happened that night. She struggled to keep her voice level.

"So why was he off work?"

"Oh, that was my fault. I'd taken.... well, let's just say I wasn't very well and Gunny took me to hospital so he'd switched off his phone and Ed couldn't get through. Afterwards, Stevie was furious. I thought this is it, Gunny's no angel, but you wouldn't want to get on the wrong side of Stevie. It's like Gunny said, they should never have taken Zane with them."

"Yes," said Nairne. "So did Stevie have an explanation of why they took him?"

"They needed a fourth guy and Gunny had let them down yeah, and Zane was so keen, totally up for it. Stevie said how could they know that it was a trap; they'd stopped lots of consignments on that road and no one had ever pulled a gun before. But you know Stevie; he's always got to blame someone else."

Nairne was shaking. She could feel her breathing getting faster and shallower, sweat was running down her back;

she felt hot and cold at the same time.

"Did Gunny tell you this?" Nairne asked. Leanne paused, then it was as if she focused for the first time. She saw the look of horror on Nairne's face.

"I overheard him and Jason talking... look....., I shouldn't have said anything; I didn't mean to upset you ...." There was panic in her voice. "Look, ignore what I said. Maybe I misunderstood yeah, Gunny's always telling me I'm not very smart."

Nairne moved over to sit next to Leanne on the sofa. She looked straight into her eyes.

"What happened to Zane?"

"I don't know..." Tears welled up in Leanne's eyes. "I thought you knew .... I thought they'd told you. Christ, if Stevie finds out..... He'll kill me!" She was hysterical.

Nairne reached over and grabbed Leanne wrists, they were so thin; it was like holding onto a bird. She squeezed tightly.

"Tell me what happened," her voice rose in anger. "Tell me right now." Leanne sobbed and attempted to pull free, but Nairne gripped tighter. She knew it must be hurting, but she didn't care. She had to know. Leanne screamed and struggled, trying to break free. She was crying hysterically. Nairne let go of one of her wrists and slapped her hard across the face. There was silence.

"All right," Leanne sobbed. "I tell you, but you have to promise, they'll kill me..." her voice cracked as her body heaved and gasped for breath.

"I promise," said Nairne.

"Zane went out on job with them, you know to get more stuff." Nairne looked puzzled. "To hijack another lorry," Leanne explained. She didn't look Nairne in the eye as she continued. "When they got there Zane went round the back with Jason, while Stevie and Ed dealt with the driver. When they opened the back of the lorry Zane climbed in and......" Leanne's body convulsed with a huge sob.

"And what?" said Nairne, grasping her wrists tighter making Leanne squirm with the pain.

"There was a man hiding in the back; he had a shotgun.... He fired it right at Zane. There was nothing anyone could do.... He was..., it was.....The man shoved his body out onto the ground and with all the confusion the driver managed to get back into the cab and they got away."

"So was he dead?" Nairne asked, tears streaming down her face.

"I don't know.... Jason said he was still breathing but….."

"But what? What happened? I need to know."

"Jason said, like he couldn't believe it, Stevie took the money out of Zane's jacket…He said the money was covered in blood….. They'd paid him two hundred pounds and like Stevie took it back, said Zane wouldn't need it. He told them to put Zane in the back of his car. Jason doesn't know what happened. He went home in the van. Stevie said he'd take care of everything." She started to cry again.

"Who else knows?"

"Only Gunny, Ed and Jason – but he legged it a couple of weeks later and of course Mr Unwin."

"How did Garrick find out?"

"Ed went to pieces, shot his mouth off, Mr Unwin was mad as hell."

"So that's why he made them all help look for Zane, it made them look innocent," said Nairne distractedly. "Leanne you need to come with me to the police." At this, Leanne leapt from the seat wrenching her wrists free.

"No, no way. You don't understand.... the police.... you can't.... no one will believe us. They'll buy them off like they did with Garrick......" the girl wailed.

"What, you mean Stevie had Garrick arrested?"

She nodded and backed away towards the door.

"But why?"

"He wants the business and this place for himself. He thought Garrick was going to cut him out and give Paul more responsibility. I need to leave. You promised. You can't tell anyone." There was fear in her eyes. "I can't go to the police, look at me, who will believe some strung out junkie? Nairne I'm sorry..." she continued to cry, stumbling for the door.

"Leanne, sit down, it's okay, I won't go to the police. Let me get you a drink." Nairne went over and poured Leanne a whisky from the half empty bottle beside Garrick's favourite chair. Leanne's shaking hands grasped the glass. Nairne glanced at her watch. It was after eight.

"The others will be back shortly. Go and wash your face. When they arrive we need to appear like normal. They mustn't find out you told me, for both our sakes." Leanne nodded.

Ed and Paul were first to arrive home. They found Leanne and Nairne sitting in the living room chatting like old friends. Paul was surprised; Leanne usually had trouble stringing a sentence together.

"Gunny asked if Leanne could stay," said Nairne in explanation. "He'll be back after nine."

"What about Pamela?" said Paul.

"No sign yet," said Nairne.

"They should have been back by now." Paul glanced at his watch. Ed smirked.

"Maybe they got held up on the way home," he sniggered.

"Ed, don't you have stuff to go and do?" said Nairne pointedly.

"No, not really," he responded.

"Dog!" said Nairne her tone abrupt and sharp. On cue, Dog rose to his feet and a low, deep growl was focused in Ed's direction.

"Yes, I guess you're right, got some paperwork to sort out next door," he said, edging towards the door. As the front door closed, Leanne looked at Nairne in astonishment.

"I can't believe you did that." A look of relief crossed her face.

"She's not to be messed with," said Paul, glancing gratefully at Nairne. "Anyway, what have you two been up to?"

"Oh, nothing much," said Nairne. "Just chatting." Ten minutes later, there was a knock at the door.

"That'll be Gunny," said Leanne hopefully. Nairne went through and opened the door.

"Come in," said Nairne.

"You're all right luv; don't want to tread mud into the house. Everything okay?"

"Yes, fine," said Nairne. "Leanne's welcome to come round anytime." Leanne shuffled passed her with a subdued thanks, as Stevie and Pamela arrived back.

"So?" said Paul expectantly as Pamela came through to the living room. "How is he?"

"You know your dad," she responded in a non committal tone. "He's fine, same old Garrick. He says it's not too bad and we took him some cigarettes, but I think he's a bit low."

"Did you ask him about me visiting?"

"Yes, but he wasn't keen, doesn't think it's the sort of place you should be going." Paul looked crestfallen.

"I'll ask him again next time, maybe we can persuade him. Anyway, I'm exhausted; we had to go through three sets of checkpoints."

"What for?" asked Nairne.

"New rules. When you cross from one region to the next, they're starting to keep a note of vehicle movements, I'm not sure what that's going to do for business." With this, Pamela made her excuses and tottered upstairs to bed.

"I could kill Ed," said Paul sitting down heavily on the sofa. "He's been making snide remarks about Pamela and

Stevie all night."

"I am going to kill Stevie," said Nairne, her tone cold and hard.

"Yeah, right," said Paul looking at her, but something about her face made him pause. "What's wrong Nairne? Has something happened?"

She hesitated, unsure of what to tell him, unsure of whether she could truly trust him, especially since what she had found out implicated Garrick.

"Tell me, what is it?"

"It's nothing," she replied.

"Tell me, I can see it in your face. What is it?"

"Okay, if you're sure you want to know, but once I tell you nothing is ever going to be the same again, not for anyone."

Paul nodded; his stomach began to churn.

"Zane is dead; he died the night he disappeared. Stevie took him out on a robbery and it all went wrong. He was shot at point blank range with a shotgun. Your dad found out from Ed and helped cover it up. All that searching was a charade to stop anyone from suspecting them."

"I don't believe you... how did you find out?"

"Leanne overheard Jason telling Gunny. Jason saw it happen. Gunny should have been at the robbery, but he was late so they took Zane instead. Leanne thought I already knew, she let something slip and I forced it out of her. She says if Stevie finds out he'll kill her."

"But why would dad cover up for them. There's no way, no way." Paul got up and began pacing backwards and forwards. "I know the stuff at the warehouse is stolen, but if Zane got killed..... I don't understand. Dad would never do that, no way. You've never liked him, you're just saying it. Okay, maybe the stuff about the robbery is true, but dad wouldn't have helped them hide it, no way." Fury and confusion flooded through Paul.

"If you don't believe me go and ask him," said Nairne coldly.

"How can I ask him? Pamela gets the only pass. How do I get to see him?"

"Pamela and Stevie won't be well enough to visit him next week."

"What? How do you know that?"

"Because I'll make sure of it," said Nairne.

THIRTY FOUR

The next few days were tortuous. Nairne was like an automaton. She functioned and communicated, but the warmth had left her. Pamela and Stevie barely attempted to hide their relationship and Paul looked so angry it was a wonder he didn't explode. The next visitor's pass was for the following Tuesday. Nairne had confided in Paul on Monday afternoon, when she spent a couple of hours in the kitchen, preparing a large spicy curry.

"That smells great," said Paul. "Can I have a taste?"

"No," Nairne barked back at him. "Not now and not later. In fact, you're going out at dinner time."

"Why, what are you up to?"

"Put it this way, no one who eats this is going anywhere tomorrow."

"You're not going to do anything drastic?" He was worried.

"No, just make them sick. Then you can take the pass and visit your dad."

"You could come with me."

"No, I have other plans."

When Paul stopped in to see Ed and Stevie he mentioned that Nairne had cooked dinner not realising he would be out so there was some going spare. The boys duly invited themselves round.

"Nairne, let me help you serve," said Pamela, entering the kitchen.

"No, it's all right Pamela, you've got your good clothes on, and you might get splashed. I'll bring it through."

Nairne took through three large platefuls of chicken korma; some cans of beer and a bottle of wine were already on the table. Finally, she emerged carrying her own plate. She had fed Dog and shut him in the living room; she didn't want him getting scraps from the table. They ate, Ed and Stevie made crude jokes, Pamela laughed, Nairne barely spoke, but when asked she provided second helpings and more beer. After they had eaten, the three of them sat and drank while Nairne cleared away the dishes.

"I better go through and help with the washing up," said Pamela reluctantly.

"No, have some more wine," said Stevie filling her glass, "I'll go." Pamela looked surprised. Stevie wasn't exactly domesticated. "It was good of her to let us come round. She's obviously wanting to make an effort. It's only right we should help out and Ed's bloody useless in the kitchen."

Ed snorted and took a slug of beer.

"Anyway Pam, you need someone to keep your wine glass topped up."

The kitchen door swung open. Nairne knew who it was before she turned round.

"I've come to offer my services." He walked over and leaned against the worktop next to the sink.

"Thanks, but I can manage," said Nairne. "Why don't you take some more beers through? Pamela might be missing you."

"There's still plenty through there and Pamela's got Ed to keep her company. I thought maybe you and I should get to know each other a bit better, now we'll be spending more time together."

"Will we?" she responded.

"With Garrick gone, it would make more sense for me to move in, look after the three of you."

"But there are only three bedrooms and they're all taken."

"I'm sure one of you could squeeze over and make room." He laughed and ran his hand down her back leaving it resting on the small of her back. Her body stiffened. She wanted to scream at the thought of him touching her. But she stayed very still and continued to wash the dishes.

"I know you've got a soft spot for Paul, but he's only a boy and I think you need someone with a bit more...experience." As he spoke, he leaned down and began nuzzling at her neck pulling her round so she was facing him. Then he felt a sharp pain just above his groin.

"I think you should stop that," said Nairne. He pulled his head back and glanced down at the large stainless steel vegetable knife that was pressing against him "Now take some beers, go back next door and we'll pretend this never happened. And Stevie, next time there will be no warning."

She felt his hand slip from her back as he backed away and left the kitchen. Nairne was shaking, her blood was pounding in her veins, and she held herself up on the edge of the sink. She wished Paul was back.

Paul returned after ten. The three adults were drunk and rowdy in the living room while Nairne sat in the kitchen with Dog.

"Hi," said Nairne casually. "Did you have fun?"

"I went to see Craigie; we didn't go out or anything. The town's pretty rough at night now. It's weird, when we came here it was like some sleepy little village, but now it's like some bandit settlement. Anyway, how did you get on?"

"They all ate dinner so I guess sometime soon it should take effect."

"But didn't you eat it as well?

"Yes, but I took mine out the pot before I added those special ingredients."

"What did you put in?"

"Oh, just some bulbs from the garden. It will make them sick and feverish, but I'll be here to look after them."

"Once I've spoken to my dad I'm sure we'll be able to sort all this out, get Stevie out of the house. My dad will tell him."

"Paul," Nairne paused and looked at him. "Stevie's talking about moving in here, to look after us while your dad's gone."

"But there's nowhere for him to sleep.....you mean him and Pamela?"

"He wasn't that specific," said Nairne her fist clenched. "He suggested one of us would be willing to share with him."

The colour rose in Paul's cheeks.

"You mean he thinks you and him..... Did something happen? Did he hurt you?"

"No, he tried it on, but all he got was a bit of a fright, I was holding this at the time." She picked up the knife which was now lying on the kitchen table. "But it means we have to deal with him once and for all. You need to make your dad tell us what happened."

At eight thirty Nairne got up went downstairs and started breakfast before waking Paul and then trying to rouse Pamela.

"Oh, no I'm not well, I've been up most of the night," said a voice from the darkness. "I need to sleep."

"But you and Stevie are going to Edinburgh this morning to see Garrick," said Nairne brightly.

"I'm too ill," said Pamela, "I can't possibly......Stevie will need to go and explain."

"Can I get you anything?"

"Just some water and can you let Steven know I'm not well," she replied.

"Maybe he could take Paul," said Nairne.

"Oh no. I don't think that would be a good idea. Garrick would be annoyed."

"Where's the visitors pass?" said Nairne. "I'll take it round."

Pamela indicated towards her handbag. Nairne slipped the pass into her pocket and fetched a glass of water. By the time she came downstairs, Paul was waiting for her.

"Here." She handed him the pass. "I'll go and see how next door are doing."

Nairne returned a few minutes later to announce that both Stevie an Ed were far from well.

"Ed's in bed, Stevie's lying on the sofa and he looks awful." She got a large glass jug from the cupboard, filled it with water and then added some liquid from a small bottle in one of the cupboards.

"What that?" Paul asked.

"Just something to make them both feel more nauseous. We need this to last a few days and what I gave them last night won't do that. But every time they take a drink they'll make themselves a little bit worse."

Paul was shocked, but she was right. They had to make sure Stevie and Ed were out of commission all day.

At ten o'clock Paul set off for Edinburgh leaving Nairne with her patients. She gave each of them a jug of water and then she borrowed Stevie's keys from his room, went over and unlocked the padlock on the outbuilding.

The lock was stiff but she managed to undo it and prise open the door. Inside, the old stone building was full of boxes and crates; Nairne ripped open the first couple of boxes containing cigarettes; the next contained whisky and brandy. On the left had side of the room there were three large wooden crates. She fetched a crow bar from her dad's toolbox and prised the lid off the first one. Tightly packed with straw, the box was too heavy to lift so she pulled back the straw and discovered long canvas parcels. Carefully, she pulled the top one out of the box, and laid it on the floor and unwrapped it. Inside was a shotgun, like Mr Cranshaw's, she looked back into the box; there were at least a dozen of them. It looked like the business had graduated from drink to guns. She rummaged in the box for ammunition; there was none. She scoured the room and eventually found two small heavy boxes containing cartridges. She took out a box. She was sweating by the time she had nailed the lid back on the crates and returned everything in the storeroom to normal. Locking the door, she took the gun and cartridges with her. Time to check on the patients, she thought. It was close to lunchtime. She would offer them something to eat.

Paul arrived at the detention centre just on time. The road blocks had taken ages. Nervously, he approached the gates and showed his pass. After being searched and enduring a wait of twenty minutes, Paul, along with a group of other visitors, was taken to the visiting area. Rows of tables with three chairs at each filled the dingy space. He spotted his dad instantly; meanwhile Garrick's eyes were scanning for Pamela's unmistakable blonde hair. Paul waved and Garrick hurried across. He went to hug Paul but, Paul pulled away.

"I know we're not supposed to have any physical contact," Garrick muttered apologetically, indicating to Paul to sit down.

"Where's Pamela? I've been so worried since she didn't show up last week, is she all right?"

"But she came last week with Stevie," said Paul. "She said you didn't want to see me."

"No, I didn't get any visitors last week, and Pamela told me you didn't want to visit me. She said you were angry with me. What's been going on?" Garrick demanded.

"I have to ask you something, dad. It's important."

"Okay, but first tell me what's been happening. I don't hear from anyone, no one visits and now you turn up here on your own."

"Look, everything's different. Pamela and Stevie....." His voice trailed off, but the insinuation hung in the air for what seemed like ages.

"That son of a bitch," said Garrick. "When I get out of here I'll.... Pamela.... what is she thinking about, after everything I've given her. Are you sure about this Paul? It's not some teenage fantasy."

Paul could feel his temper rising.

"Dad, forget about Pamela. Look, she told me she was seeing you every week. So every Tuesday she and Stevie set off together. He's running the business; he's all over Pamela like a rash. Ed and Gunny are always talking about it and last night he practically tells Nairne he's moving in. Dad, they set you up."

"What do you mean?" Garrick was reeling from the news.

"That night Gunny phoned you – why didn't he call Stevie?"

"He tried, but the mobile was off."

"And Ed? It's a bit of a coincidence and how did you manage to get there before Gunny? He lives much closer. You'd told Stevie he had to move out hadn't you?"

"Yes.... but Stevie wouldn't, he hasn't got the nerve...."

"Why didn't you turn him in when Zane got killed?"

Garrick recoiled as if a shotgun blast had just hit him.

"What did you say?" he stalled.

"Dad, I know Zane's dead. I know how it happened. Why did you cover it up?"

"How do you know? Who told you?"

"It doesn't matter; tell me why you lied for them."

"Oh, for Christ's sake Paul, you know why, you're not stupid. They were out doing a job for me. If I'd told, then I would have been implicated. It was a stupid mistake, he should never have taken the boy with him. He knew that, but Stevie's reckless; he's out of control." Garrick spat the words in a hushed voice, the anger in his tone apparent. "You have no idea how much I regret it. He was only a boy."

"So why didn't you tell Stevie to go then, why did you continue to employ him?"

"Look, the damage was done by then, and he knew too much about the business."

Paul hesitated, there was more to this. His father looked nervous, guilty.

"What else? I know Stevie killed that man outside the pub. I know Zane saw that, but then you knew that as well didn't you?"

Garrick's face flushed.

"I did what I thought was best. That boy would never have stood a chance against a bloke like Stevie."

"So what does Stevie know? What's the secret dad, tell me. It's okay for you in here, but I'm stuck at that house with this guy and I need to know what's going on. Tell me, or this is the last time you'll ever see me."

Garrick looked unsure. Paul was not going to let go. The boy was grown up now, maybe he deserved the truth.

"Okay, but you have to understand I did it for you and Pamela. You can see how it's going, survival of the fittest isn't that what they say, a man's got to look out for his own. You've got to make decisions on the spur of the moment; you've got to deal with the consequences."

"Dad, just tell me!" Paul's voice was sharp.

"I warned Stevie that Daniel knew about the stolen goods. A lorry driver got hurt. He died. Daniel made the connection with the warehouse. He was going to turn Ed and Stevie in to the police. He warned me so I could tell you to stop working there. He didn't realise I knew about the hijackings." Paul tried to interrupt, Garrick held up his hand. "I told Stevie to get his story straight and get rid of any evidence, but no, he decided he'd shut Daniel up. You know what happened."

"Stevie pushed him into the river? Stevie killed him?" Paul whispered back.

Garrick nodded.

"What could I do? I've tried to do what's best for you and Pamela and for Nairne and her brother but....." Garrick broke down.

Paul sat back and stared at him.

"I had to keep quiet, but once I get out of here Tony will help me out. He's connected. If I could speak to him, he could make all of this go away. Pamela said he was away on business, but when he gets back.....We'll get rid of Stevie, he'll pay for what he's done. Then you and I will get the business back on track, proper family affair and young Nairne, I know you're keen on the girl, we'll be fine just the three of us."

"Dad, Tony hasn't gone anywhere, he won't take our calls; he doesn't want to know. It serves you right....How could you? They opened up their house to us, gave us somewhere to live and it's like Nairne said, everything just turned to shit... you destroyed everything....."

"Now wait a minute young man," Garrick took the high moral ground. "You weren't so fussy when I had money to spend on you. Okay, so it's unfortunate what happened, but Daniel Grear was a self righteous fool. He would have seen me go to jail and for what, for getting people what they want. Supply and demand, isn't that what I always say?"

"Yes," said Paul, lowering his head and staring at Garrick. "But that's the problem, the Grears didn't want any of it, Daniel knew what was coming so he did his best to protect his kids. He offered to share that with us, but it wasn't enough, was it? It's never enough!" Paul pushed his chair back, the legs scraped noisily on the floor, eyes turned to stare.

"Paul, son, I know you're upset, but that place is perfect, it's a fortress, we need to hang on to it, don't you see?"

"I'm not your son, and it's not our place to hang on to," said Paul, striding across the room. Garrick called after him, but he did not turn round.

THIRTY FIVE

Paul returned to find Nairne sitting in the kitchen. A shotgun and an open box of cartridges lay on the table. The house was silent. He stood staring at the gun.

"Nairne, what's going on?"

"Don't worry." She raised her head. "I haven't killed them yet." There was an expression of such hatred in her eyes that Paul felt the hairs on his neck stand on end.

"Are they still sick?"

"Yes, I gave them some soup for lunch; they'll not be up before tomorrow."

"Where did you get that?" he gestured towards the gun.

"Oh, that's what they sell now, didn't you know? It came in handy today. I got Ed's confession on tape. I thought he was the most likely to crack and once he saw the gun he was quite forthcoming. You know, Leanne was right about Zane, it wasn't instant. They watched him bleed to death in the back of Stevie's car, after Stevie retrieved the money he'd paid Zane for taking part in the job.

I didn't realise Ed could be so...communicative. He told me where Stevie hid the records for the business. Interesting reading." She indicated a large pile of paperwork on the table. "Looks like your dad's mate Tony is helping them get started. Apparently, your dad drew the line at guns and drugs so Tony was happy to see him go. All that stuff out there, Tony paid for everything, the new vehicles and the wages. They owe him everything."

Paul sat down at the table.

"Shit, what are we going to do? Ed will tell Stevie what you did."

"Ed's unconscious. I gave him some more medicine. I

doubt he'll wake up again today. Anyway, he's locked in his room and tied to the bed. I told him that if I heard a noise or he tried to leave the room I'd shoot him. We've got the confession; we'll give it to the police."

"But Ed will say you threatened him. There's still no evidence, the car's gone, we don't know where they hid Zane's body and Stevie will have an alibi. And what do we do if they don't believe us?"

"Can your dad help? What did he say?"

"He's as bad as Stevie; I don't want to talk about it."

"Tell me what happened," insisted Nairne.

"Okay," Paul braced himself. "He admitted he knew about Zane, but he couldn't turn them in because Stevie knew too much."

"What, about the business? It was only stolen goods, that's not exactly the crime of the century. My brother got killed!" she exclaimed.

"There was more to it. Your dad found out about the business. They killed a lorry driver months ago. He was going to turn Stevie in. Dad warned Stevie and......" he trailed off.

"He killed him!" She was on her feet and reaching for the gun.

"Nairne, no!" Paul grabbed it and snatched it out of her grasp. "Then you'll be just like them. What would your dad have done?"

"He'd have gone to the police."

"Okay, but we don't have any evidence, even with the stolen goods. With Tony on their side they'll be able to buy their way out of trouble or go to jail for a while then they'll be back here."

"What are you saying?" Nairne asked.

"I don't know – we need someone more powerful than the police...."

"What, like Tony?"

"Yes, everyone thinks he's more powerful than the police. So we need to make Tony think they're his enemies, that they've double crossed him....

"Okay, so let's set them up. Let's destroy all the stuff and tell Tony that Stevie blew all the money."

"But Tony won't take my calls." Paul replied.

"No, but he'll take a call from Gunny. We'll tell Gunny that Stevie and Ed have run off with all the stock. We'll say they bought a lorry and cleared the place out. He'll run to Tony. When Tony comes down here and finds it's all gone he'll go mad."

"Yes, but we could get caught in the cross fire," said Paul.

"Then we won't be here when he arrives," she replied.

"You mean leave here?"

"Yes....., no....., I don't know. This was my dad's place; he'd have wanted me to stay."

Paul leaned across the table and took her hand.

"Zane's not coming back and I know your dad chose this place because he thought you'd have better chance here, but..."

"I know," said Nairne. "Even if we get rid of Stevie and Ed, there will be others. This place has too much going for it, I don't want to live here knowing what happened to dad and waiting for the next person to come along and try and take it from me. What about your dad and Pamela?"

"I don't have a father," said Paul. "And as for Pamela, I think she's made her bed. Where will we go?"

"I don't know," said Nairne. "But we'll find somewhere. Lots of other people are in this position. We'll manage. Before we go there are few things we need to take care of."

The next morning they rose early. There was a lot to do. Nairne continued to give her patients homemade soup and the three of them continued to feel sick, dizzy and generally unwell. Stevie demanded a doctor but she explained that when she called the surgery they said there was a forty-eight hour flu going round and that they should drink plenty of fluid and stay in bed. Paul called Gunny and told him not to come round, no point in everyone catching it. Gunny was pleased to have a couple of days off.

Nairne phoned Mr Elliot from Kersmains farm. She remembered him from her father's funeral and he kept pigs. Two hours later he turned up in his land rover with a trailer on the back.

"Now are you sure about this, young lady?" he asked, as he loaded Mona, Lisa and Goat into the back of the trailer. "They're fine animals and I feel terrible only offering you this for them." He held out an envelope full of notes.

"No, I'm sure," said Nairne. "It's too much work and I know you'll look after them. Would you be interested in these as well?" She pointed over to four crates of rather excitable chickens. He hesitated.

"I'll throw them in for free. They're good layers."

"Only if you're sure." He turned to Paul. "Maybe I should have a word with your dad," he said.

"Oh, he's out," said Paul. "But this was his idea."

"Okay then," said Mr Elliot, never one to turn his nose up at a bit of good luck. Nairne felt a pang of regret as she watched him drive away. Soon there would be no going back.

It was a windy day so they set the bonfire on the far side of the house, out of sight and smell of their invalids. The cigarettes burned quickly, next were the guns; the boxes and handles burned leaving the blackened metalwork, which they dumped into the river. They emptied the bottles of alcohol and hid the bottles in the woods. They had held back a few bottles and cigarettes; they could be useful to barter with later. The boxes of ammunition were trickier.

"We'll bury them," said Nairne. She set out with the boxes in a barrow to find a suitable spot. While she was away, Paul emptied his father's Range Rover and began to pack. He took the tools from Daniel's shed, cans of petrol, a small bottled gas stove and a tent that had seen better days. It was getting dark by the time she reappeared.

"They'll never find them," she said. "Now there's the water supply, the power and the phones." Paul was confused.

"Once Gunny goes to Tony we need to make sure Tony actually visits so we need to steal their mobiles and cut off the phone. That way he has no choice but to turn up."

"But why the power and the water?"

"If Tony is more lenient than we think I want to make sure there is nothing here that Stevie can use. I've already unplugged the freezers so the food will be off by tomorrow. It won't take me long to destroy the water pump and tank and the wind turbines. Without them this place is useless. Come on, I suppose we better check on the patients."

Ed looked terrible. He felt sick all the time. His throat was dry and he had a fever. He was thirsty, but after each drink he felt worse. He was also scared. He didn't realise how fear could feel, but when she had pointed that gun at him....

Pamela was no longer the picture of female perfection. She was clammy and shivery; when Paul took her in some water, she was tearful and complaining.

"You have no idea, I feel terrible."

"I know," said Paul. "But I'm sure it will pass. Guess it's just lucky Nairne and I haven't got it." He smiled encouragingly as he left the room.

Stevie was not such a good patient; he was lolling on the sofa next door, with a blanket over him. Each time Nairne went in, he would shout and complain.

"I need a bloody doctor," he yelled, trying to prise himself off the sofa. His legs felt like jelly and his balance was terrible.

"I told you, it's flu," said Nairne. "The earliest the doctor can come is Friday and chances are you'll be better by then. Ed and Pamela are both looking better." She poured him some tea and left him a bowl of soup next to the sofa.

"I bet you're bloody loving this," he sneered. He grabbed her arm and pulled her towards him. She struggled against his grip, but he wouldn't let go.

"When I'm back on my feet I think it'll be time to teach you a few things about how to look after a man," he grinned. Nairne reached over for the tea and tipped it on his lap. He squealed in pain as the burning liquid seeped through his clothes.

"Bitch! You'll pay for that!" he snapped as she pulled herself from his grasp.

"So will you," she laughed. Stevie tried to stand up, but his head was spinning. She walked towards the door.

"You get back here and clean up this mess," he howled.

"Make me. You're just piss and wind," she responded looking down at his soaking trousers. "You're nothing, and soon you'll get to find out what pain feels like."

"What is that? A threat?"

"No, it's a fact," she responded as she slammed the door behind her.

Stevie lay back. Anger flooded his veins. He would teach her….

Moments later the door opened with a crash and Nairne stepped back into the room. This time she was holding the shotgun. She pointed it at him, from only a few feet away. He stared, a look of disbelief on his face as he struggled to push himself into a sitting position.

"So, are you going to, shoot me?" he sneered.

"Maybe," she replied. "Maybe I'll start with your knees, or a bit higher up..." She lowered the barrel.

"You haven't got the nerve."

"I want you tell me how you killed my dad."

The question shook him. How could she know about that?

"You're crazy."

"No," she responded. "Garrick said you killed him, but I want to hear it from you."

"Okay then, but you shouldn't believe everything Garrick says. I did hit him and push him into the river, got this for my trouble." He held up his forearm, which bore the scar from Dog. "But I didn't kill him – Garrick finished him off when he went down there and did his heroic rescue bid. Garrick was right – survival of the fittest, that's the way the world works, and your dad and Garrick just didn't have what it takes. Your dad was soft, so was that half wit brother of yours and you – you haven't got the nerve."

The recoil from the gun shoved Nairne backwards into the wall, her shoulder seared with pain. The explosion in such a small space rang in her ears, as the two barrels blasted a hole in the wall above Stevie's head. Ed's heart leapt into his mouth, he lay in his room and whimpered like a child. Pamela, who was asleep next door jolted awake. Paul who was outside dropped the stuff he was carrying to the car.

A shower of bricks and plaster rained down on Stevie.

"I told you, you haven't got the nerve!" His face contorted, as he tried to push himself onto his feet. He felt giddy. The room swam in front of him. His legs buckled uselessly.

Nairne lowered the gun and laughed at him; she turned and slammed the door shut behind her.

THIRTY SIX

The next morning they rose early. It was still dark. Paul called Gunny; it was obvious from his tone that he had woken him.

"What's wrong?" said Gunny, trying to focus.

"Gunny, it's Ed and Stevie, they've done a runner, taken all the stock, everything; it's all gone. I heard a truck, it woke me and when I got outside, they were just leaving; they've taken everything. I don't know what to do. I tried Tony but I just got his answering service."

"Shit, you're kidding me," said Gunny.

"No, they're gone, taken all their clothes. The place has been cleaned out."

"Right, okay, right," said Gunny, panic in his voice. "You sit tight, I'll call Tony."

"Can you come round?" asked Paul

"No way! Shit!" said Gunny. "I don't want to be anywhere near here when Tony gets here. Look, I'll call him, tell him you had nothing to do with it then I'm out of here. Shit, those bastards, they must be crazy....." the line went dead.

"We've got about two hours," said Paul. "Let's get organised."

Nairne went out to the shed, and armed with a torch and a hammer, she destroyed the wind turbines. She pummelled the gear boxes until they were no longer recognisable. Next, she took ladders out to the house, climbed up, and smashed the solar panels, pulling the cables from them. She had already dug up and broken the water pipe to the tank, now she disconnected the water pump and pierced holes in the bottom of the water tank. She could hear the precious liquid trickling away. Back inside, Paul made breakfast. They ate in silence, and it was strange how she felt scared and elated at the same time.

"Are you going to check on them before we go?" Paul asked.

"No, I'm sure once they get thirsty enough they'll get out of bed."

After a last look round the place they went out to the car. Dog jumped in the back while Nairne and Paul climbed in the front.

"Here goes," said Paul.

"Yes," said Nairne. "Here goes." The engine clicked into life and they drove down the driveway and along the road. Paul pulled in to a small clearing and they waited. Forty minutes later a black Range Rover with tinted windows cruised by and turned into the driveway. Paul reversed onto the road and set off.

Stevie woke. He had been aware of noise outside, his head hurt, and he moved slowly, into a sitting position. He felt terrible, but not sick. Unsteadily, he got to his feet and lurched across the room. He switched on the lights. Nothing happened. He pulled open the curtains; it was still dark outside. He stumbled into the kitchen; God he was thirsty. He reached for a glass and turned on the tap. Nothing happened. He shouted to Ed. There was a mumbled response.

"There's no power or water, I'm going next door to see what's up." Pulling on a jumper and some boots, he slipped out the back door and walked round to the house next door. The house was unlocked.

"Paul, Nairne...." he shouted and waited, but there was no response. "Pamela!" He heard a noise from upstairs. He tried the light switch in the hall. Nothing. Pamela appeared at the top of the stairs in her dressing gown.

"Oh Steven, I feel terrible. I've been so sick." He ignored her and stumbled into the kitchen. Pamela came through the door behind him. She put her hand on his arm. "What's wrong?"

"I don't know," he said. "The power is off and so's the water. Where are they, Paul and Nairne?" He pushed past her and started to look round the rest of the house. Everything seemed as it had before.

"Maybe they've gone out," she offered.

"Where to? It's only half past eight. We haven't been well, and they wouldn't just leave us."

"Maybe they're out seeing to the animals."

He stormed out the door and headed across the yard throwing open the door to the pig shed, then the chicken coup. Pamela stood on the doorstep.

"What's wrong Stevie? What is it."

"They're gone," he hollered across the yard. "The animals are gone." He rushed round to the outbuilding. The padlock still hung in its place.

"Where's Garrick's Range Rover?" he demanded.

"I don't know," said Pamela defensively. "I told you, maybe they've popped into town. Calm down Stevie. You're scaring me."

"Something isn't right. I knew it last night, all that stuff with the shotgun, but she didn't actually hurt me….. She was laughing at me......"

"Who was? What are you talking about, what shotgun? You're rambling."

"Nairne, she laughed at me, like... like I was nothing.... I need to get the keys." He lurched back into the house, reappearing moments later; he fumbled with the lock on the door, his fingers scrabbling to turn the key. He flung open the door. The building was empty except for an envelope with his name on it. He tore it open. Inside was a single sheet of paper with the words. "You were right, it is survival of the fittest and you didn't make the grade." He crumpled it up and threw it to the ground.

"That little bitch, she's stolen… she's taken the lot…. Wait until I get a hold of her…."

Pamela stepped back from him, fear in her eyes. Both

their heads turned as they heard the car approaching up the driveway.

"See!" said Pamela. "I told you they'd just popped out." Stevie gasped as he saw the vehicle and recognised the number plate.

Paul turned into Corn Market.

"I'll only be a moment, it might not work, but it's worth a try," said Nairne as she jumped out the front seat and crossed the road. The police station was still in darkness; she pushed the envelope containing the records and Ed's confession through the letterbox and returned to the car.

"I'm not sure there will be enough of them left for the police to prosecute," said Paul. "Not after Tony gets there."

"Maybe not, but at least we tried."

"Which way?" said Paul.

"North," said Nairne. "Let's go north."

RACHEL MEEHAN lives in rural, southern Scotland and has been writing fiction for a number of years. Water's Edge is her first novel.

She lives with her partner, and their house is situated well above sea level where they grow much of their own food and generate some of their own electricity.

Read an extract from

Power's Out

(Book Two: Troubled Times Series)

ONE

The rain lashed against his face, stinging his skin as he pulled the hood tighter and kept his head down. The house was barely visible and just as it had been described: single storey, with thick walls and mean windows. Smoke rose from the chimney. It was too dark to see, but he could smell it.

The quiet country road leading nowhere was silent. He was so close he could almost taste success. Sixteen months of searching, of dragging his useless body along bleak roads, through one nowhere village after another, always too late, always the same, 'yes, they were here, but they left some time ago…..' But he had learned patience and he could wait a little longer.

He knew that he made an interesting spectacle with his left leg distorted and his gait awkward. And then there was his face. He saw the way people recoiled when he turned to speak to them, and they saw the scarring, the melted skin, the distorted flesh, but at least his sight was intact.

The wooden cattle gate was secured with a rusty bolt and he struggled to undo it with the twisted fingers of his left hand, each finger broken, each break a vivid memory of pain searing through his body. Before then he had never truly understood pain. He'd seen others in pain, he had inflicted it often enough, but he had not grasped what it did to a person's soul.

The yard was muddy and his boots sank into the ground, sliding beneath him. He steadied himself on the gate, closed it behind him and walked over to the front door. He knocked loudly and waited. A light flickered from within, casting dancing rays through the small dimpled glass panel as he heard the key being turned and the door opened, slightly.

"I'm sorry to disturb you, but I wondered if I could take shelter in one of your outbuildings, just for tonight? I'll be no trouble, but it's a bitter wet night and I've walked a long way."

The woman peered at him, although it was difficult to see much with the light from the candle, but she could see that he was soaked through. It was rain rather than snow that fell, but the air was chilled by a strong northerly wind. A man could freeze to death out there. He was not the first stray to come past her door looking for help and no doubt he would not be the last. She considered his request. He could have sneaked into one of the outbuildings without her knowledge, but he had come and asked.

"I have money," he said, fumbling to get his hand into his pocket. She saw that the other hand looked damaged.

"I have no need of your money," she responded. "You can bed down in that building there on the corner, there's plenty of straw and it should be dry at least."

He nodded in thanks and walked off across the yard. She noticed his limp and shook her head sympathetically.

Morning brought daylight of sorts; dense clouds hung over the landscape and he woke to find her standing over him as he lay in the straw, his blanket wrapped tightly round his body. He did not know how long she had been there.

"Would you like some breakfast?" she asked, her voice gentle. He nodded and struggled to get up. His limbs were stiff and awkward and as he pushed himself to a sitting position she saw the left side of his face. Instinctively, he reached up to cover it.

"No need to worry about that, I've seen worse," she said. "Come into the house when you're dressed and ready and I'll get you something warm to eat."

He knocked as he entered the room, aware instantly of the warmth. A wood burning stove blazed away in the corner and the woman, her back to him, stirred a pot of porridge. He coughed.

"Just sit yourself down, I'll bring this over," she said, ladling some of the steaming mixture into two bowls. She placed one in front of him and then sat down at the other end of the table.

"Thanks, this is very kind of you." He looked directly at her. She was old, sixty-five, possibly older, a farmer's wife, solidly built, with short, grey hair. She wore sensible clothes made for the outdoors. Her hands were strong; he looked at how she grasped the spoon; these were hands that had done work.

"You live alone?" he enquired.

"Yes, that's right," she replied. "My husband passed two years ago, he's buried out there, on his land, as he would have wanted it. Just me and the animals left now."

"It must be hard to keep this going alone. Is it safe out here on your own? You should be careful letting strangers into the house." He smiled as he spoke.

"It is as safe here as anywhere else I reckon. It is not the place that creates danger, but the people, and there's not many that pass this way. And you, what brings you out here in winter? It's easy to be caught out there and perish from the cold. Are you on your way to somewhere?"

"I'm looking for someone," he replied.

"Family?" she asked. "There are a lot of folk who have lost their families, even more so since the conflict started. But from your voice I'd say that you are not from Scotland."

"No London, although I've lived here a few years now. Enough time to put down roots, enough time to that feel this is home. I even fought for it." He pushed up the sleeve of his left arm exposing a tattoo, a St Andrews flag and the number of his unit.

"And is that what happened?" She indicated to his face and his hand.

"Yes, that's what happened when they took me prisoner, an Englishman fighting for the wrong side. But I was one of the lucky ones."

"It's a sad day when we treat our own country men in such a way," she sighed. "So who are you looking for?"

"My nephew, he moved to Scotland with his father after the London floods. I don't know what happened, but the place they were staying was deserted when I went to see them, after my military service. The unit didn't have much use for me once I was crippled." His tone was bitter. "His father was gone, but I heard that my nephew had left and was headed north. He was travelling with a girl. His name is Paul. He would have been seventeen then, closer to nineteen now. I haven't seen him for several years, not since I left London, but he's the only family I have left and I know my brother would have wanted me to look out for the boy. I've been searching for months, and even been close a few times, but they keep on moving and I never seem to catch up. I'm beginning to think it's a fool's errand."

"Your nephew, you say? That is a long time to look. You must have been close."

"Yes, his father was my only brother. We were always close until the migration started. I'd already moved north a few years earlier, but my brother had business interests. He was reluctant to move, one of those who didn't believe anything like this could ever happen. He thought all this talk of climate change was nonsense."

"Well, I wish you success in your search," she said, reaching over and taking the empty bowl from him. She went over to the sink and began washing the dishes.

"I don't have any coffee," she said. "But I still have some tea if you want a warm drink before you get back on the road."

"Thanks, that would be great."

He sensed a change in her, a tensing, a distance, which had not been there before. She filled the kettle and placed it on top of the stove.

"I don't suppose you've seen any travellers that fit my

nephew's description?" he asked, watching her intensely. "I heard in the village that there were a couple of youngsters camping out this way."

"As I said, not many people pass this way, but if you let me know where you plan to look next I'll keep my eye out and if I see him I'll let him know you're looking for him. You must tell me your name so I know who to say."

He rose from the chair and walked over to the small book shelf next to the dining table. Glancing along the shelf, a book on animal husbandry caught his eye. He picked it up and flicked open the front cover.

"That's funny; I used to know a man called Daniel who had this exact same book." He laid it down carefully, the front cover open, showing the inscription.

She did not respond. She placed the cup of tea on the table.

"Don't let it get cold," she said, returning to the sink and continuing to tidy.

He walked up behind her. She heard his steps, felt his presence get closer, and felt his arm reach out to her. She did not turn around.

"Your name?" she asked again, her voice steady. "You didn't tell me your name."

"It's not important," he replied. "Just tell me what I need to know and I'll be on my way. No one will blame you. As I said, it's a dangerous place for a woman to live on her own; what else could you do?"

"As I said, it is not the place that brings danger, it's the person. Is that not right? And you will do whatever you want regardless of what I say."

"Aren't you frightened?" he asked.

"Of you? No. To what end would such fear serve me?"

Lightning Source UK Ltd.
Milton Keynes UK
UKOW05f0610101013

218817UK00001B/2/P